T0354705

Screams
of Burning
Horses

Michael Dean Kiggans

Screams
of Burning
Horses

SCREAMS OF BURNING HORSES

iUniverse books may be ordered through booksellers or by contacting:

iUniverse
1663 Liberty Drive
Bloomington, IN 47403
www.iuniverse.com
844-349-9409

Because of the dynamic nature of the Internet, any web addresses or links contained in this book may have changed since publication and may no longer be valid. The views expressed in this work are solely those of the author and do not necessarily reflect the views of the publisher, and the publisher hereby disclaims any responsibility for them.

Any people depicted in stock imagery provided by Getty Images are models, and such images are being used for illustrative purposes only. Certain stock imagery © Getty Images.

ISBN: 978-1-6632-6496-1 (sc)
ISBN: 978-1-6632-6497-8 (e)

Library of Congress Control Number: 2024914478

Print information available on the last page.

iUniverse rev. date: 09/26/2024

For the Bee

דבורה

I am quite content to be the pillow of his mind.
Sarah Barnhard Faraday
Michael Faraday: A Biography

Contents

Take from all of today's industrial nations all their industrial machinery and all their energy-distributing networks, and leave them all their ideologies, all their political leaders, and all their political organizations, and I can tell you that within six months two billion people will die of starvation, having gone through great pain and deprivation along the way.

However, if we leave the industrial machinery and their energy-distributing networks and leave them also all the people who have routine jobs operating the industrial machinery and distributing its products, and we take away from all the industrial countries all their ideologies and all the politicians and political machine workers, people would keep right on eating, possibly getting on a little better than before.

R. Buckminster Fuller
Utopia or Oblivion: The Prospects for Humanity

. . . what we must strive for at the present moment is that every electric power station we build shall actually become a stronghold of enlightenment and that it should be devoted, so to speak, to the electrical education of the masses. . . .

. . . it must be realized and remembered that we cannot institute electrification when we have illiterates. Our commission will endeavour to put an end to illiteracy—but that is not enough. It has done a good deal compared with what existed before, but it has done little compared with what has to be done. In addition to literacy, we need cultured, enlightened and educated toilers; the majority of the peasants must definitely realize the tasks confronting us.

V. I. Lenin
The Eighth All-Russia Congress of Soviets

Screams of Burning Horses

Cigarettes and Coffee
PART I

1.

Jackson Banner stared out into the weary gray, early morning rain, and the huge substation switchyard, listening to the incoming high voltage transmission lines sizzling. He stood motionlessly in the doorway of the shed; his scarred white hardhat tilted naturally askew above his right eye. The hard rain spattered loudly and rhythmically on the roof and concrete apron outside the shed.

He was dressed in brown: thick quilt-lined jacket half-zipped, revealing a brown, black, and white flannel shirt and thick black turtleneck underneath, with brown corduroy pants bloused loosely over his laced and zippered black boots. Even dressed as he was, he was still cold. His weathered, acne-scarred face—framed by a *Varmer Joiles* beard, with long thick brown hair pulled into a tight bun at the base of his skull—showed his tiredness in the storming, bitter weather. His black wire-rimmed glasses teardropped symmetrically over the bridge of his nose and set cheeks. There was a weary slouch in his heavy shoulders as he stood. His arms were folded, relaxed together against his chest, one hand holding a thermos cup of hot coffee and gripping a slow burning cigarette with the other.

He was 24 years old.

The rain beat concentric rings upon the concrete. Raindrops spattered his boots and the lower part of his bloused pants. He took another drag on the cigarette, slowly inhaling the thick luxuriant smoke through his nose, and then exhaling it slowly and smoothly out of his mouth, the plumed smoke dissipating in the rain. He smoked the cigarette steadily in seeming thoughtful silence as he watched the unending downpour. When he reached the filter, he flicked it onto the concrete in front of him, where it hissed and died. His throat felt raw and he suddenly began coughing. The freezing, windy weather made him feel cold and mean to his bones.

"You all might as well come on in and sit down a spell, Jackson," Rick Pitts drawled loudly in his thick Arkansan voice behind Banner. "B.S. and Sammy won't be heah a while."

Banner grunted without turning around. Thumbs hooked into the belt-loops of his pants, he stared at the empty two-lane highway that ran parallel lengthwise with the substation. He wondered what Little Turtle must have thought seeing "Mad" Anthony Wayne and his legion troops come marching through the Tills Plains here nearly 200 years ago. Banner dimly made out the slightly rolling flatlands to the east. Spring mercilessly was howling its annual arrival into Ohio this year; the rain would melt the snow and churn the fields quickly into thick mud. He also knew he was going to be soaking wet later on when B.S. and Sammy and the rest of the men showed up for work. He shivered at the thought; maybe it was because he was raggedly tired.

Jesus.

Banner thought about the Bee waiting at home for him.

Suddenly, a lone car appeared on the horizon, coming towards him, its bright yellowish headlights cutting harshly through the dark. Banner felt relieved when it hissed on by the substation: he wasn't ready for anything; especially not working.

2.

Banner, Rick, Tower, and Ringo had driven north from the Cape Kennedy Space Center 27 hours ago. They had performed and completed one of the largest high voltage substation maintenance jobs the company earned the contract to do.

The last day of the finally completed job, Jackson Banner lay worn and exhausted in the cold motel room bed and stared at the bare white ceiling—too tired to take off his sweat- and oil-stained clothes; too tired to reach down and unlace his hot screaming feet from his boots; too tired to take a shower—and thought about the last transformer that he had worked on. He was glad to be alive. Through the long night, staring up at the bare white ceiling—it might have been the inner lid to his coffin—smoking one cigarette after another, he listened to the lonely pounding sweep and gentle roar of the Atlantic's waves washing along the shore as if it were the eternal song of God.

B.S. Archwood telephoned Banner's motel room at three in the morning and without even a cheery hello started babbling as if he were drunk again about another job that just came up: an emergency. B.S.'s voice whined into Banner's stunned ear like a mosquito that wouldn't go away: "I jus' got word that you all finished up today. I heard what happened down there today too an' I wanta talk to you about it later. Listen, I need you to pack up and leave right now and get the hell up here to Attica, Ohio. And bring the rest of the crew with you! If they're out carousin' aroun', go get 'em right now and sober 'em up! I need ya up here, Christ, we're in a hell of a mess! Got terrible trouble up here, a bad son-of-a-bitch! Bastards're carryin' guns and shooting out insulators and blowing out transformers on poles all over the gawddamned countryside."

What?

"Ah shit, keep that to yourself and lemme tell 'em myself, got it? Hey! Lemme give ya the directions where to meet ya at," and B.S. rattled off the directions while Banner desperately tried to write them down on the motel's stationery. He would find how to get there by flipping through the road atlas anyway.

After B.S. finished talking, Banner wanted to scream into the receiver, "But it's three o'clock in the gawddamned morning!" but instead he mumbled resignedly, "Sure, we'll be there," because he had no choice and he knew it. B.S. had already got hold of him, and without another word B.S. hung up, leaving the loud buzzing dial tone coursing through Banner's ear.

Oh fuck.

He suddenly wished he were home with his warm, loving wife. He hadn't seen her in two solid months. Gawddamn B.S. anyhow. He called the Bee after B.S. hung up the telephone. Banner told her he'd be only two, two-and-a-half hours away from home.

"But are you coming home after you finish there?" the Bee asked sleepily.

"Probably," Banner sighed, and there was silence over the line. That was not what she wanted to hear. Two hard long months on the open road was getting on his wife's nerves. And his. He especially didn't feel like telling her what had happened on the last day of the job down here. It'd be like that July 4th weekend when he had come home with his wrist all bandaged up and explaining that to her. Or when they found out that Phil Lazarus had nearly been killed after coming into physical contact with a live 7200-volt fuse.

And what's she going to think when he does tell her?

"The job in Florida's finished," Banner told her. "But I'm gonna tell B.S. that I'm gonna go home after we finish up there in Ohio. My Gawd, it's only a couple of hours away."

"I know," the Bee sighed. "I just want you home. I want to see you."

"I know. I want to be home too. So do the rest of the guys."

There was another silence. Banner didn't know what to say to her; to soothe her. He had calculated the days they actually lived together since their marriage over two years ago—they added up to 46 days: a Wednesday here, a Sunday and Monday there, and then on the road. The only communication they had left to them was the use of a telephone every night. They had barely enough time to consummate their marriage the way it was.

"I love you," he said seriously to her, meaning it and furious with himself. This, he realized now, was no way to live. "I'll be home soon," he told her.

"I love you too, Jackson," the Bee said. "Just be careful driving."

"I will. I'll, I'll see you later."

"All right, I'll see you."

"Yes," he said, and hung up. Every conversation he and the Bee held over the telephone went nearly the same now. The more he traveled the more homesick he grew. He felt torn every working day, not knowing how and what to decide.

"*No! No! The hell Ah will!*" Rick howled when Banner with a death-head's grin and sickened eyes gave him the glad tidings from B.S. after waking him up from an exhausted sleep in the other bed; but he had no choice either, and he knew it, too. "Oh, Gawd!" Rick groaned.

None of them did. It was back on the road again. They all checked out of the motel a half-hour later, laying aside all morning plans for a crisp shower, huge breakfast, and leisurely journey home.

Now it was only time for cigarettes and coffee.

Rick and Banner drove a six-wheeled truck, while Tower and Ringo drove one of the company's ten-wheeled oil rerefining rigs.

Over the citizen's band radio, Tower and Ringo cried and moaned and bitched all the way north as the white broken lines of the interstate highway receded behind them. At the neon-lit gasoline stations, road-side rest areas along the interstate, in the glittering, roaring, jumping truck stops, they kept up a plaintive, chanting litany that hammered at Banner until he thought he was standing before the Wailing Wall in Jerusalem. He got tired of listening to it, but then, as everyone else on Channel 19 listened to their sniveling, the truckers began wailing laments too, and he and Rick couldn't help but laugh: it was like listening to country western music. There was nothing they could do about getting out of this particular job, except quit the company, and none of them could afford to do that; none of them.

Weeping, Ringo longed to go home and see his wife Naomi and his three young children: "I ain't seen 'em in two months you know," he screamed at Banner. "My kids don't have an old man," and Banner pitied him, but they were all in the same boat. Tower was totally stinking drunk: along the highway, he had left a broken trail of empty beer cans, like the metaphorical fairy tale Hansel, crying and incoherently mumbling that life was unfair, unfair. Rick drowned his own bellyaching silently and stoically by chainsmoking his own rolled cigarettes. Banner tried to keep up with Rick by smoking filtered Old Golds and found he couldn't do it. Almost in yogic concentration, Rick kept his eyeballs peeled the whole trip for the state highway troopers and listened intently to the citizen's band; he didn't want to be pulled over any time during the long trip north. When Banner took over driving for a while to let Rick rest, Rick would gather his cherished banjo from behind the passenger seat and sing old bluegrass and gospel songs, mumbling in between them, "Another job to go to. Ain't no rest for the workin' mon."

Banner fell introspectively silent as he drove through the night. He was worried about what B.S. Archwood had told him over the telephone. The faint static on Channel 19 filled the cab with its soothing noise. Every once in a while, he heard two truckers shout greetings to one another, only then to fade out into the reassuring static as the distance increased and they fell out of range. The only lights during the nighttime were the truck's cutting headlamps, with the white center strip of the interstate highway gliding by him like a discontinuous linear function in calculus; the green interstate highway signs and illuminated uphill mileage markers; the green, blue, and white numbers across the dashboard, the citizen's band and A.M.F.M. radios; the red glow of his unseen cigarettes, and the stars surrounding him from horizon to horizon.

The cloverleaf intersections and towns flickered by in rhapsodies of color, only then to be swallowed in the overwhelming, lonely darkness.

Night turned into day into night again as they raced northward, stopping only for gasoline, breakfast and supper, and 10-100s along the interstate highway.

The weather had changed viciously when they plowed through the mountains on I-75 south of Chattanooga, Tennessee. It was snowing like hell in the mountains, blizzards and gusting winds that terrorized them all, especially Tower and Ringo as they kept mourning for their mortality, the snow and wind turning everything around them into pure whiteness. "Gawd*damn*, turn the *heat* on in this friggin' truck," Banner chattered, as the white, blinding snowstorm screamed and howled at them through busy Tennessee and all of Kentucky to Cincinnati, where it turned into a cold, miserable, sharply windy rain. They were freezing by the time they finally pulled into the sleeping town four hours later.

It was 0500 hours when they parked the overworked trucks on the deserted main street, leaving them idling asthmatically; the wind buffeting. The nighttime pristine air and cold heavy rain made everything shine and shimmer on the pavement. A small, cramped diner wedged between a general hardware store and a Christian bookstore was miraculously open, its red neon SORRY WE'RE OPEN sign buzzing on and off. The four men ran inside and sat hunched and frozen at the counter and ordered coffee right away. Banner nearly gagged from the overpowering stench of the cooking grease that permeated the air. Tower mumbled, "I want a waitress to go with nothing on her," and belched loudly. Banner shook his head. They were tired and mean-tempered, all of them drained from being on the road and lack of sleep, knowing they had finally made it. Banner's eyeballs ached and his face felt tight and cold. He couldn't believe the change of weather from south to north.

Two grizzled old farmers who sat at a small table behind them kept staring at the scruffy-looking crew, one of them peering over the top of a local newspaper that he held.

Tower kept slipping off the stool; Banner had to grab him by his jacket to keep him upright. It was hotter than hell inside the diner. Banner couldn't see a thing with his glasses fogging from the heat. They ordered breakfast, all of them wanting steak and eggs, hashed browns, orange juice—tomato juice for Tower—sourdough toast, glazed doughnuts, and coffee. Banner ordered his medium well and scrambled.

The waitress, who doubled as the cook, poured their coffee and served the doughnuts and juices. Rick and Ringo wolfed down six doughnuts apiece before the breakfasts were served, keeping the young woman on her toes and slightly frazzled from their incessant demands of more. Banner silently drank his coffee and watched her ass. She finally finished cooking the food and served the steaming hot plates on the counter in front of them. They tore into their meals and ate like starving animals.

Except Tower: he had had his eggs cooked "frogeyes." He took a woeful, basset-hound look at them and then stumbled out the door, where they all heard him barfing painfully on the wet sidewalk.

Ringo began laughing loudly, almost hysterically, in a high shrill "hee hee hee hee hee."

Banner said loudly, deadpanned, "What a crew. What a fucking crew," and shook his head sadly.

The waitress, who had gone to the door and was helplessly watching Tower upchuck, gasped at Banner, a look of outraged indignation stamped upon her face.

Banner looked at her with raised eyebrows and lamentedly exclaimed, "Oh, excuse my terrible participles," a maddened and nerve-tired glint in his eyes and his voice, while Rick and Ringo laughed and laughed, and laughed even harder each time they heard Tower.

They suddenly stopped laughing when they saw Banner hungrily eyeball Tower's uneaten breakfast. The steak sat on the plate, floating in its red juices and staring at him, beckoning him like one of the sirens of Lorelei to savor the tender meat. Tower had no use for it. When he grabbed the plate, Rick and Ringo as if on cue reached over and attacked the food, scraping the food on to their plates, but Banner had stabbed the steak with his fork, declaring it as his own. "That's mine." They left Tower's plate almost spotlessly clean. They then finished gobbling the food, even picking up crumbs from the counter and wiping their faces afterwards. They groaned and belched contentedly, gulping down last cups of coffee and sucking on toothpicks.

They paid for the meals. Banner stoically paid for Tower's uneaten breakfast; he would get it out of him later. He had had his battered thermos filled with hot, strong, black coffee—no cream, no sugar—with steam boiling out the top: just the way he liked it. It had to keep him going for the next unknown hours: you never knew how long it was going to be before the next meal, especially when you were out in the field.

He heard one of the farmers mutter disgustedly, "Sweet Jesus Christ," as he stepped out into the cold sheeting rain and Tower's undigested beers, and nearly lost his footing.

"Gawddamn it, Tower!" Banner yelled, shaking his foot over a prone and still dry heaving Tower, puke spattering everywhere. "Jesus Christ!"

Rick and Ringo were bent over against the building, holding their sides in hysterical laughter. They were too tired to think straight; been on the road too long. In the rain, above the buffeting wind: "You know where we're goin'?" Ringo shrilly asked.

"Yeah. B.S. gave me the directions. Jesus *Gawd*, Tower, oh foul, *foul!* Can't even *hold* ya gawddamned liquor!"

"Who's gonna meet us there?" Ringo asked, still laughing.

"Somebody from the utility, I reckon," Banner answered, disgustedly looking at Tower and his slimy boot. "B.S. and Sammy are gonna be there, too. They'll probably be up here with a couple of the other guys. You animals ready?"

"Yeah."

"Sure."

A weak grunt from a pale and shaking Tower, who managed to stand on wobbling legs.

They climbed into the trucks, all of them soaked from the rain.

Banner sat heavily in the passenger seat, shivering inside his jacket. Muttering lowly, "Christ, can you believe it, all over my friggin' shoe," cleaning his boot with a dirty, oily rag he picked up off the floor.

"Heh heh heh heh," Rick snickered, and revved the engine. "What're we gonna do on this job?" he asked. "B.S. say?" He was hunched inside his jacket too, rubbing his hands vigorously and yawning, aware bloodshot blue eyes staring at Banner. He wore his customary garb: jeans, flannel shirt, black leather jacket, motorcycle boots, and small woolen brown cap over his thick, long-braided hair.

Banner shook out a cigarette and lit it with his Zippo, inhaling the smoke slowly through his nose. He shrugged finally: "Don't know," he lied smoothly. "All B.S. did was give me the directions to get to the substation. I could hardly get a word in edgewise."

"Mm-huh," Rick said slowly, reaching inside his jacket and pulling out a small sack of tobacco. "Well, you don't mind waitin' a few minutes, do you? I just ain't ready yet to bust my testicles." He then took his sweet time rolling the entire contents in deliberate concentration as Banner shivered and wearily watched him and the hard rain and cold wind.

The truck's heater made him sleepy. The cigarette burned to the filter.

For ten minutes, while Rick rolled the tobacco into almost perfect cigarette form and put each one inside a crumpled cigarette pack— "Christ, will ya *listen* to that poor slob," Banner yelled at Rick—Tower was drunkenly screaming over the citizen's band radio what the hell was taking so long. Rick grinned deliberately through the diatribe; he didn't like Tower much. Ignoring the sotted, streaming outbursts, Banner asked, "How many ya got there? Enough to last ya for a while?"

"Yeah, until the next time, mon. Ah got plenty."

"Well then. You all ready to go?"

"Sure," Rick said, grinning mirthlessly. He lit the last cigarette he rolled, inhaled deep and hard. The aroma penetrated the darkened cab. Wordlessly he gave Banner the full, crumpled pack, who shook out one, then returned the pack.

"Okay," Banner said. He accepted the truck's lighter from Rick, sucked the rich smoke into his lungs and then handed the lighter back to Rick. He let the smoke slowly out through his nose, watching it flare gently out in a great cloud all around him. Then he wearily grabbed the citizen's band microphone from the truck's dashboard. "Let's get going," he drawled over the radio.

"It's about fucking time," Tower screamed back at him.

"I'm just a hair over pissed off, Tower," Banner calmly said into the microphone. "You owe me two ninety-five for breakfast and a new pair of boots."

Forty minutes later, after driving around lost in the rain for 30 of them, they finally arrived at the substation. The high voltage transmission lines had run parallel with the road for three miles when they turned off the major east-west highway to follow them. They drove another three miles on a paved, narrow county highway following the power lines and then found the darkened, imposing old switchyard, 500 feet long and 250 feet wide, surrounded by a 10-foot-high wire-meshed fence and topped with strung barbed wire all the way round the perimeter. Part of the transmission lines branched off a darkly-silhouetted Blaw Knox-designed line tower and entered into the substation. The rest of the transmission lines continued to parallel the road beyond the substation, the tall steel, single-circuited tangent suspension corset-typed towers standing like straight, silent soldiers in formation, the cables sagging in a perfectly wide catenary between each tower.

They found the entrance gate already wide open. The signs that stated

DANGER
NO TRESPASSING
HIGH VOLTAGE

and

ENTRY LIMITED
TO AUTHORIZED PERSONNEL
ONLY

on the gate looked as if it had only recently been shot full of holes.

"What the fuck is going *on* here?" Rick asked, surprised.

"I don't know," Banner answered, frowning and immediately not liking the looks of the surroundings.

Oh boy.

"Drive on in and park by that shed."

It was raining even harder.

3.

The high voltage transmission lines along the Blaw Knox-designed towers continued to crackle and sizzle in the rain.

So here we are, Banner thought, standing motionlessly in the doorway, still watching the empty highway, waiting for a sign of B.S. Archwood.

Somebody farted loudly behind him.

"'Scuse me," Rick drawled. "Steak and eggs."

They had pulled into the switchyard at 0545. No one was around; it was deserted. The shed they occupied was a large storage area. A dozen labeled drums full of 10-c dielectric transformer mineral oil sat in the rear of the shed. Two hot sticks in aluminum tubing leaned into a corner. Two ladders and an old table and four wooden chairs and a dangling fluorescent light over it were in the middle. The light didn't work.

Tower and Ringo sat at the table. Rick leaned against one of the ladders, directly behind Tower, and was watching him intensely. Ringo was stuffing his face with a Dolly Madison cupcake and a cup of lukewarm chocolate (acquired in a battered and dying vending machine at the only gasoline station in the small town).

Tower silently and morosely stared red-eyed at the table; red-headed, long red beard flowing away from his reddened face, wearing two dirty white sweatshirts and denim bib overalls, hunched deeply inside his jacket, hardhat tilted low on his forehead. A useless paper cup of cold coffee with cream and sugar sat on the table in front of him. Banner half-expected fruit flies to be drowned in it. A burning cigarette dangled uselessly from Tower's lips. He looked as if it would take superhuman effort to lift even a 12-inch open-ended adjustable wrench.

Each time it looked like he was going to take a nose-dive into his coffee, Rick slapped his hardhat with his own, jarring him awake with a snarling start.

"You motherfucker Pitts," Tower growled.

"Better watch it, or we'll sick Sammy on ya," Rick warned, laughing. "Asides, ya shoulda remembered what happened to ya in Philadelphia."

Tower groaned, contrite and suddenly miserable.

Banner finally went back to the table, then sat down heavily in one of the chairs. Rick bummed a cigarette from Banner. They sat silently and slowly smoked. The smoke hung inside the shed like the rain outside, thick and dense. Banner sipped his coffee, then lit another cigarette when he was finished with the other one. His throat still felt raw; tired, depressed, he felt as if he were catching a cold. Two, two-and-a-half hours from home: the Bee.

"Jesus, you guys smoke too much," Ringo said, holding his nose.

"Ah totally agree with ya there, Ringo," Rick said. "But Ah do everything in excess. Eat, shit, fuck, smoke, and ain't none of 'em necessarily in 'at order." He shook his head. "And work. Ah work too much too an' ain't gettin' paid very good for it either. Ain't that right, Jackson?" he asked Banner.

Banner sighed resignedly: "Yeah," was all he could muster for the moment. He took a drag on the cigarette. "So you all may as well enjoy life now while you got it. You ain't gonna enjoy it when B.S. shows up." He sipped his coffee, then grimaced at the cup. "You all might as well relax a while before they get here. I don't know what the hell is up, but I don't like the looks of it. There's a dead substation out there for some reason. And I don't know why," he lied. "Jesus, this coffee tastes like it came from the bottom of the pot left on a stove for a week! Christ, it's wretched!" Then he slipped into silence for a while, slowly sipping the coffee anyway.

Beggars can't be choosers.

When he finished the strong burnt coffee, he stood and walked to the doorway again, flicking the butt on to the gravel outside and looking at the rain and the dark substation switchyard. He suddenly realized he was exhausted from the long trip north and the lack of sleep. He just wanted to go home; to get away from it all. Cape Kennedy haunted him; that last, scheduled, final transformer he worked on.

He stared at the switchyard. The first thing he noticed when they had driven inside through the open gate was the sustained silence. It was unnatural; the silence lay heavily in his ears. Only the high voltage transmission lines on the towers were crackling.

The three-phased high voltage lines arched in from one of the Blaw Knox transmission towers and were attached to the dead-ended, arc-horned strain insulators at the top of the interconnected steel-latticed structure. Then the lines came straight down to the buswork on stand-off insulators and were attached to tubular three-phased copper conductors and spanned out parallel lengthwise on the bus side of the switch rack.

Three sets of dead-tank construction primary oil circuit breakers sat side by side, each set containing three individual oil circuit breakers for A, B, and C phases. They were permanently attached to the concrete foundation and coupled together by a lift rod that opened the breakers when they were switched out. On both sides of the primary oil circuit breakers where the lines came down from the buswork to the disconnect switches, all the disconnect switches were opened and locked.

Behind each of the oil circuit breakers a huge silver-painted Westinghouse-designed transformer the size of a two-car garage stood on a concrete foundation also, now silent, the primary and secondary shining insulators jutting authoritatively into the air.

The primary lines ran beneath the opened disconnect switches above the large insulators on the oil circuit breakers to the top of the insulators on the transformers. There they snaked down through the center of the insulators and to the copper windings wound around the iron core inside the transformers. The copper was wound tightly around the iron core, the primary and secondary copper windings not touching each other, but separated by insulating washers and spacers, impregnated gums, and wrapped cotton, the copper windings around the laminated core.

(And when electricity was applied, on the primary side of the windings, there existed high voltage and low amperage. The primary winding of voltage and amperage induced itself on to the secondary winding in *a perfect step-down mathematical ratio*, where the voltage was lower and the secondary amperage higher.)

The power lines then rose out of the secondary insulators on the transformers to another part of the steel-latticed structure, an almost exact duplicate of the primary side. Three sets of secondary oil circuit breakers, each silent set with its disconnect switches opened and locked, parallel to the ground, sat across from the respective transformers.

A long, low, white building which Banner figured housed the switchgear differential, circuit, and linear coupler relays, kilowatt, voltage, and amperage meters, and operating handles to open and close the breakers, stood silent, dark, and locked.

Jackson Banner stared at the large switchyard. The substation was dead. There was no electricity flowing through it. It gave him the willies. The silence seemed almost ominous. He heard the wet high voltage transmission lines crackling and buzzing relentlessly at 60-cycles-per-second outside the substation, on the transmission line towers, and on the primary bus. He wondered what had happened, why B.S. Archwood said it was bad.

"Hey, Rick," Banner said enthusiastically. "Let's go outside and look around, see what we got here."

"It's fucking *raining*, mon," Rick answered. "Ah don' wanna get wet."

"We're gonna get wet anyhow when B.S. shows up. And I'm already soaked."

"Okay, mon," Rick drawled. He slapped his hardhat on his head and grinned.

Banner turned and looked at the other two men. "You guys stay here. Don't let Tower go to sleep," he told Ringo. He shook out another cigarette from his pack, stuffed the pack back into the breast pocket of his shirt, zipped his jacket tighter, then lit the cigarette, blowing the smoke into the rain.

"Ah'm ready," Rick said, the grin still on his face, blue eyes wide and reddened from lack of sleep. "Ah'm too tired to care 'bout anything. Let's just go and check the mothers out. So what if Ah get wet."

"Oh yeah," Banner muttered, and he and Rick stepped outside.

4.

The rain felt cold.

The deep-white graveled foundation crunched and shifted beneath their boots. Banner hunched inside his jacket, silently cursing the cold and the rain and the situation he found himself in. They walked warily up to the nearest large transformer. Rick grabbed hold of one of the radiators as Banner read the nameplate information on the large tap changer compartment.

"This big bitch is dead all right," Rick said, scanning the gauges quickly; expertly. "Look," and he pointed to the liquid level gauge, "it's not even readin' low, and the sudden pressure relay device is popped out. *Son*-of-a-bitch."

Banner bent down and immediately looked at the bottom three-inch-diameter drain valve and saw that the plug was gone and the valve handle fully opened. *Shit.* He suddenly noticed a huge oil stain on the rocks, barely discernible from the rain. He inhaled the rich aroma around him, and the dielectric mineral oil seemed to be suspended around and through him. "*Wow*, somebody drained this transformer," Banner said, suddenly awake.

Rick grinned and laughed. "Oh *mon*, we may be in some *trouble*."

Each knew what the other was thinking. They walked to the other two silent transformers and found that they also had been opened and drained, the pressure relay gauges popped out, and the level gauges reading "Low."

"Whaddaya think?" Rick asked.

"I think we're gonna be here either filtering oil, or finding out all of 'em's blown, gotta be taken out of here, and new ones put in," Banner told him matter-of-factly. Inwardly he was angry, because he knew it was going to be a long, strenuous, gut-busting job, especially in the rain, which was soaking him.

Jesus.

"I wonder who drained 'em?" Rick asked somewhat thoughtfully.

Banner shrugged and sighed, feeling the rain. "Kids, maybe, but I kind of doubt it," he said. "I think it's somebody wanting to sabotage the sub. Look at them bullet holes in those signs when we came in."

They stared at each other.

"Oh, Christ," Rick laughed nervously.

"I don't think the transformers are blown," Banner said. "They woulda probably blew up if somebody pulled out the sudden pressure relays and then opened the valves. Let's go check the breakers," Banner said.

They crunched silently over to the primary gray-painted cylindrical oil-filled tanks, noting that the oil-float level gauges indicated oil in all three single-phased tanks. Two three-foot-high red porcelain insulators jutted out of each breaker. On the side of the breakers on top of the manual operating cabinet, a semaphore was positioned behind green glass, indicating that the breaker had been tripped open. The secondary oil circuit breakers were smaller than the primary ones, and they too were filled with the ten-c mineral oil. They had been tripped open also.

"The sub's dead all right," Banner said, pointing to the opened line and bus disconnect switches above them; to the manually-operated brightly-colored red air-break handles in the closed and locked grounded position next to the galvanized columns.

"You got that right," Rick told him, and shook his head, looking around. "Ah'll bet they went out on differential. I think you're right. Whoever did it didn't mess with the breakers. Shit. Well," he said, squinting, looking up into the roiling gray clouds, "there ain't no more use in standin' out here any longer. Let's get the hell outta this rain. Ah don't need to get any more wetter than Ah have to."

Banner grunted and they turned away, heading toward the shed. Banner felt the rain go down the back of his neck, pouring off his hardhat. He was soaked.

"Fuck Ah'm cold," Rick mumbled, shivering inside his jacket.

Banner threw his useless cigarette on the ground. *Busting our asses all the way up here for this*, he thought. He felt in his gut that someone deliberately sabotaged this station.

Jesus, we're in trouble now.

Ringo stood in the doorway to greet them, munching on a Baby Ruth, his pudgy cheeks swelled out like a squirrel storing acorns for the winter. "Where the hell did you get that?" Banner asked him, acting surprised.

"Back in town."

"Christ, don't you ever stop eating?"

"I'm a growing boy!" Ringo declared, clearly enunciating his words, began haw-hawing, looking like a haunting caricature of Captain Kangaroo hiding behind thick-lensed, black-framed glasses that enhanced his myopia.

Tower was still sitting at the table, his long red beard draped over his chest, hardhat down over his eyes, meaty arms folded across his belly. Rick put a finger to his lips, then slapped his wet hardhat over Tower's, splattering raindrops everywhere. "Huh? What?" Tower asked, snorting, startled, coming awake, sitting straight up, eyes the same color as his beard. "You motherfucker Pitts," he grumbled—Rick laughing—and grabbing with shaking hands his cigarette pack.

Ringo said wistfully, still looking outside: "It's sure raining out there."

"Be glad it ain't snow," Rick told him, looking outside with Ringo.

"Why's that? What for?"

"'Cause you're gonna be bustin' your ass out there, Ah do believe."

"Oh yeah?"

"Oh yeah. There ain't no oil in those transformers. Sides that, the pressure devices are popped. The units might be blown, so we might havta replace 'em all." He looked at Banner and winked. "Mebbe that's why B.S. wanted us up here so fast." Banner shrugged.

Tower groaned, listening to Rick.

"Oh my aching gonads," Ringo wailed, sighing loudly. "What did B.S. get us into now?"

"The nameplates say each of 'em holds 2000 gallons of oil, so multiply by three," Banner told him. "If the transformers are still good, and if they bring the other rig, that means vacuum-dehydration, vacuum-filling, changing tons of Fuller's earth, we're gonna *be* here a while. Maybe two or three weeks. Definitely two." He fell silent. "Especially in this friggin' weather."

"Ah, gee," Ringo sniffed forlornly. "And we're gonna be stuck here with Dellasandro?"

"Life's nothin' but one big disappointment after another, huh, Ringo?" Rick asked breezily, but a pinched look was etched upon his sallow face.

"Yeah, it's just full of 'em," Ringo answered rather mournfully, and affectedly stifled a sob. He knew he wouldn't be seeing his wife and kids for a while yet.

"Well, you all may as well enjoy it now while you can, you ain't gonna be pretty soon. Sides that, it looks like somebody *deliberately* opened those bottom valves out there on those big bitches, and drained all the oil out. Somebody has fucked with 'em. Ah think we're gonna be in trouble, Ah jus' know it." Tower groaned again. "Ah got a queasy feelin' 'bout this one." They sat down in a mute state of depression, except Banner, who stood in the open doorway again, gloomily looking at the transformers.

"*Damn* I don't feel like doing anything," he said tiredly. "I got more better things to do than waste my time here filtering oil. For Christ's sakes, we just worked the last two months sixteen hours a day, seven days a week! I didn't even get to go to the ocean!"

"Life's a bitch, Jackson, mon," Rick told him, reached into his shirt pocket, and pulled out one of his homemade cigarettes. Rolling it lovingly between his fingers, he said, "Yeah, just one big disappointment after another. Just grim, heh heh heh. You all know that by now. You know what they all say: 'Tomorrow's a vision, yesterday's a memory, but today is a bitch,'" and he laughed and lit the cigarette.

Banner sighed loudly, then turned and faced the crew. They all looked back at him in tired resignation. "Jesus, the *work* we're gonna be doing."

"Tell me all about it, mon," Rick answered him. "Ah been doin' it a lot longer than you have." There was a long silence as Rick smoked the cigarette. They heard the rain still pounding around them, and loudly on to the shed's roof. "You only been here a coupla years."

Banner grabbed his thermos, and screwed the red plastic cup on top of it. His nerves were shot. He was truly exhausted. "I think I'm gonna sit in the truck for a while and listen to the radio, see if I can hear 'em on the air." He was silent for a moment. "Christ I'm so tired of it all," he said wearily. "I don't know how much more of this I can take. That last transformer down there on the base just about did me in." He shook his head. "Just make sure Tower stays awake."

Banner knew they were all tired, just like him. He knew that this was going to be another long project, almost like the one they had just finished at the space center, and there was going to be another one to do after he was through here. There seemed no end to it; what had he signed up for?

Jackson Banner walked out the door—into the rain—wanting to go home.

The World's Finest Craftsman

1.

February 0330 hours, a year-and-a-half ago

It was a thick black night with no moon. The stars shone brightly against the velvet darkness, pinprick lights that gazed down upon the old earth in all their frozen epic patience of time and grandeur. The air was crisp and cold. Snow lay on the ground, pristine and sparkling white.

Jackson Banner finished his cigarette before he climbed out of his battered Jeep. In front of the huge, dark blue building the old red fire-truck pumper, now converted into an oil rerefining unit that carried 3,000 gallons of 10-c transformer mineral oil, idled loudly. Two of the large white six-wheeled trucks were idling also with their parking lights casting bright reds and yellows upon the snow-covered ground. Plumes of white smoke were billowing out of the exhaust pipes in a constant thick stream, rising and dissipating rapidly in the air. Banner shivered deep in his brown quilt-lined jacket, hardhat in hand and his large thermos in the other.

Above the yellow entry door of the building hung a large rectangular white sign that said in black letters: **THROUGH THIS DOOR PASS THE WORLD'S FINEST CRAFTSMEN**. It always made Banner feel good to see the sign. *We're a breed apart from the others*, he thought.

He opened the entry door and stepped inside; then very nearly stepped back out. "Christ," he muttered. The building had been constructed out of galvanized aluminum, and it was colder inside. Banner felt as if he were inside a meat locker. He saw his exhaled breath virtually hanging in the cold stillness.

The building housed the company's equipment. The office was inside a 60-foot long, 12-foot-wide trailer. A concrete floor had been poured out twenty feet from the side of the building, and the trailer was parked directly next to it. It sat behind the huge sliding entrance door's path all the way to the rear of the inside of the building, leaving enough room for the trucks to go in and out. The rest of the interior was a poured floor of large, loose gravel. There were dozens of 55-gallon drums stacked neatly and tied on pallets the whole length of the rear of the building, most of them full of used rerefined 10-c mineral oil. Against the farthest wall, opposite the trailer side, were the marked drums of the askarels, painted yellow and DANGER PCBs stenciled upon them. They stood in a 20-foot by 20-foot concrete pit with 18-inch-high concrete walls around the perimeter.

On the concrete floor near the entry door between the office trailer and side of the building lay spare parts for the oil filtering equipment that were used on the various projects that came up. Labelled rows of different-sized and -manufactured insulators stood upright, resting between propped horizontal boards. Large short-circuited capacitors stood in rows next to the insulators. Threaded pipe fittings of varying lengths and shapes lay in huge bins. The crews' lockers, an old table with a dangling burned-out fluorescent light that hung from a long extension cord off a ceiling beam, and the portable chemical toilet stood on the concrete foundation towards the rear.

Ropes, ground cables, hot sticks, chains, lengths of extension cord, and wooden ladders hung on the wall. Empty and full nitrogen bottles stood in a roped-off area next to the door, the hoses and fittings hanging on the wall behind the bottles. 200-pound boxes of sacked Fuller's earth lay on pallets behind the trailer, and behind the Fuller's earth were the bags of floor dry absorbent material, and 50 boxes of empty oil sample glass jars. A small brick oven was in the center back of the building. Here the men heated the jars before taking them out on jobs. They washed, dried, then baked and boxed them before each trip.

Sammy Dellasandro's 1963 Corvette was parked away from

everything. It sat next to the front wall, a sheet covering the body of the car. The propane-powered tow motor was parked a few feet away from Dellasandro's car.

The building was still cold.

The only light that emanated inside the unheated building came from the interior of the trailer. Banner stepped hurriedly to the light, slapped his hardhat on his head, opened the door and walked inside, the heat smothering him instantly. His glasses immediately fogged.

Sammy Dellasandro sat behind Archwood's scarred trailer wooden desk, dressed in pressed work pants and neatly pressed brown work shirt, with his brown jacket opened, unzipped, and laundered clean. He had his feet propped up on top of the desk and was leaning backwards in the old oak swivel chair. His hardhat was down low over his face, his long thick, black curly beard bursting out from beneath his hat. His arms were folded across his chest.

Banner shivered as he felt the warmth come back to his body. Another old wooden desk butted up against Archwood's. He sat down behind the desk, took off his glasses and cleaned them with a snot-dried red bandana. After putting them back on, he poured some of the hot black coffee from his thermos into the red plastic cup, the steam boiling up at him, the aroma wafting into his nostrils.

On the wall opposite the desks a huge green board was filled with magnetic tiles. On each white tile was the name of one of the workers. Next to the white tiles were yellow ones, and on these were the names of the cities and towns with the states abbreviated alongside. Red tiles denoted the industrial customers. Light blue tiles designated calendar dates. Banner noted that Rick Pitts and Gordon Short were working at the Coleman Company in Wichita, Kansas, and from there they were to head to Getty Oil in El Dorado. The Fryman brothers were in Knoxville, Tennessee. Leroy Chessan and Ringo were in Pennsylvania, with stops in Maryland, Virginia, West Virginia, and Kentucky before they were scheduled to return. They were going to be out for four weeks. Banner, Dellasandro, Archwood, and Tower were grouped last, with Monesson, Pennsylvania marked on a yellow tile, and the name of the steel mill next to their names.

Banner looked at the date. They were to take oil samples and ratio the turns on 70 transformers, de-energized one at a time, and if any transformer needed oil added, the crew was supposed to take care of it, by rerefining the 10-c mineral oil inside the transformer only once, then move on. Archwood and Dellasandro were to ratio the transformers. Banner was stuck with Tower: they were to draw up the transformer data sheets, take the oil samples, test them, and if any needed topped off and filtered, Banner and Tower were supposed to do it. Work 16-hour days. Banner hoped the job wouldn't last too long. It was figured this Monesson job would last two weeks with four men doing it. Banner figured if he were lucky, all the transformers' oil levels would be normal. But he knew his luck was low and the odds were naturally against him anyway. Steel mills, like other industrial concerns, usually forgot all about their electrical power systems until something happened that needed looked at.

The day before yesterday he had just returned from a week in Detroit, Elkhart, Kankakee, and Chicago. Archwood had told him he was going to Monesson with them because he was short of manpower and they were behind in the work log. They were always behind.

Suddenly, Dellasandro reached and tilted his hardhat back over his head; he looked as if he were surprised to see Banner sitting across from him. "You're a half-hour late, college boy," he sneered. "What's your excuse this time?"

"Where's B.S.?" Banner asked, ignoring Dellasandro's jibe.

"He ain't here neither. And that red-headed juicer is late too. I think them two went out drinkin' last night, and they're probably drunk."

"No doubt," Banner said wearily, and sipped at his coffee.

A suspended hostile silence enveloped the room. Dellasandro stared at him with amused contempt in his steely, mocking eyes. Banner pulled his cigarette pack out of his shirt pocket, dug another Old Gold out and lit it. He brought the smoke through his nose before exhaling it out of his mouth.

"What time is it?" Banner asked a moment later, and in reply, Dellasandro farted loud and long, all the while smiling sweetly at him. "Merciful Jesus!" Banner gagged when the aroma reached out and embraced him. He waved his hands in the foul air. "Holy Christ, Dellasandro, you're rotten through and through. Somethin' must have crawled up your ass and died there the day you were born. Jesus," Banner said disgustedly, and quietly stood, cup and cigarette in his cold hands to Dellasandro's harsh laughter.

He walked back to the laboratory in the next room to get some air.

Here was where he spent his time when he was not on the road. The laboratory was jammed with 10-c and askarel oil samples to be tested, in boxes and inside a huge black metal cabinet against one wall. A small bench had been built to house the test equipment. Shelves above it held the chemical apparatus, the beakers, distilled water, the chemical solutions to mix the oil; small propane tanks for the Bunsen burner; gram weights, and charts and graphs to use when necessary. Maybe a week went by when Banner would do nothing but analyze the oils. He would slowly and methodically analyze each one, sometimes testing an oil sample two or three times just to be sure that the results were correct, then type up a transformer data sheet and list everything that the men had checked off, then pass the sheets to Archwood for his inspection with the preliminary recommendations. The clock on the wall showed

0330, and suddenly Banner felt tired, despite being up and only having had six hours' sleep.

Dellasandro suddenly loomed next to him in the laboratory's darkness. "Well, what time is it, college boy?" he asked.

"3:30," Banner answered.

"Oh yeah? Well Ah'm gonna give 'em five more minutes to show up. If they ain't here then Ah'm gonna leave without 'em. An' you're comin' with me, college boy."

"Thanks a lot. You're all heart."

"Yeah, I know." Dellasandro looked at Banner for a hard moment, then shook his head. "I don't know 'bout you, college boy. A guy with your education workin' here and bustin' your ass for peanuts. I think you're more stupid than the rest of us."

"Tell me about it," Banner said, becoming depressed at the thought of having to work with Dellasandro again. There wasn't any relief in sight. *Where the hell were B.S. and Tower?* Dellasandro just grunted in reply, then turned and stalked out the door and into the cold, slamming the door loudly behind him. Left alone, Banner felt the sudden silence squeezing him.

The only sound inside the trailer was the quietly gurgling water fountain.

2.

Ever since leaving the university, the dean of the Arts and Sciences College wrote to Banner every three months, reminding him he only needed one more course to graduate.

He had left one of the letters in his briefcase and had forgotten all about it until one day he was wearily reminded of it again when Dellasandro began rummaging through the briefcase looking for some transformer data sheets and inadvertently found and read the letter with an undisguised malicious glee.

"Well well well," Dellasandro exclaimed sarcastically to everyone inside the suddenly silent trailer. "We got ourselves a college boy. And the fucker never even graduated. He's just a fuckin' drop out just like the rest of us."

Banner's face flamed in anger and shame as he reached out and grabbed the letter.

"What's the matter, college boy? School too tough for ya? Haw haw haw!" and Banner cursed him savagely. So ever since that day, Dellasandro needled him constantly about being a "washed-out four-eyed college boy who just cou'n't hack it, haw haw haw."

Banner now sighed and took a deep drag on the cigarette. He heard Dellasandro outside, rummaging through the bins of pipe fittings. His incessant sniping about Banner being a "college boy" rankled within him, and he felt disillusioned about the whole experience.

He had dropped out of the university, needing only one more course to study in order to obtain his Bachelor of Science degree in mathematics. There had been a lot of pressure put on him by his immediate family: what are you going to do when you graduate? Do you have a job lined up? How come your grades are so poor? Why are you taking all these courses in philosophy? What good is it going to do you? He didn't know what to do. He majored in mathematics during those four, full, hard years and at the same time was desperately acquiring thirty hours in philosophy, trying to obtain a bachelor of arts degree in that subject. But the end of the four years arrived rather quickly, and his relatives were clamoring for a decision to be made by him.

He had failed ordinary differential equations two times previously and decided to study it again his last spring quarter at school. When he was a first quarter sophomore, he had signed up for the mathematics course, but found that he could not keep up with it because of the other courses he had registered to take: a first course in elementary Russian and Latin, which he studied for two years; the calculus physics of heat and mechanics and subsequent laboratory courses; and another mathematics course—the first rudiments of the theory behind analytic calculus—intermediate real analysis. These other courses demanded a lot of time and energy out of him, and he became hopelessly swamped and ended up drowning in a plethora of numbers and abstract equations run riot, and so he abandoned the ordinary differential equations class.

The second time he had signed up for the same ordinary differential equations course he found himself in the same situation: taking other courses that demanded too much of his time and sucked the energy out of him, and he had to abandon it again. He wanted desperately to learn the subject matter because he was fascinated by the methods of solving the equations, but he had flunked the final examinations because he couldn't properly prepare for them, and it ate into him that he couldn't devote the time to study this art.

That last spring quarter he was a senior in the university, but he did not feel like one. He knew, deep inside, that he was not ready to face the world outside the atmosphere of scholarship, but it had been rapidly approaching him, and he had to take a stand. He didn't know what he wanted to do when he got out. He had felt the same way when he graduated from high school; he grimly registered for the mathematics course and was determined this time to master it.

But the mathematics professor—a short, stocky, muscular, grinning handle-barred mustached man with a heavy German accent and sparkling laughing black eyes—upon the first day of class, distinctly told the hushed and rapt class of 35: "There are two things I do not like . . . hah . . . hah . . . hah. . . . I do not like mathematics majors . . . taking a course in ordinary differential equations . . . when they cannot pass the same course . . . by the same author two times before . . . and I do not like to teach mathematics majors . . . this particular course . . . when . . . to paraphrase Dickens very loosely if I may . . . hah . . . hah . . . hah . . . ordinary differential equations is a far, *far* more important course to the electrical engineering people . . . who now occupy these seats in this classroom."

The class was sheer hell. The professor covered every bit of the material he said he was going to cover. From the first day of class to the last, he copied his notes laboriously from the ever-present papers in his hand to the dusty blackboard in a slow and meticulous scrawl with the chalk squealing in screaming protest. He repeated the scrawl in a chanting monotone, not answering any questions because he did not like to be interrupted; everything was so obvious after all. After filling the blackboard with the painful-looking writing, the professor would go to the other side and in utter silence erase the entire blackboard, with the same fixed frozen smile upon his face, seeming oblivious to the class, then start over again continuing with new material. This strict procedure was carried out rigidly for an hour every day, beginning at four o'clock in the afternoon, five days a week, for ten weeks straight.

Every day the professor assigned forty problems—whether in the textbook or from another—that were to be finished that night and handed in at the next classroom session in ink, all polished and tight, much like the method found in Landau's *Foundations of Analysis*. The professor always diligently graded the homework papers and handed them back to the students the following day.

Most of the students' papers were heavily marked with corrections and annotations, but Banner's never were. There was no remark, no check marks, nothing to be noted that the professor had even looked at the problems, except for the number of points that the professor had given him, which was a correct 40-out-of-40. Banner never really knew if his homework assignments were correct; it confused him.

After the sixth week, he finally asked the professor if the assigned papers were graded correctly, the professor looked at him through those sparkling and laughing eyes and just answered in his thick German accent: "Yes, Mr. Banner, do you have doubts about your own mental ability?"

Banner looked at the smug face of the mathematics professor and suddenly knew what he had to do. It was as if he had just wakened. He knew he understood the subject, and still looking at the professor, said very quietly, "Well then, I don't need this. I can finish it some other time. I already know enough mathematics." Banner left the man's office, which was silent as the man behind his desk, and Banner stepped outside the mathematics building, not looking back.

He finished the rest of his course work in English literature and philosophy that last spring quarter and took all the final examinations, but dropped the ordinary differential equations course for the third time. He had passed every course he took in university during his four years there, but by not finishing, this had lowered his grade-point-average in his major and he knew he would not receive his degree. The last day of school for him—the last day he would reside in Gamertsfelder Hall—he handed in his final examination essay on hermeneutical phenomenology even though he knew that it did not matter now; nothing really did.

"The hell with it," he said aloud. "I'll do it on my own."

When he came back home, he felt burned out, educated but knowing nothing, and he did not know what to do. What now? What was next? He felt oddly displaced, falling nowhere near the standard psychological bell curve of normalcy or insanity. There was nothing to look forward to—no successful career or diploma in hand—with the world poised and ready for him even though he was not. He kissed graduate school goodbye, and realized he would never teach mathematics in a university, nor go back to school for any reason.

He was only 21 years old.

During that same month of June after he had left the university, he received his job back in a franchised restaurant as the only cook on the graveyard shift. The manager was elated that Banner wanted to return because he was doing the cooking himself, and therefore had no chance to chase the waitresses around, trying to seduce them. Banner plied his craft diligently: one didn't need to use the calculus to grill hamburgers or know Russian to read the waitresses' checks dangling on the wheel or use phenomenological reductionism to converse with anyone.

Nothing had changed; the Newtonian outlook of the world still prevailed in the restaurant business. He fed the nighttime people their ghastly, peasant food: the drunks; the lonely and lost souls who prowled the American streets looking for unknown salvation or a warm place to stay; the late-night movie-, theater-, and concert-goers; illicit lovers whispering to each other in the corner booths; teenagers hanging out in the booths too, laughing and chattering and usually stoned on something.

Even the waitresses were the same: eternally harassed and bitter from the suggestive sexual aggressiveness of the male customers; their daily lives torn and wrought with strife over broken marriages, broken families, broken dreams, demanding children, demanding lovers who beat them when drunk; and old junked and rusting cars that usually never ran right and not enough tips to make it through the week for gasoline money.

Banner listened and endured all this with stoic perseverance, usually leaning against the back grill while cooking his French toast for his break and sucking on a toothpick as a waitress sobbed on his shoulder about her endless problems, or listened to the inane chatter of the girls as they created the delicious strawberry pies for the next day.

And all the while he was silent and thought that the whole lot of them—himself included—were nothing but *sudras*. The old philosopher's voice always echoed in Banner's mind: "Man is the measure of all things," and Banner would laugh out loud at the ghostly thought, and the girls would look at him askant.

At four a.m. he cleaned the kitchen counters until they were spotless and shining under the fluorescent lighting to be ready to go for Gertie, the morning cook. He then, perfunctorily, washed all the dishes and the kitchen utensils, heated up and greased the doughnut machine, stoned the grills, emptied out the grease traps and if he had to emptied out all the old grease from the deep fryer vats and heated new ones in, and then finally, achingly, mopped the floors.

Life was a bitch.

He drove to his family home after working all night in the restaurant and was in bed by seven o'clock; his stepfather gone to another ironworking project; his mother still in bed; his younger brother still sleeping off another heavy nocturnal dating session that he had with his girl-friend. Up usually by noon, he ate breakfast and then wearily got out his manual typewriter and pounded out meager résumés and cover letters of his life thus far; and to the telephone directory, where he looked up the names and addresses of different manufacturing firms so he could fill out employment forms. He felt he had to do something more worthwhile than feed people who roamed during the nighttime hours.

After spending a whole day driving around the small city filling out applications and handing in his résumés and listening to the same haughty line everywhere he went, "If we need a person with your particular expertise, we shall give you a call," he would—chilled and weary—go back home to bed and sleep restlessly until an hour before getting ready to go to work again and start the whole process over again. After a while, he figured out what corporations wanted: people who were

21 years old and had 10 years' work experience, and he laughed at the thought. A hundred years ago that may have been true.

At the end of the first week in September, however, he received a telephone call from one of the companies he had applied to, and the man on the telephone identified himself as Algis Jasper III. Banner had an intuition he was going to be hired, no matter what it entailed. Someone had taken notice about him and wanted to have a friendly chat with him about his future. Banner made an appointment with Algis Jasper III for the next day, Saturday, at three p.m.

That Saturday afternoon Banner drove through the small town he had grown up in—through his detached teenage years—and by the manufacturing plant on the western edge of the town near the busy Penn Central railroad tracks to meet Algis Jasper III for his allotted appointment. He noticed for the first time that the plant was a huge, bright, blue-painted three-story building covered in old galvanized aluminum. The name of the company blazed in large white and blue letters amid a scarlet-colored hexagon, the large bold sign painted on the front side of the building. When he pulled on to the coarse, graveled driveway, he saw a few cars in the parking lot. He parked the Jeep near the plain office entrance. Concrete steps led to an oak door surrounded by blue galvanized aluminum.

A young blonde-haired girl, cramped behind an arsenal of secretarial equipment on her desk and seated next to a massive telephone board, turned to him as he entered and asked, "May I help you?"

"I'm here to see a Mr. Algis Jasper," Banner said to her.

She nodded, smiling, and punched a button on the board next to her without even looking at it. "Hello? Mr. Jasper, a young man is here to see you. Just a moment, sir," she said into her tiny headset. She looked up at Banner. "Is your last name Banner?"

"Yes, that's right," Banner answered quickly. "Banner. First name's Jackson."

She smiled pleasantly at him. "I like that name," she murmured to him, then spoke into the headset: "Yes, sir, it's him. Yes, sir." She looked at Banner again. "He'll be with you in a moment, Mr. Banner," she said. "Why don't you have a seat and relax until he gets here?"

"Thanks," Banner said. He sat in one of the hard chairs in the small lobby and immediately noticed framed colored photographs on the wall across from him depicting a sequence of events of a high voltage substation structure under construction. Banner was impressed as he looked at the pictures, the substation taking shape in front of the camera's lens. Another photograph had a large McGraw-Edison transformer sitting on a wooden raft on a river surrounded by a tropical jungle, with three Indonesian natives standing next to it and in front of a tall red-faced mustached man who was leaning on a cane and frowning into the camera. Banner was again silently impressed with the pictures, and he wondered idly what he could possibly do here.

At that moment a tall, elderly gentleman—for gentleman was the first thought that came to Banner's mind—with a thick thatch of white hair, huge walrus mustache, and a mottled, reddened face appeared in the doorway next to the girl's desk. Banner immediately identified this man as the same one in the photograph on the raft, but thirty years older. He was dressed in total white, like an old Kentucky colonel, with a fine gold watch chain hanging in front of his suit, and a small pink carnation in his lapel. He leaned on a cane and peered at Banner nearly a minute before he nodded silently. Banner rose and silently shook the man's finally proffered hand. The old man's hand was still calloused and hard.

"Mr. Banner?" the man asked softly.

"Yes, sir."

"I'm Algis Jasper. Why don't we go to my office where we may have a quiet talk." He had a slow Virginia drawl and southern gentlemanly manners. He turned, said, "Thank you," to the girl behind the desk, and motioned to Banner to follow him.

Banner followed Algis Jasper through an office with partitioned cubicles, each jammed with books, papers, desks, and other assorted paraphernalia. They then came through a darkly paneled hallway. Stopping by a glass door that led out into the brightly lit manufacturing area, Algis Jasper tapped on the glass and said: "This is where the company repairs transformers, and also, mind you, we rewind transformer coils here, and electrically test all the equipment before shipping them out by truck or rail. We rebuild transformers, weld them together where they need it, repair them, refilter the oil in them, *et cetera, et cetera*. It's all interesting work, but you won't be doing any of it here."

Won't?

They continued walking through the hallway. Through an open door after passing the shift foremen's office and engineering pools, they came to a huge warehouse with metal shelves that rose thirty feet in the air, where insulators, gauges, capacitors, and small 75- and 100-k.v.a. transformers lay in crated boxes on pallets. In the middle of the dark and cold warehouse, a 60-foot-long trailer sat in a pit on its wheels, its doors just an inch above the concrete floor that surrounded the trailer.

"Come on in," Jasper said, opening the door for Banner. Banner noticed the different odors that permeated the entire building. The interior of the trailer was cool and fresh, while out in the warehouse the mineral aroma of transformer oil soaked into the wooden walls, floors, and roof of the building. The difference between the inside of the trailer and outside assaulted Banner immediately. It was quiet inside the interior.

Jasper told him: "Let's go to my office. There's no one here right now.

There's a crew working in Barberton today on an emergency call-out, and they'll be working late."

"What happened?"

"Three transformers in an old substation in a cement factory blew up at about two o'clock this morning. We were called up to supply them with a new temporary substation so it would be ready by Monday morning. I got Archwood and Dellasandro, Rick Pitts, and Phil Lazarus working over there. They've been at it since early this morning. They're a good bunch of boys. They might get done tomorrow if everything goes right. They'll be working right through the weekend."

Jasper then walked the length of the crowded trailer and opened the door at the far end. Banner followed him inside. He sat across from Jasper and watched Jasper sit delicately in his high-backed oak swivel chair with his hands resting upon his cane, a twinkling look in his gazing eyes.

Behind Jasper, a poster-sized photograph in a large oak frame depicted a massive transformer—with a conservator tank above the top of one set of tubed radiators and surrounded by a wooden substation structure with another transformer sitting next to it—engulfed in complete hellish flames while pouring oily, thick, black smoke into the sky. The substation structure was also engulfed in flames. The violent picture struck Banner—heart leaping; a thrill down his spine—as it starkly stood out amid the dark-paneled walls of Jasper's office.

Jesus.

Jasper cleared his throat twice in two great harrumphs. "Let me ask you something, Mr. Banner," Jasper drawled slowly in a kind voice. "I was looking through your college transcript and was intrigued by the courses you took. Not many people, I myself included, would probably have had the stamina and patience it takes to go through the material you've covered, believe me when I say this, I never graduated from high school. I see you've dropped out, and I know why since you wrote about it in your cover letter, and now you're looking for something to do. Tell me, do you have plans to finish?"

"Yes, sir," Banner answered. "I don't know when though." He didn't want to think about the university, or the mathematics course right then.

"I see," Jasper said, and looked at a copy of the transcript that lay upon his clean desk, and then pointed to a space on the paper. "There is one course here that you took while in school which absolutely stumps me though. I never learned this, in fact I have no desire for it whatsoever, although my good wife has a propensity toward what I think is a cultural aberration." Algis Jasper chuckled lightly to himself. Banner permitted himself a little smile, too, though not having any idea what the old man was thinking.

"Why, good sir," Algis Jasper harrumphed, "did you take this particular course, Dance 120: The Ballet?" Algis Jasper had looked down at the transcript to squint and read it aloud. He suddenly raised his eyes and his bushy eyebrows leaped up, and looked at Banner. "Did you actually take *ballet* lessons?"

"Yes, sir," Banner answered, suddenly embarrassed. "But I don't see—"

Algis Jasper held up his hand. "Please let me continue, sir." He laid his hand back upon the table and looked at the transcript again. "Even though you only had average grades in school, and I can see why you had average grades, Christ, look at these courses you took. The biological and chemical sciences, and even a few physics courses. You have quite a tremendous background in mathematics and philosophy, and you have had at least six quarters' worth of laboratory analysis in these science courses you took. To tell you the truth, sir, I need a good chemist. But the ballet dancing, this *gawddamn ballet dancing* intrigues me. Why did you take it?"

Jasper looked at Banner, as if trying to figure the young man out.

"Well . . . I wanted to improve my co-ordination," Banner answered as Algis Jasper listened closely, and he knew that he had to give a correct answer to this one: the final examination.

"I was never any good on my feet, so I thought the ballet would help me achieve some sort of balance. I was never very well co-ordinated to go out for any of the high school sports, especially football and basketball. I couldn't go through all the drill routines without messing them up in some sort of way. When I began university, I thought I would enroll in the ballet to see what it could do for me. To see if I could achieve a greater sense of balance."

"Has it?"

"I think so," Banner answered truthfully, looking back at Algis Jasper in the eyes, and thought, *where is all this going?*

"That's interesting, sir, that's very interesting," Algis Jasper stated, smiling slightly and looking pleased with himself. "I like the reason you say you took these lessons. Yes indeed, I like the very idea. It will come in handy, believe me. Very pragmatic of you, very good insight."

"What's that?"

"The ballet lessons. You see, what we do here a great deal of the time in this service division is work inside live high voltage substations. When you find yourself in a substation and working around the live high voltages that you'll encounter in your work, you have to be careful at all times and take your time in doing your work, but doing it at a measured pace. One false move or wrong step you take in a substation and you may lose your life just like *that*," and Jasper slammed the palm of his hand on to the top of the desk loudly, making Banner's mind jump with a thrill that went from his throat to his constricting balls, "and you won't even know it happened."

Jasper stared hard at Banner. Banner was silent.

"Now your ballet lessons will come in handy some day when you take oil samples out of energized pop-top transformers for example. Even so, your ballet will come in handy just even being in a substation when you're surrounded by all the hot buswork and hanging cables. Believe me, you'll want to be careful in substations."

Algis Jasper chuckled. "Well, sir, what do you think so far?"

"Well, I don't know," Banner said. "What exactly do you do in the substations?"

Algis Jasper looked at him for a long moment, with both hands resting upon his cane, gazing at him kindly and with tolerance. The boy, indeed, was going to be "educated." He cleared his throat twice again, then leaned forward.

"We work as the service division of the company whose building we now presently occupy. If there are transformers going out to be installed somewhere, in some factory or a manufacturing outfit or even one of the power companies, we are sent down on the job to electrically test the units themselves, the insulators, the oil, then run our vacuum-dehydration units and bring the dielectric up in the transformers as high as we possibly can, then fire them up when everyone is clear and ready. That's one of the things we do for the company. Most of the time though, we get emergency calls from our customers with bad problems. We then dispatch a crew out to take care of it. It could be anything, and we always have to be prepared for it. Sometimes we'll have to move the transformer out and bring it back here, and install a temporary one in at the same time. It costs a company time and money to be down. That is why we have a good reputation, and an expanding one I might add, because we have all the best available men we need to handle any one of these jobs. But I need more men. We're open for business 24 hours a day here, seven days a week, 365 days a year. We'll go anywhere anytime we're called."

Jasper paused, looking at Banner. "Do you understand, young man?"

"Yes, sir."

"Good. Listen, and I'll tell you where we're headed in all this. This company, with whom I have been associated all my working life and am now part owner, has always put out high quality, rewound and repaired transformers, oil circuit breakers, new switchgear, and our own custom-made capacitor racks and banks. We are proud of our record here. But the service division of this company is still relatively young, it's only being formed into something definite just two years ago. It was formed for the express purpose of assisting the transformer company here, but now we're also involved in servicing industrial companies that are now beginning to realize how important their high voltage electrical equipment is. They usually have no electricians who are qualified to even open the gate of a substation let alone work on a transformer."

Algis Jasper paused another moment, coughed mightily twice into his fist, then settled back into his chair. He laughed softly; once.

"You see, Jackson, what we do here is still virtually in its infancy. There will be a lot of work for you to do here. If you join this organization, you'll be getting in on the ground floor of a fast-moving company, because the service division is going to grow very big in three years. You'll be right in the middle of the transition. We're going to move out of this building and into another, though still tied to the company here. It's going to get big soon. There will always be work here for you. Regardless of lay-offs, recessions, depressions, people will have to have power. This society is based on electricity. This is where it all starts, and industry most of all needs it."

He paused again.

"What do you think, sir?" the old man asked softly. "Would you like to join our band of men and get some work experience in you? Look, you're 21, you just came out of school, but you did make it through for the four years. Nobody can take that away from you. And look at what you accomplished there. You have taken some pragmatic courses to get yourself into an industry. How many students receive an education like this nowadays?"

He leaned forward slightly.

"Let me tell you, son, I always respect a man who wants to get an education. Education does not stop with textbooks in college. Colleges today just try to prepare you to face the world, and they do a pretty lousy job of it if you ask me. If you want to go back to school anytime you work for me, you can go and take as much time as you need to go through it. I'm looking for intelligent, bright, good men with good heads on their shoulders to work for me. You'll learn a lot on this job, believe me. You'll learn about the job but you'll also travel across the country and see how other people earn their keep and how they live. Sir, I think you'd be a damn fool to turn me down."

Algis Jasper sighed softly, then continued: "There's only one hitch to the whole thing. You'll be coming up just like everyone else, right at the ground floor. Just because you came out of college doesn't mean you start ahead of everyone else. You don't. I can only offer you, like everyone else who starts here, three dollars an hour, all the overtime you can handle, and an expense account of 100 dollars a week. That's three dollars for breakfast and lunch, and seven for dinner. You're allowed 13 dollars a day for meals. I'm going to increase that amount in the future. At the end of the first month, we check on your progress and give you a quarter extra per hour. End of the second month, you'll receive an American Express card in your name and the company's, two gasoline credit cards, and a telephone credit card. Then each year thereafter we negotiate on wages, man-to-man. There's no union here. I realize the wages aren't that great yet, but you can and will be able to move up quickly in this organization. I have a suspicion that Archwood is going to make you a crew leader in a little while. You're the first one we hired off the street, you know. All the rest of the men came from within the company, out there, in the shop. I keep hearing stories to the effect that it's a great honor to be in this service division. If it is, then I want to congratulate you in case you join up."

Algis Jasper looked at Banner with raised eyebrows, and again offered his right hand. Banner knew that the old man had snagged himself a new employee, like a dancing bass hooked on the end of a fishing line.

Monday morning Jackson Banner found himself in the trailer with the other workers. They all sized him up silently. B.S. Archwood sat behind his desk, looking worn and haggard, an old railroad engineer's hat covering his long blonde hair, a cup of cream-colored coffee in one hand and lit cigarette in the other.

He took one look at Banner and asked, in a tenor's voice: "You Banner?"

Banner nodded.

"Follow me. Rick, you too," and Archwood got up and walked outside into the warehouse, carrying the coffee with him as Banner and Rick Pitts followed.

"You have to know something," Archwood told him in the middle of the warehouse, stopping in a deserted aisle and facing Banner. Rick stood silently next to him. "We're known as the 'Green Berets' of the power companies around here. We usually end up doin' the work that our other competitors refuse to do, and especially the power companies. If something's never been done before, believe me, Banner, this service division is gonna find a way to do it. We're given the impossible ones and we take 'em because of the challenge, plus it'll always give us more information if we ever run across a similar problem like it, plus we make a hell of a lotta money on the impossible jobs."

Archwood looked at Banner, searching his face.

"You gotta lot to learn, and not too much time to get it. I'm gonna let Rick show you around, learn the ropes. We all just got back a couple hours ago from Barberton, and we're all tired as hell, so we ain't gonna be doin' too much today. Right now, I'll leave you in Rick's hands."

Rick nodded, grinning, tapped Banner on his shoulder, and they left Archwood without saying a word. Banner didn't know what to think.

During the first week of his new employment, he and Rick wandered through the company's transformer yard, picked out large transformers with their primary and secondary insulators still attached, climbed them, short-circuited the phases on the insulators, then ran through a variety of electrical tests. Banner learned how to use the test equipment and interpret the data by flipping through the manuals that Rick provided. He learned how to inspect a transformer, to identify the many parts and the functions of each, and learned how it operated.

Banner was shown how to draw mineral oil samples out of the transformers. He learned how to retrieve the dense, highly aromatic and toxic askarels out of the sample taps of askarel-filled transformers, being very careful not to get any of the polychlorinated biphenyl molecules on the ground or on his skin, Gawd forbid if such a thing happened; your skin burned with an invisible fire. In an hour's time, the American Standards and Testing Materials procedures for analyzing the 10-c mineral oils and askarels were outlined to him. He thus performed the tests, utilizing the techniques he remembered from the laboratory courses he had taken in school: color, sludge, viscosity, specific gravity, specific resistivity, dielectric, acid neutralization, and interfacial tension.

During that first introductory week, he was shown—while actually on a job in an old energized high voltage substation inside the middle of a roaring, dirty, drop forge foundry—what to do to prepare a live, humming transformer for oil rerefining. And while there, there was the ever-present thought that the substation was live: the old transformer still energized and literally hot from the heavy load demand of the drop forge's machinery, its' old dirty insulators and cables energized, the whole unit continually humming at 60-cycles-per-second, looking benevolent, no moving parts but actually "alive," and potentially fatal if he came into contact with the exposed parts that carried the high voltage electricity.

"Electricity is like Gawd, mon," Rick Pitts told him, grinning. "Omnipresent, it's ever'where in space. Invisible, 'cause it can't be seen. Omnipotent, 'cause Ah been jolted before with four-eighty an' Ah *know* what power is. Think about it awhile. It's the Ark of the Covenant."

Banner soon found out.

He realized that working at the drop forge foundry was nearly the same in every other industrial firm he found himself in. He found out, during his first six months of employment with the company—throughout the cities and towns in America—that most of the work he performed was long, physically demanding, and requiring such mental awareness that he was left utterly exhausted at the end of a working day. Working in the energized substations took a lot out of him, especially staying alert in the face of exposed copper buswork in transformer vaults or outside in old substations near dangling copper cables. The knowledge that the high voltage substations were live and operating the instant he worked on the equipment was always on his mind, knowing he had to be totally aware of it at all times. He did not ever want to feel what alternating current was like.

And here he was, who took on the jobs no one else wanted because it was too dangerous—working on energized high voltage equipment—risking his own life because he never knew what condition the high voltage substation equipment was in when he came upon them. His work, too, was always full of surprises, and he always had to be ready for anything. The adrenalin flowed, the senses were heightened, the danger always invisibly there, staring you in the face: it was the romance of the job he liked, the anticipating thrill of being around the live, humming, raw, controlled fire of electricity, working on the equipment while it sang around him, knowing that no mistakes were allowed, just perfection the first time around.

All his moves had to be true.

He found *samadhi*.

Like this: taking oil samples out of the rounded tops of 75-k.v.a. single-phase transformers, one transformer at a time, and there are nine transformers that form the substation, with bare copper conductors spanning from wooden poles, ringing the transformers, hanging eye- and waist-level, branching off and attached to the high voltage insulators. It is a real nightmare: you are the fly amid the web of energized lines, and the spider of electricity was always there waiting to get you.

The rounded lids of the transformers are each held down by a large metal ring that is sealed also to the rounded tanks. They are each joined together by a long-threaded bolt, flat washer, and hexagonal nut screwed tightly against the ends of the open ring. The primary 480-volt insulators are white, but the years' accumulation of grime from the industrial firm has turned them almost brown in color. They are energized. All the transformers are energized, all humming loudly in rhythmic frequency, nearly a chant, each of them used to light the interior of the factory. The insulators stick out just below the rings.

With gentleness, being meticulous and with bated breath, you perform a *pas seul*, your mind concentrating upon the task at hand. The first transformer: holding finger against the washer, gently unscrew the bolt, loosening the ring. The screwdriver, taped from the handle to the last sixteenth-of-an-inch of the straight edge, is inserted and gently but forcefully rotated counterclockwise. While you do this, you also watch the ring and insulators out of the corner of your eye. Ease the bolt straight out and away from the transformer and grab with two fingers the washer and flat washer in a tight grip and gently step away in a half *glissade* from the transformer. You do not want to drop the pieces on to the insulators, Gawd forbid. You put the bolt, flat washer, and nut back together and pocket it.

Then, wearing dielectrically-tested lineman's rubber gloves for hot electrical work, you pry away the stuck ring from the transformer. It suddenly pops up—*Jesus Christ*—and you catch and hold it clumsily and tightly frozen in the air, and look at the humming transformer. The lid did not move, and you did not strike the insulators prying the lid away. *Wow.* You lay the ring on the ground in a *plié*, straighten up in the second position, where your working foot is naturally extended to the side, just like you were taught in ballet, and gulp in a great breath of air.

Your partner just grins at you.

Then you take an oil sample bottle and give it to your partner, who you know is glad you're doing all the work and not him. Ready for the *pas de deux*, you step over to the transformer, stand between two primary insulators on the rounded tank—again in the second position of the ballet—and careful of the bare copper cables which surround you. Gripping it tightly, you lift the lid slowly and carefully straight above the tank, exposing the energized, humming internal copper windings and iron core beneath clear yellow ten-c mineral oil. You then tell your partner to go ahead and get the sample, but be damned careful, because the transformer is energized, and don't let go of the fucking bottle. Your partner slowly dips the bottle into the top of the oil and brings it up three-quarters full, which is good enough as far as you're concerned, and you put the lid back down over the exposed tank, carefully, making sure you do not get near the insulators. You then proceed to return the ring to its rightful place and bolt it tightly against the transformer's lid and tank, at all times concentrating your mind one step at a time on the project at hand and remembering that the transformer you are working on is energized and humming loudly in musical monotone, so keep your tools and your hands away from the gawddamned insulators.

Now there are eight more transformers to do, just like this one.

Indeed yes: dance maneuvers had to be played out while working in a live high voltage substation. Electricity always flowed through the path of least resistance, and he sure didn't want anything to come between him and ground; 1/10th of one ampere of electricity across a person's chest was enough to kill, stopping the heart. Banner understood why Algis Jasper had hired him: not for his mathematical expertise, or his other college courses, but for his knowledge of the ballet.

The ballet lessons came in mighty handy; yes, indeed.

Like this: performing another *pas seul*, crawling on your belly, with your face pressed to the ground, hardhat trying to slide off, your body squeezing between an old grimy brick building and a bank of energized, single-phase transformers hooked up for three-phase operation. You reach ahead with a pair of channel lock pliers in one fist, a quart glass sample bottle in the other to drain oil from the transformers so later you'll be able to perform the A.S.T.M. tests upon the oil in the warm security of the laboratory. Then you crawl to the next transformer, your hands blackening from years' accumulation of dirt and wet, thick, black grime that lay everywhere and upon everything—*hey, do I really need to do this?*—your work clothes absolutely filthy and heavy from the grime, knowing your skin's pores are filled with it, breathing and getting it stuck in your sinuses; then, on top of it all, crunching over old sharp thick glass shards that lay beneath you from the broken windows of the old building above.

There is no way to avoid it.

The bottom drain valves of these particular transformers face the building, the secondary cables running from the insulators and hanging very low to the ground, so old that bare copper wire shows through the frayed and grimy sheathing. Then deliberately you crawl slowly and carefully—your partner telling you to keep your ass down low—beneath the old cables and maneuver slowly into a sitting position, eyeballs oscillating back and forth, not moving your head, watching where you put your hands, arms, legs, shoulders, checking yourself out.

Ballet lessons indeed.

You sit between the humming, uncaring transformers, your back against the blackened brick-roughened wall, resting your ass gingerly upon the broken glass, your knees to your chin, knowing not to move unnecessarily, watching where you are. Now you begin to understand how a soldier feels in combat with unseen danger lurking about, waiting to get you. You look at the gauges on the transformers and the nameplates if you possibly can, dictating the information to your partner, who stands and watches you on the other side of the transformers, hoping you won't fuck up.

Or—and this one they promoted him as a crew leader afterwards—like this: in a West Virginia chemical refinery on the Ohio River, with the raw smells of benzene compounds percolating through the air, the engineers there had tried unsuccessfully to get the major electric power companies to come and obtain six askarel samples located in a deep dark, long water-filled tunnel that usually was filled with chlorine gas. The service division of the electric companies absolutely refused to do it. Meanwhile, the Environmental Protection Agency in Washington, D.C. was throwing a tantrum for information and analysis, and as a last resort B.S. Archwood was finally contacted and he gave Banner the job, telling him only to collect the six askarel samples and not to come back without them.

Banner drove south through Ohio and on into West Virginia the following day not knowing what to expect. When he saw what he had to do, he could see why it was refused. He didn't want to do it either, and silently cursed Archwood for getting him into this mess.

The engineers made him don a skin-tight scuba diving outfit and fitted him with oxygen tanks and mask, and had ropes secured to clamps that fit around his thin-rubber-gloved wrists. As they lowered him into the dark pit by ladder, he found himself in water up to his knees. He looked around the pit with a flashlight strapped to his hardhat, the only light that existed in the depths. He found six 250-k.v.a. transformers sitting closely side by side along a wall on a concrete pad, three feet above the water.

Open copper buswork lay exposed all around him though well above the water against the walls and—*oh my Gawd*—he was standing on sheathed, live 25,000-volt cables that ran to the transformers. No wonder the service divisions of the electric power companies told the chemical refinery's engineers to go pound sand.

It so happened that there had been no chlorine gas in the pit that particular day, but the refinery's engineers took no chances, even as they monitored the pit. Banner left the suit, the gloves, the oxygen bottles, and mask on anyway. He didn't want to take any chances either.

He gingerly stepped off the power cables, wondering who the hell designed this place. It took him nearly an hour to retrieve the oil samples, inspect as best he could the leaky, sticky-sided transformers (in which he thanked God that he didn't have to breathe the foul odors of the dielectric chemical this time), and record the data off the nameplates and gauges. He knew full well these transformers, though in need of maintenance, could never be repaired sanely. Meanwhile, he took very great care in not screwing up and being fried in the water from accidentally bumping into the exposed buswork or any part of the conductors on the transformers. Lord only knows all he needed was to have the oxygen tanks touch the hot copper bus.

Ballet lessons indeed.

From this impressive performance, as the memorandum written by the refinery's engineers went up the chain-of-command stated, the service division received all the contractual work from the headquarters of the chemical refinery. There were three other large refineries in three other states, plus other divisions scattered throughout the northeast sector of the country. Algis Jasper III was absolutely delighted by the good news. Archwood came up to Banner when he arrived back at the shop and asked him how he did the job, questioned him in detail about it—Dellasandro had stood by Archwood's side, silently brooding and ominous—then told Banner that he was a damned fool for trying such a stunt, but congratulated him anyway for a job well done. Archwood then and there decided to make Banner a crew leader.

Banner shrugged, said, "Okay, great," and received a dollar-an-hour raise from the company. He was then earning $4.25 an hour, and the rest of the men considered him a "Green Beret."

3. February 0335 hours

Where has all the time gone? Banner thought to himself, standing in the laboratory. This particular job in February he had to work with Archwood and Dellasandro, and it wasn't going to be pleasant with Tower along. The clock on the wall read 3:35. He took a deep drag on his cigarette, then slowly and smoothly exhaled the smoke out his mouth. The trailer door suddenly burst open and Dellasandro poked his bushy, bearded face through. Cold air flowed through the trailer.

"What is it now?" Banner asked sourly.

"Count your lucky stars, college boy," Dellasandro told him, his mocking blue eyes glittering at Banner. "Archwood and your buddy just showed up outside. Let's go," he snarled, then slammed the door.

He never found out that Banner had taken ballet lessons. *Thank God*, Banner thought.

He sighed, then swigged the hot black coffee in three burning gulps, walked over to the desk where he first sat, and recapped his thermos. Did he have everything ready to go on this trip? He slapped all four pockets of his brown pants: keys, change, Zippo, wallet with two hundred dollars, comb, bandana; then checked his shirt pockets: Cross pen and pencil and Old Gold cigarettes. His briefcase was still in the Jeep; he would have to go get it.

The trailer door burst open again next to him, with Archwood stumbling inside and cursing, "Gawddamn it, can't even pick up mah own feet." He saw Banner sitting at the desk and cracked a grin. "Well, I see you're all ready to go." Archwood still looked three sheets to the wind.

"Oh yeah yeah, I'm ready all the time," Banner answered, grinning mirthlessly and lighting another cigarette.

Archwood went over to his desk and began rummaging through the drawers. He looked as if he hadn't had any sleep yet. There were dark circles under his bloodshot green eyes, which accentuated his high hollow cheeks. His shock of blonde hair kept trying to fall over his right eye, and he was forever sweeping it back over his head. "I thought I left them fuckers in my desk," Archwood whined loudly, still plowing rapidly through the clutter.

"What are you looking for?" Banner asked.

"My smokes." Banner watched Archwood dig deeper, then saw his face crack into another grin when he found the pack. He tore off the cellophane, opened the pack, and shook a cigarette out.

Banner reached over with his Zippo and let Archwood bring it to life.

"Thanks," Archwood said, and started coughing from the smoke.

The door flew open and Dellasandro marched into the trailer, a mean look etched upon his dark face, and he glared at Banner. "I just put your buddy in the fire truck. Maybe that'll sober him up while he's driving, haw haw haw." He looked at Archwood and yelled: "You ready to *go*, fireball? Ya got your lungs and your liver and your *balls* back together for this trip?"

"Yeah, yeah, for Christ's sake," Archwood answered impatiently, taking rapid puffs on his cigarette. "Listen, I'm gonna stop at that doughnut shop before we get on the freeway. I'm gonna need a cup of coffee."

"Jesus, that's what ya get for drinkin'," Dellasandro yelled, laughing. "Ah'm gonna go to Shenandoah. Ah'll just meet you girls at the truck stop."

"Well, you just drive slow so I can catch up with ya," Archwood told him. "I'm gonna have Tower stop there too. Ain't no use being fucked up any more than we already are."

"Well, you do what you want, B.S.," Dellasandro said. "Ah'll meet you down there. College boy, you follow me," thumping Banner on his hardhat.

Ouch.

As Dellasandro stepped out of the trailer, Archwood yelled out, "You do only the speed limit until I catch up with ya, ya got it?" and shook his head when the door slammed shut. He and Banner looked at each other in silence. "Go on, get outta here, Jackson," Archwood said quietly. "We'll catch ya in no time."

"Whatever," Banner answered tiredly. It was going to be a long and harrowing four-hour trip. He just knew it. He hoped Archwood and Dellasandro roomed together. He sure didn't feel like sharing a room with Dellasandro.

The air was still crisp and cold when he stepped outside. The stars still shone: majestic, proud, and so damned uncaring. The front six-wheeled truck was idling hard, the smoke billowing rapidly out of the exhaust pipe. Banner caught a glimpse of Tower slumped over the steering wheel inside the old red pumper truck, his head buried in his folded arms. Banner shook his head.

Jesus.

He opened the passenger door to the second six-wheeled truck and put his thermos and hardhat on the floor between the seats. Leaving the door open, he walked over to the Jeep and dug his black briefcase out of the back seat; then locked it. He put it on the passenger seat of the truck, shut the door, then walked around and climbed in behind the wheel. He immediately turned on the heater, the headlights, the citizen's band radio, and the interior cab light that dazzled his eyes relentlessly.

"You ready, college boy?" Dellasandro's cold voice suddenly crackled over the citizen's band; then the static hissed on the frequency.

Banner grabbed the microphone, squelched the volume and answered, "Just wait a minute."

"Whaddaya think this is, tea time?" Dellasandro's voice crackled back at him. "Let's go."

"Then go on," Banner answered flatly. "I'll be with you in a minute." He put the microphone back on to a magnetic hook on the dashboard. The bright brake lights on Dellasandro's truck still shone loudly on to Banner's face. Everything inside the cab had a red glow. Banner shivered as the warmth from the heater finally filled the interior. He reached inside his jacket and pulled out his cigarettes, knowing he was going to smoke them on the way. Then he picked up the thermos, poured another cup of coffee into the hard plastic cup, and set it on the motor mount beside his road atlas. The steam wafted wispily upwards. The citizen's band radio was still hissing.

He looked at the briefcase. He couldn't remember if he had put the book inside. He unzipped the whole perimeter of the briefcase, then flopped it open. A battered and well-thumbed Spiegel's *Applied Differential Equations* in the second edition lay on top of a loose ream of yellow-lined paper which was filled with Frobenius-type equations. He was now studying it again on his own, and doing it at his own pace. He was determined to get his degree. He flopped the briefcase closed and zipped it shut.

Jackson Banner picked up the microphone again, killed the interior cab light, and then spoke into the microphone, squelching the static: "I'm ready now. Let's go," and put the microphone back on the dashboard.

"Yeah," Dellasandro's voice crackled back at him. "Let's go."

Cigarettes and Coffee
Part II

1.

The six-wheeled truck was parked next to the shed, its deep, dark blue color glowing bright through the rain amid the dreary grayish landscape, the company logo glaring out at Jackson Banner in a bright yellow background and large blue lettering on the back door and sides. A huge, muscular, bronzed arm with a powerfully clenched fist taming three long snaking bolts of lightning adorned the rear sliding door of the truck, painted on by Rick Pitts a year previously.

Banner climbed into the cab behind the leather-covered steering wheel—turned the ignition's key to listen to the citizen's band radio; turned the windshield wipers on once to wipe away the rain—and slumped back against the seat and silently watched the rain spatter rapidly back on to the windshield. He felt exhausted from the long trip and lack of sleep.

It was cold inside the cab. He felt colder after being out in the rain while exploring the substation. It was coming down hard and the mist from the rain chilled the early morning air. Listening to the downpour made him sleepy, but the static and faint tones emanating from the citizen's band sounded like bizarre electronic music that kept his nerves on edge.

He couldn't get that last transformer out of his mind.

The company, after many long months of bidding and compromise, had wrangled the contract to perform work at the Cape Kennedy Space Center. It was during the time before the Space Shuttle program began in earnest. Half of the high voltage electrical power system grid on the base had been shut down, out of service since the end of the Apollo program. With the new Space Shuttle program coming up, the engineers put out the bids to test and restart the system. The electrical power grid was fairly large, and the work involved started with testing the large

Westinghouse-designed transformers and oil circuit breakers within the two huge main switchyards, then moving on to test the equipment in the double-ended distribution substations scattered over the base.

Banner and Rick ended up in the Vehicle Assembly Building, the headquarters' building, the central instrumentation facility, the operations and checkout and flight crew training buildings, Pad A at Launch Complex 39, isolated radar sites, and other outlying areas on the base. They tested every transformer and took oil samples, and wrote up the reports every day for the company and the N.A.S.A. engineers. All this was preliminary before the actual work. When the reports were analyzed, the space center presented a list of the transformers to be refurbished. B.S. Archwood sent Banner and Rick down south again to work on the 50 askarel-filled transformers that needed to be rerefined. Tower and Ringo had the other job of working in the two main substations.

The contract stated that the askarel rerefining work would be done while the transformers were still energized: on-line. Banner didn't like working with askarel—no one in the company did—but Archwood thought he and Rick were the company's best workers to handle the harsh chemical.

"Good luck," Archwood told them. "Be careful. Don't fuck up," giving the two young men that look of his. "I want at least a transformer done a day."

Banner didn't like filtering transformers while they were on-line anyway, but he especially didn't like rerefining energized askarel-filled transformers. It was too dangerous, but the company already had the reputation of working on these types of live high voltage transformers with no interruption of electrical service, and word spread throughout industry.

All the transformers at the Cape were still hooked live into the electrical distribution grid of 17,000 volts.

A lot of time and effort went into filtering a transformer of this type. Most of the time was spent getting to the indoor substations and setting up the rerefining system. Plastic sheeting was laid upon the concrete foundation surrounding the transformer and the pumps and motors lay hooked together by the oil hoses upon the sheeting. Full drums of askarel had to be brought to the site (sometimes they were on the 16th floor of the Vehicle Assembly Building one day and the 24th the next) and used to preload the portable rerefining equipment with the toxic dielectric fluid, and usually to top off the energized transformer to the "High" level marked on the liquid level gauge. Aprons, goggles, rubber gloves, and respirators were worn when handling the equipment. A half-hour later they were finally ready to begin the process.

Askarel was the trademark name given to a nonflammable dielectric fluid and was an excellent insulator as it had a high resistance to acids, oxidation processes and bases. It was molecularly made up of trichlorobenzenes and highly chlorinated biphenyls, with glycidyl phenyl ether and 3,4-epoxycyclohexylmethyl-3, 4-epoxycyclohexane carboxylate as the stabilizing compounds. These compounds under tremendous heat produced highly distinctive aromatic hydrocarbons.

Since the basic structure of askarel was a pentachlorobiphenyl molecule—the dreaded P.C.B.s—hydrochloric acids were produced when a transformer filled with this dielectric was under load. This was one of the reasons why Banner despised working with this chemical and was leery of it, as his skin would feel as if it were on fire, invisibly burning, for days afterwards if he wasn't careful in handling it.

It also weighed nearly 13 pounds per gallon, and lugging the equipment hither and yon through industrial areas took up a lot of time and energy. Usually, you were already damned exhausted even before starting the filtering process. Because the chemical was six pounds heavier than water, to filter this type of transformer, you had to pull the contaminants from the top of the fluid, through the filtration system, and push the refined chemical through the bottom valve. (It was just the opposite for 10-c mineral oil.) It wasn't so bad if the transformer was de-energized, as sometimes was the case, because then you didn't have to worry about getting air bubbles up through the iron core and copper coils and causing the transformer to fail. It was when the transformer was still on-the-line, pushing hundreds or thousands of volts and amperes through themselves, that you had to be careful.

Banner and Rick took two full months to complete this aspect of the job at the Cape Kennedy Space Center and had not deviated from the set-up or filtering process. It was a bright sun shining morning that last day on the job (for Tower and Ringo had finally finished in the two main substations) and already they had congratulated each other on a job well done. Banner had everything hooked up correctly to the transformer—an energized 17,000-primary-volt Esco unit with an enclosed primary and secondary air circuit breaker attached on opposite sides—and routinely gave Rick the go-ahead to start the generator in the truck.

The liquid level gauge on the transformer read "Normal," so they proceeded to fill the transformer to the "High" mark. This assured them that plenty of new askarel from a 55-gallon drum which sat in the truck would fill the filtration rerefining system first and then the transformer. Banner engaged the electrical start on the filtering system while Rick, still in the truck, stood over the drum of askarel holding one end of a steel pipe connected to a hose as it sucked the chemical out of the drum and in through the filtering system and then to the top valve of the transformer. When the needle reached the "High" mark on the liquid level gauge, Banner shut off the filtering system. He closed the top valve on the transformer, disconnected the hose, held it straight up so no askarel would spill on to the ground and plugged it. Then he took the same hose, lowered it, and unplugging it, quickly attached it to the bottom valve, spilling nearly a thimbleful of the chemical on the plastic sheeting already in place. Rick walked over at the same time holding the end of his plugged hose, then unplugged it and attached it to the top valve of the transformer.

"Gawddamn," Rick drawled. "Ah can hardly buhlieve we almost got this son-of-a-bitch done."

"You said it," Banner answered.

They were both grinning and nearly delirious at finally nearing the finish. This particular transformer had a borderline low dielectric. Two hours on this one, with one change of dry filters, Banner thought, and they'd be through.

"Ready?" Banner asked.

"You bet," Rick answered, smacking his lips and rubbing his gloved hands together, looking at the gauges on the humming transformer.

Banner reopened the top and bottom valves on the transformer, checked that the valves on the filtering system were open, and then turned it on. Two seconds later the transformer failed with a powerful internal explosion, blowing hellish black smoke and intense orange flame through the sides of the attached circuit breakers. On the opposite side, away from them, the long gooseneck pressure relief device blew smoke and fire out simultaneously; then everything came to a stop. The sound of the explosion echoed in the distance.

Both young men stood frozen for an instant, in shock and surprise. Banner's first reaction was to close the transformer valves, while Rick shut off the filtering system. The transformer stood silent three feet away. It had poured electricity in through a large white warehouse facility and two other smaller buildings. Before the explosion Banner heard the hum of conveyor belts and other machinery inside the warehouse. Now there was nothing. The only eerie sound came from the generator. His ears rang.

It had happened so fast that Banner was not prepared for it. He stood against the perimeter fence staring wide-eyed at the transformer. Banner was still in shock; he tried to figure out what went wrong. He always was on the alert for potential hazards and errors and made sure he did everything correctly so nothing like this could happen. But it did.

He saw people stream out of the building, staring and pointing at the two young men. A minute later two fire trucks came roaring up, men hopping out and unreeling hoses. The base security personnel sirened up to them, and leaped out of cars, shotguns and pistols drawn.

"Where's the fire?" one of the firemen shouted, running up to them.

"Ain't one," Rick answered, his voice slightly shaking. Then he laughed once and grinned.

"Well, gawddamn, somebody said there was an explosion here!"

"That's right," Rick said, and pointed at the transformer. "This bitch blew up all right. But there ain't no fire. The motherfuckin' oil saved our gawddamned *lives*, mon."

Paradoxically it was true. No doubt about it, if it had been 10-c dielectric transformer mineral oil instead of askarel, they would have been dead, with smoke and flame and parts of themselves roiling into the clear blue morning sky. 10-c mineral oil burned at 400°; askarel caught fire at 4000°. But the synthetic dielectric oil had saved their lives because the toxic fluid was inherently nonflammable and extinguished the explosion and flame almost instantly. Banner never liked working with the chemical because of the hellish vapors and its burning effects on his flesh and its potential carcinogenic factors, but he came to respect it for what it was.

He found out later why the transformer blew up.

The space center's electrical workers later that same day cut open the welded top of the transformer and found that though Banner and Rick had filled the transformer to what they thought was the "High" level mark they had only filled it to the "Normal" level. The liquid level gauge had given them erroneous information because the cork that floated on the oil had been twisted out of place; there had been no way to know this otherwise. With the gauge pointed to "Normal," it was actually reading "Low." When Banner saw the gauge read "High," the askarel that he filtered in to the transformer was where "Normal" would have been.

After switching the hoses to filter the transformer and restarting the system, the machinery pulled air in through the top hose, through the filtering system (all the while pushing the askarel inside the filtering system itself through the bottom hose and opened transformer valve), until air went shooting through the inside of the transformer, forming massive bubbles up through the energized core, creating a fat spark and resulting explosion, which blew itself out through the circuit breaker cubicles and a 12-foot flame out of the pressure relief device.

It was madness, he finally realized. That night, while listening to the ocean washing along the shore, he realized how dangerous the work he did truly was. He knew all about the hazards involved in high voltage electrical work, and how it was much more so because most of the work done was completed while electricity still flowed through the equipment, and it had to be kept uppermost on one's mind. There were no allowances for error. None. It wasn't worth it; not any more, he thought.

He remembered that initial blast—surprising him to his soul; he thought he was going to die—sounding as if someone had fired a large shotgun directly next to him. It still echoed in his mind. He had felt as if he were suddenly on fire too, a sickening sensation descending through him, senses pulsing with quick adrenalin. It was like being in a dream, not real but actually occurring; like a green soldier in his first battle, the baptism of fire.

It had happened to him once before, and the blast from the transformer brought it back to him in clear and painful memory.

One hot summer night he and the Bee were visiting his parents and they were ready to leave at midnight. Stepping out on the front porch, Banner saw a barn only two houses from them suddenly enveloped in flames. It was on Old Man Martin's property. Banner used to work for Martin when he was a teenager, bailing hay and storing it in the lofts and taking care of the horses Martin had quartered for others.

The barn exploded into hot dry flames and was fully consumed within minutes. Banner ran over to the barn, helpless to do anything, and was surprised to find Old Man Martin in front of the barn door holding two shotguns and two bandoliers of shells, tears and rage streaking his ruddy face. He threw one of the shotguns and a bandolier at Banner and yelled above the roar of the flames: "Horses're on fire an' they're runnin' out the door! Shoot 'em!"

And it was terrifying to see, and he never forgot: flaming horses, roasting live flesh, jammed into the entrance, screaming in pain, twisting and kicking and bellowing in the roar of the engulfing fire. Old Man Martin and Banner discharged the weapons into them, the shotguns loud and ringing in Banner's ears. He was filled with shock and pity at the carnage before him; Old Man Martin was never the same afterwards.

The screams did not leave Banner for a long time.

That night as he lay on the cold motel room bed listening to the ocean and Rick's drunken snoring in the other bed, he remembered the screaming horses and shuddered; for he felt the same way when the transformer blew up, the blast taking him back to the dying, screaming horses and feeling as if his skin were on fire.

2.

"It's madness," he said aloud in the truck. "I must be out of my friggin' mind. It's time to do something else."

Before the second phase of the space center job, he had returned to the university that he had attended for four years and took the examination for the ordinary differential equations course he'd been independently studying. When the test was over, he knew he had passed the course because the professor (one who had taught Banner calculus during his freshman year) graded the paper while Banner sat across from him in his office and nodded while looking it over. He didn't make a mark on it except for a big red A on top, and congratulated Banner.

"Young man," he said, looking at Banner over the top of his steel-rimmed glasses. "This is the finest paper I've ever had to grade. You really understand this subject. Congratulations. You've passed the course with flying colors. Which means, of course, that you've finally got your degree."

And all the way south Banner had a big grin on his face, relieved that he was finally through; that he didn't have the weight of the unfinished four years around his neck like a millstone anymore.

But after the last transformer blew up right in front of him, the frenzied control—the state of ecstasy; of *samadhi*—he had carried within him while earning a living working in high voltage substations suddenly snapped, and he saw that he had to get out of this line of work.

"I think I'll teach math somewhere," he said to himself. "I'm tired of all this."

The endless hours on the road, driving through rain and snow and sleet and enduring hot, dusty weather or the dripping humidity of the southernmost states were taking its toll upon him. The cold motel rooms with the cold motel room beds with the chained color television sets, the roughened, coarse towels and washcloths, the stationery with the motels' letterheads, and the Gideon Bibles looked all the same now; the meals in the truck stop restaurants, the dining rooms of the hotels, the vending machines in gasoline stations and the manufacturing plants all tasted the same too.

There was hardly any joy in eating steak and eggs for breakfast, even though he ate like a starved animal this early morning; it was still the same, reminding him of all the ghastly food he had once prepared for people who came to the restaurant where he once worked. Coffee felt as if it were eating a hole through his guts. Dinner anymore he could barely order: he never knew what he wanted, and he wanted to gag just reading the menu. And when the waitress served the evening repast, all he could do was sit and stare at it, his mouth watering at the aspect of eating it—like a rabid dog—but his stomach recoiling at the thought of another ghastly restaurant meal.

There were times when the only thing he could eat was the old, scalding, urine-colored broth that dispensed out of battered vending machines inside industrial plants, and scalding, watered-down chocolate that filled old weakened cardboard cups. He would live on that for days at a time when stuck working in one area, the only real meal being chewy French toast he would gag down early in the mornings back at the hotel dining room.

He realized that it was all getting to him, and this last incident in Florida seemed to show it to him loud and clear.

The citizen's band still poured out static and crackled wildly. Transmitting distances were shortened by the inclement weather, but Banner heard people chattering over the frequency. He flipped slowly through the rest of the twenty-three channels, idly listening to the loud and ghostly voices of America around about him six miles. Most of the channels were empty of traffic except for the eternal hissing.

He flipped back to Channel 19 and heard, "Break, break, break," like a 200-pound Donald Duck, "where's that Lickety Split?"

"Oh shit, they're coming," Banner groaned, recognizing Archwood's handle. He sat straight up and scanned the wet shining road.

"C'mon you Lickety Split, where are you?"

"I don't know where the hell I am!" a whining voice answered distantly. It was Archwood all right.

"Did you turn down that Old Smith Road?"

"No!"

"Why, yay-yus, haw haw haw, you missed it, di'n't ya, haw haw haw. Ah bet ya even that four-eyed college boy missed it too, haw haw haw."

You son-of-a-bitch.

"Break, break, break."

I am not up for it, Banner thought, leaning over the steering wheel and staring at the still empty highway. *I am not up to listening to Dellasandro and not ready to put up with his bullshit.*

He shut off the citizen's band when he heard Dellasandro break again over the frequency. He turned the ignition off then, felt the sudden weight of the rain all around him, and recapped the thermos and put it on the oily littered floor.

"Damn," he sighed. "Back to the grindstone." He slapped his hardhat on tightly to his head, climbed out of the truck, and walked back to the shed.

"Uh oh," Rick grinned, looking at Banner's scowling expression. "Ah fear trouble's comin'."

"With a capital D," Banner told him.

Tower shook his head slowly upon hearing the news. "Oh shit," he wailed, pulling at his beard, "I'm screwed again."

"You all sober now, Tower?" Banner asked him, almost feeling sorry for him.

"Barely," Rick grinned.

"I got some coffee in my thermos in the truck," Banner told Tower. "You better drink some fast."

Letting out a loud sigh, mumbling incantations to himself, Tower zipped up his jacket and stood unsteadily and shuffled out the door without looking at anyone and looking abjectly at the ground by his feet.

"Poor bastard," Banner said as Tower disappeared.

"Hee hee hee hee," Ringo snickered. His hands were folded across his belly, feet propped up on the table, and he leaned precariously backward on his creaking chair. "Hee hee hee," he went on, then paused and let out a huge belly laugh like Santa Claus, which then disintegrated into childlike affected weeping.

"Upon my soul, Ah think he's hysterical," Rick grinned at Banner.

Banner only grinned.

"Yes, suh, Ah do believe the man is hysterical. Cheer up, Ringo, things can only get worse from here on out," and Rick started laughing too. "Ah, damn, anybody heah ready to bust their ass?" he asked harshly, and he too stood by Banner, who still watched the road. They all knew that as soon as the others arrived, it was going to be intensely physical to get the job started, whatever it would entail.

It was still dark, but lighter than when they first drove into the substation, the sun shining above the clouds somewhere. The daylight seemed not to penetrate through the thick heavy cloud cover. There was only constant rain, cold wind, and tired aching bodies from the foul weather.

"I hope I don't catch a cold," Banner told Rick. He felt as if he were coming down with one. *Dear God*, Banner thought, *not now. I don't need one.*

"You mean pneumonia," Rick said.

"Whatever. I don't need anything right now to aggravate the hell out of me."

"You're gonna have Dellasandro."

"Don't remind me."

"Ah need a warm woman, clean sheets, and a week off."

"Well, you *are* getting married next week."

"Yeah," Rick said, grinning. "Ah'm in love."

"Uh-huh," Banner said, smirking. "It's love all right."

"Whaddaya mean? It is love."

"'Wovon man nicht sprechen kann, darüber muß man schweigen,'" Banner said, quoting Wittgenstein, pointing a finger to the sky.

"Christ, you and your philosophy!"

While they were in Florida working on the space center grounds, Rick met his new love in a strip joint next to the motel where they stayed. Her name was Jackie Love Storm—which was the same name she used in her act—and Rick fell in love with her the first time he saw her do her bump-and-grind routine. "Ah'm in love, Ah'm in love," he kept telling Banner at work, impatiently waiting for the long day to end, hot and fevered during the last half-hour of labor. Every evening after work he would be inside the strip joint watching her, drinking beer and wooing her later while the other girls stripped up on the stage.

Then one night a month later, Rick told Banner (Banner never went with him, but tried to kill time through Gibbon and Plutarch while listening to the ocean from the motel room bed), Rick convinced her to go out with him. The first thing he did was actually showed her how, uh, well-endowed he was, and they balled all night long on the beach under the shining stars and listened to the waves pounding on the shore.

"Ah'm in love, Ah'm in love," he sang to Banner. "Ah ain't nevah seen a woman could screw lahk she could, mon, honest to Gawd. She tu'ned me every which way but and wouldn't let go. She loves my cock. What a hell of a ride, yes suh. Mah Gawd," making Banner ache badly for the Bee a thousand-and-some miles north.

When Rick found out that the huge work project was nearly completed and that he would only be there another month—"Oh shit," he yelled, "what am Ah gonna do? Ah need mah woman!"—he proposed to her, giving her a big shining diamond ring, a dozen white roses, a pair of sheer black stockings, and (to Banner's unending surprise) she accepted.

Next week Rick was flying back down to Florida. Banner was going with him to act as best man. Everything had already been pre-arranged with Archwood the previous week before this job came up. He had finally gotten over Darla, his now ex-girlfriend from Ponca City. Banner was happy for him and hoped everything would work out for them both, even though he thought that love was certainly strange. He had not yet met Jackie.

He heard an engine running and shifting gears above the rain, and he spied the indicating lights of a cab and trailer on the distant tops of the rolling plains. A heavy-duty convoy: another truck was following it, the company's first oil rerefining rig, and there was a third truck behind it too, a 40-foot oil tanker. Behind the tanker, there were three other rigs, each carrying a large transformer upon low-boy trailers, similar to the ones in the switchyard.

"Christ, we're gonna be here all week," Rick moaned.

"And the next," Banner said disgustedly. "And maybe the week after that. Christ. Look, Archwood's with 'em, following behind the last truck. I sure hope these transformers ain't blown."

"You and me both, brother. Ah wonder who's all gonna be here."

"Who knows?" Banner answered resignedly.

Tower suddenly appeared around the corner of the shed, holding a badly wrinkled- and grease-stained paper cup of coffee. He too looked at the trucks coming closer. A lit cigarette dangled from his lips. "Shit, man," he croaked, still looking hung over and starting to shake as he stumbled into the shed, "I ain't ready. I ain't had no breakfast."

"That's what you get for orderin' eggs staring at you," Jackson Banner told him sourly.

"I shouldn'ta drank them beers," Tower lamented, sitting blearily at the table, staring into his coffee.

"It's too late to repent of your sins now, bitch," Rick said, deadpanned. "They're already here. We gotta get to work."

Ponca City
31 December
2300 Hours

1.

Jackson Banner was cold and tired.

He and Philip Lazarus had been at the oil refinery since 0630 that same morning and spent the whole freezing and windy day outside, rerefining 10-c dielectric mineral oil inside the old, energized substations near the tank farms. Rick Pitts had left his Monza for Lazarus to use while he was back in Ohio, and so he and Banner had driven the car from the Holiday Inn to the refinery every day now for the past two weeks, leaving the huge oil rerefining rig at the plant. They now sat in the plush front bucket seats of the idling car, the heater on full blast, tucked inside their clothes and stamping their numbed feet. The radio was on, rockabilly music vibrating loudly inside the car and through Banner, the seeming endless jangling sounds of electric guitars buzzing through his teeth.

A steaming cup of coffee sat on the dashboard, fogging the windshield in front of Banner.

He also heard, above the loud music, heavy rumbling through the air, as the furnace clicked on inside the big rig parked next to them. It heated the transformer mineral oil as the oil filtered through the 800 pounds of Fuller's earth in two huge steel tanks at the rear of the rig. As the furnace operated, black smoke billowed streaming into the cold night, the wind dissipating the smoke as the smoke came trailing away from the leeward side.

Lazarus sat in the passenger seat, staring at the rig, lit cigarette dangling from his long fingers. His hardhat was tilted back from his forehead; his long curly blonde hair splayed out from beneath it. Archwood had nicknamed Lazarus "Spaniel," because Lazarus' small purebred Cocker, Misery, had the same long curly blonde fur on top of her head. Lazarus was wiry and toughened, fair-skinned, but looked somewhat old and somber for his 24 years. He had just wakened two minutes ago when Banner slipped in behind the steering wheel. Now they sat in silence, both tired and numb, with the cold permeating the car even with the heater on full blast.

"How many hours we been on this transformer?" Lazarus asked, his clear tenor in his chest.

"16-and-a-half hours," Banner mumbled, teeth chattering. My Gawd he was cold: *Oklahoma in the wintertime.*

"How many gallons of 10-c do we have left?" Lazarus asked.

"'Bout 20 gallons."

"Christ man, we gotta change filters in an hour."

"Great. Fantastic. Tell me about it." Banner closed his eyes. Working in this icy, windy Oklahoma weather chilled his bones through to the marrow. All day long his body felt physically beaten, raw and numb from the damning dry cold that swept off the unseen Rockies and through the Great Plains. The air pierced through his sinuses and up between his eyes, giving him an immense headache all day; the hairs froze like needles inside his nostrils. He wore two pairs of long underwear beneath a flannel shirt and blue jeans, and two pairs of woolen socks covered his cold feet. He didn't feel like changing Fuller's earth filter cartridges again for the umpteenth time today.

Every day for two weeks now, he and Lazarus worked 16- and 18-hour days trying to complete this vast project of work in the huge oil refinery, but as each day slowly passed, they found themselves getting farther and farther behind. Archwood telephoned their motel room every night, screaming nearly 1500 miles away as to why they weren't on schedule. Banner became quite tired of trying to reason with Archwood, and let Lazarus finally do all the talking.

The refinery's electrical foreman, "Ironjaw" Parker, had a list of 200 mineral oil transformers that had to be tested. As Banner and Lazarus went through the laborious procedure of analyzing each oil sample, they made notes of what had to be done to the particular transformers that needed the oil rerefined in each of them. Banner then made the calculations as to how much time and how much Fuller's earth they needed to perform the strenuous tasks—four tons of the mineral had been shipped to the refinery—and they would proceed on one of the energized transformers. Sometimes, if they were lucky, they finished two transformers a day, but most of the time was spent rerefining one transformer which took two or three days, or one that took a week.

Plus, there was the added attraction of changing the gawddamned soaked cartridges that always took a lot of precious time. Banner sighed and inwardly groaned when he thought about the cartridges.

Oh, Christ bless me, he thought.

Two 200-pound cylindrical cartridges—three feet in diameter; three feet tall—filled each of the two tanks in the big rerefining rig, and they weighed much heavier after being soaked from the high acidic mineral oil. The cartridges were hoisted out of the tanks by cranking on a chain hoist, and the men always hoped that they wouldn't bust their knuckles against the heavy cartridges as they guided them out of the tanks.

After dumping the soaked contents into an approved dumpster, they added new sacks that lay in the inside of the cartridges and emptied 16 bags of Fuller's earth into them, no chance of any of them baked and dried before use, so that they could have had the added advantage of improving the oil much faster. All the sacks sat under a huge tarpaulin to protect them from the Oklahoma elemental weather—it was the only protection the men had—and when they needed the Fuller's earth, they loaded as many as they could into the rig before starting on another transformer.

If you were good at changing out the tanks, Banner thought, *you could do it just within an hour.* The coffee always tasted good afterwards, the cigarette a luxury item, but your body screamed in anguish, drowning in the aroma of the 10-c mineral oil; life's blood.

After this, one complete pass on the energized transformer was performed. Depending upon the size of the unit, the time varied when to check the dielectric and acidic neutralization number against the oil flowing into the rig versus the rerefined oil flowing out. If it were the same, the whole process of unloading and reloading the Fuller's earth tanks were looked upon in stoic suffering and dread. Because it always had to be done, again and again and again; this was surely the rolling stone of Sisyphus.

And it usually occurred often enough that rerefining oil was looked upon as a long and laborious task. There were so many things to do to get started and finished. Sometimes, Banner thought, you could be on one transformer for a week or two (and sometimes three), attempting to lower the n parts per million of water out of the oil by vacuum-dehydration. And when one calculated the ungodly amount of Fuller's earth that had to be used on a particular transformer with a low dielectric and high acid level, it seemed overwhelming to find out how many times one was going to have to change the tanks.

And this was just a very small portion of the work involved.

Here at the refinery, Banner and Lazarus couldn't get away with any short-cuts. "Ironjaw" Parker was always there to have the mineral oil analyzed when the two young men felt they had finished with a transformer. They could only move on to the next one after Parker was satisfied with the results. When he found a dielectric just barely over the minimum standard, he made Banner and Lazarus stay on the transformer another day.

Banner got sick of working in the refinery after the first week, putting up with the foul odors of the different raw chemicals that flowed through the refinery's system, the bleak nasty weather, the militaristic hard-nosed attitude of the electrical foreman, and Archwood's unreasonable questions. He was also mad at having to spend Christmas and now New Year's Day away from home and the Bee and celebrating the holidays by busting and freezing his balls off in the Oklahoma winter.

He silently cursed Rick for going back to Ohio.

Lazarus turned to him and suddenly grinned. "Boy," he said, "it's a good thing we opened that port-lid, huh?"

Banner snorted. He grabbed the hot cup of coffee and sipped at it. "You ain't kiddin', buddy," he answered. "Christ Almighty I was scared. I about shit myself up there."

He put the cup back on top of the dashboard, then reached inside his brown jacket and pulled out his cigarette pack. He wiggled his finger inside it, trying to feel for a cigarette, and found he didn't have any more. Disgustedly, he crumpled the pack and tossed it on to the floor. He didn't figure he smoked all of them already; he was hungering for a smoke.

Wordlessly, Lazarus offered Banner his own pack: Marlboros in the crush-proof box. Banner gratefully took one, lit it a moment later with the Monza's cigarette lighter, sucked on it hard, and then blew the smoke against the steering wheel.

"Damn I wish I had more cigarettes," he said, tapping the wheel. "I shoulda bought some this morning before we got here."

"Don't worry about it, Jackson," Lazarus told him. "I gotta whole carton in the cab of the truck."

"Thanks," Banner said, and he took another drag on the cigarette. He was tired and edgy, and wished he could get out of the cold.

The particular transformer they were working on was an old cast-iron gray Westinghouse unit, standing nearly ten feet high, squared all the way round, and having two-inch tubed radiators spanning three sides of the unit. It was also covered with thick black oily grime from the refinery's immediate atmosphere. Earlier that same afternoon, when

Banner and Lazarus went to find the number of gallons of mineral oil the transformer contained, they had found the liquid level gauge broken. The round glass had been shattered, and instead of the needle gauge reading "Low," "25-C," or "High," the needle had been twisted 180 degrees from the markings on the gauge. The oil and winding temperature gauges were not working either, both pegged at the maximum temperatures.

Banner told Parker about it after the initial inspection, but all he cared about was the condition of the oil. "You let me worry about the little stuff, mister," Parker told Banner. "You just take care of bringin' the acid level down in this transformer. Got it?" and walked away from the young men, leaving them alone for now. Banner hated the man's guts.

"Whaddaya think? Think it's full of oil?" Banner had asked Lazarus.

Lazarus shrugged. "Beats hell outta me," he answered, grinning. "Lemme go get the ratchet and sockets. We might as well take the port-lid off and see what we got. Okay?"

"Yeah, yeah," Banner said. "I'll go climb this thing."

Lazarus left him and climbed into the back of the tractor-trailer rig. Banner glanced up at the transformer and saw that the high voltage insulators were encased in metal at opposite ends of the unit which led into the primary and secondary switchgear circuit breakers, so he knew he'd be safe on top.

The transformer was literally hot; energized, he could feel it hum beneath his hands as he grabbed on to two of the hot radiators. He boosted himself on top of the unit, his boots wedged between the radiators to give him support, and lay prone on top of the hot metal. His hands were covered with grime and his jacket was coated too. His knees burned upon the lid. *Jesus*, he thought, *I can't even keep clean on this miserable job. And this gawddamned transformer is hotter that hell. They must be puttin' one hell of a load on this baby for it to be so hot.* He had to keep shifting his weight from one knee to the other because the metal burned through his clothing. *Christ,* he thought, *you could fry steak and eggs up here.*

Lazarus yelled from below, "Here, catch these," and Banner caught a thrown ratchet, an open-ended adjustable wrench, a flathead screwdriver, a roll of cloth tape, and two sockets that came flying at him. He found that the nuts and bolts holding the gasketed port-lid were 9/16th of an inch in size. He then began the tedious task of removing the nuts, bolts, flat washers, and lock washers, being careful to screw each item back together again and placing them far away from the port-lid; his hands and fingers burning from the hot metal lid of the transformer.

Meanwhile, Lazarus was busy attaching the hose connections to the top and bottom drain valves of the transformer, working silently and efficiently. Both of them were tired and cold and had gone without lunch. Banner's ears were freezing beneath his hardhat, his fingers numb and almost useless. When he finally removed all the bolts and nuts that held down the port-lid, he took the screwdriver and pried the lid away from the old, crumbling gasket.

He then carefully lifted the lid up and away from the exposed, internal iron core and copper windings of the transformer, put it on top of one of the sets of radiators, then carefully peered down into the interior of the loudly humming transformer to see where the oil level was.

What he found scared the living hell out of him: "Holy Mother of God!" he yelled, jumping back and waving frantically at Lazarus, who stood in the rear of the rig, watching him. "Fill this bitch up with oil, Phil! Jesus, the thing ain't even half-full!"

Lazarus immediately started the rerefining equipment by flipping a switch. Pure yellow mineral oil began splashing noisily on to the exposed, slowly smoking iron core and copper windings. No wonder the transformer was so damned hot!

"Damn man!" Banner shouted, and he started shaking. *Keep a clear head; let's get it straight.* He should have known better, but how else could they have found out? Yes, the transformer was hot, but that could have been from the load of the refinery's machinery. He never expected the transformer would be hot from not enough oil to keep it cool. The transformer still maintained its steady hum as the oil splashed in, and he worried about the air bubbles that invariably formed inside. He didn't waste any time climbing down to the ground. He pounded futilely upon the copper winding's temperature gauge, but it was out of order, or maybe it hadn't been, pegged at 120 degrees centigrade.

Jesus.

He still heard the oil pouring in on top of the core of the transformer when he climbed into the back of the rig. Lazarus stood in the back too, his eyes big and face pale, and trying to manage a grin. Banner paced up and down the center aisle between the machinery: the piping, the vacuum-dehydration unit, the huge silver-painted furnace, the two huge Fuller's earth tanks looming to the roof of the rig with Lazarus standing in between them, and the Alsop dry-pack units in front of the tanks. The interior of the cramped rig reeked of the sweet aroma of 10-c mineral oil; the machinery seemed to shine with it. Some of the fittings connecting the piping network dripped continuously. He felt energized; the adrenalin had really flowed when he took that lid off and saw the smoking core.

Jesus Christ, he suddenly realized. *I can get killed on this job.*

He walked up to Lazarus, and stood next to him. They both stared at the transformer. "You know somethin', Phil, we're crazy the way we work around high voltage," Banner said in a quiet tone. "Man, that transformer coil was *smoking*, ya know what I mean? It can still blow up."

"Uh-huh," Lazarus mumbled, because seeing Banner up there in a troubled situation reminded him of his own near-misses. Lazarus was lucky to be alive, and he knew it.

"Well, I better go check the oil level."

"Yeah," Lazarus said, and shut down the machinery as Banner went to climb the transformer again.

In the Monza, Banner mumbled something to himself.

"What say?" Lazarus asked, turning away from gazing at the truck and looking at Banner. Banner just shook his head slightly, then reached for his cup of coffee. The disc jockey on the radio announced he was going to play Al Stewart's "Year of the Cat." Banner knew his teeth were going to chatter along with the song.

"I didn't say anything, Phil," he said. "I was just rememberin'."

2.

Jackson Banner had been with the company only a few months when Lazarus got into trouble the first time. Rick had told Banner what happened. B.S. Archwood and Lazarus were at a local roller bearing mill for a couple of days to rerefine mineral oil in three transformers.

They found themselves in an old, dirty, loudly energized substation outside, sandwiched between the black-sided steel mill and a building that housed massive forging presses and large metal lathes. The galvanized structure and porcelain stand-off insulators of the small substation were blackened from the many years of industrial grime. The three single-phase transformers sat close to each other, each over ten feet high with the primary and secondary insulators poking up on top. The stand-off insulators on the switchrack's bus were not too far above the transformers. The low-profile rust-colored structure was very dense and close, full of thick, bolted girders, struts, and crossbeams. The top valves on the three transformers were attached on the sides just below the secondary insulators, all within easy reach.

Lazarus stood on one of the rungs of a wooden ladder and was in the process of loosening a stubborn one-inch plug off the top valve of the middle humming transformer when he suddenly realized he had put his right hand on one of the secondary 480-volt insulators for support. It scared him so much he froze, still grasping the pipe wrench with his other hand on the plug, sweat breaking out and shining on his pale face. It had happened so quickly, without thought.

B.S. Archwood, who had been supervising every aspect of the job, yelled, "Shit," when he saw what Lazarus had done. "Jesus Christ."

Lazarus stood on the wooden ladder, looking very frightened.

"Just take your hand offa there," Archwood said.

"But . . . but . . . but what if it . . . if it gets me," Lazarus finally managed to say in a cracked voice.

"It ain't gonna get ya," Archwood told him. "Look," he said, "if it was gonna kill you, it would have done it as soon as you touched it, right? You're on a wood ladder. Insulation."

"Yeah," Lazarus said, but he didn't sound convinced. His eyes were like saucers.

"Pull your hand off then, damn it, it ain't gonna kill you now. If it was, you'd already be dead."

Lazarus took a deep breath, shut his eyes tightly, and quickly jerked his hand away. He kept his eyes shut and let go his breath, though he clutched his chest with his hand. He was still alive.

"Well, you look okay," Archwood told Lazarus, relieved, his own stomach starting to hurt. Nerves. He wanted to puke.

Lazarus finally let out a sigh, then stiffly climbed down the ladder, clutching at the sides as if they were the only link between life and death. He was still pale and began to shake. The sweat still shone brightly on his face.

"Gawddamn," he mumbled, "gawddamn that was close."

"Relax, you're on the ground now."

"Gawddamn, man," Lazarus said, shaking his head. Archwood thought he might have gone into shock. "Gawddamn."

Archwood gave him a cigarette and lit it with shaking hands. "You all right?" he asked.

"Yeah, I think so," Lazarus answered. He shook his head again, then tried to manage a grin, and looked at his hand.

"Yeah," Archwood said.

Then Lazarus suddenly stifled a sob. "Gawddamn," he said again, "that was close. I coulda met my Maker."

"Yeah," Archwood said, still somewhat queasy. "You all right?"

"Yeah, I'm all right."

"Good," Archwood said, clapping Lazarus on his shoulder. Then he said, "Screw this motherfuckin' job," and proceeded to drag up and they packed all the equipment and left. They both got silently drunk in a tavern and stayed until it closed. Lazarus was happy to be alive. Archwood later puked until he had nothing left and then had the dry heaves. Everyone knew it was stress.

Then one Monday morning nearly a year ago, as Banner walked through the shop and into the trailer, L.A. Ross, the company's resident electrical engineer, unexpectedly greeted him, pale and whitened round face staring at him with a shocked expression in his eyes. Banner immediately wondered what had happened. Ross stood next to his old and shining desk, drumming the ends of his fingers rapidly on the wood. "Phil's in the hospital," he said first thing to Banner. "He's under heavy sedation."

"What happened to him?" Banner asked loudly. There was no one else in the trailer and his voice seemed louder because of the cramped quarters. He felt a sickening thrill go through his body, from his throat to his balls. He grabbed on to Ross's sports coat. "What'd he do? Almost get himself killed?"

"Damn near," Ross answered. He looked straight at Banner. He cleared his throat, as was his habit just before he talked. "Yesterday, he was drawing oil samples out of the bottom of some 50-k.v.a. transformers that were on a pole in the middle of an alley. Before he filled up the middle transformer's mineral oil in one of the glass sample bottles, he had taken off his hardhat to reach the small bottom sample tap because from what I suppose his body couldn't fit between the cables and the transformer. Well, when he backed out to put the bottle away in that brown sample case, you know, the back of his head near his right ear touched a 7200-volt bushing, and the electricity went through the back of his skull and travelled down through his body and blew out his right elbow. They say you can see the hole where it went in and went out. But when it happened, he was knocked unconscious thank God, and when the firemen arrived, he was up there with the back of his head resting against the bushing. Well, all the power around there was knocked out too, and the firemen got Phil off with a hot stick. He had a weak pulse. He was still alive. Can you fucking believe it? They gave him c.p.r. on the way to the hospital. The doctors in the hospital jumped on him as soon as they wheeled him into emergency, and they brought him back. When he regained consciousness, the first thing Phil asked was, 'Where am I? What happened?' Well, I guess as soon as he asked that, he suddenly realized what really did happen to him, and he . . ."

Ross's voice faded out in a crack, and Banner watched him intently.

"Well? What? What happened?" Banner asked.

"Well," Ross said, letting out an involuntary giggle; he never farted in public, "well, Phil went into deep shock again, and he damned near died of fright. The doctors revived him again, then sedated him. He's been out now nearly 72 hours."

"Jesus." Banner shifted back and forth on the balls of his feet. "Jesus. Did somebody tell his old man?"

"Yeah. Algis Jasper went out and told him and he and Phil's old man flew out to Ponca City from there. They're out there now."

"Oh, man," Banner said. "What about B.S.? Where's he at?"

"Rick was the one who called him yesterday. B.S. went half-cocked and began drinking and crying after getting the news. I ain't never seen the guy so upset before. He feels real bad about Lazarus getting hurt. He feels somehow responsible, he keeps saying, I just put him to bed before coming over here. I've been up myself almost 36 hours."

"Okay," Banner said, shaking his head.

Poor B.S., he treated Lazarus as if he were his own son. Archwood had always bailed Lazarus out of some heavy situations before, but nothing like this. There was nothing else that Archwood, or anyone else, could do. Banner grimly accepted the fact that he was needed in Oklahoma; back on the road again.

"I'm gone," he told L.A. Ross.

The Bee was almost in shock herself when Banner returned home, repacked his clothes, his toiletries, and told her that Lazarus had almost gotten himself killed on the job. She listened in stunned silence when Banner told her he was leaving immediately for Oklahoma. He didn't know when he was coming back.

"Oh God please be careful," she said quietly as she hugged him in tight arms. "Please be safe."

"Don't worry, I'll be all right," Banner reassured her, and kissed her good-bye.

The jet was in the air by a quarter after nine that same morning.

More cold beds. No warm body to snuggle warmly against during the nights. The huge jet flew to Chicago. There he transferred to another after a two-hour layover at O'Hare International, and finally flew to Wichita.

The drive in the rental car from Wichita to Ponca City was still the same: south of the spacious Flint Hills the rolling dry plains stretched for open miles everywhere that the eye could see. The interstate highway revealed itself as a straight and gray slab of ribbon that merged into the dark gray southern horizon. The miles were all the same. He had been down this way before after he had been with the company a few weeks. Then, as he drove farther south, the familiar tiny pinpricks of flame glowed in the darkened distance, and he knew he was near Ponca City. Conoco was the major employer of the people who lived there; it was a large oil refinery with an even larger oil tank farm. The white-painted tanks bloomed around most of the town in huge flowering symmetry.

That particular year, when Lazarus got hurt, the company had been contracted by the town to perform mineral oil analyses on their pole-top transformers located in back and side street alleys. Lazarus had volunteered to stay for the job when they finished the Conoco work. Lazarus had begged B.S. to let him stay in the town, because he now had a girlfriend, and he didn't want to leave her. Finally, B.S. quit haggling over it and relented. He made Rick stay also.

Rick was ecstatic over the situation too because he also had a girlfriend, named Darla. Rick and Lazarus went out every morning to retrieve mineral oil samples from the pole-top transformers, record the data from the nameplates on the transformer data sheets, and work a slow, leisurely eight hours. For a month the two young men milked the Ponca City job for all it was worth.

Then Lazarus got hurt, almost killed, and Rick seemed shell-shocked from the day's events after talking with Ross.

"Discombobulated," Ross told Banner.

Before Banner left Ohio, Ross gave him directions and the address to the trailer which Rick and Lazarus had rented by the month. When Banner drove through the quiet town at dusk and by the huge refinery's complex and on out east of town, the night sky deepened quickly into a purplish color. A cool breeze blew lightly across the plains. It was sweet pure air, not the shimmering haze of the oil refinery.

The 60-foot trailer was located in a run-down mobile home park. Rick's Monza was parked in front of it. Banner found the curtains drawn. Soft light seemed to emanate from the trailer. He parked the car behind Rick's, stepped out, stretched, and inhaled the fresh Oklahoma air. When he walked up the wrought-iron steps to the front door, he heard Rick mumbling inside the trailer.

Now what's the matter? Banner asked himself, and knocked on the door.

"Is that you, Jackson?" Rick's muffled shout came drawling through the door.

"Yeah, it's me," Banner replied.

"Come on in, mon," Rick shouted again.

Banner opened the door. A lamp dimly lit the dark-paneled walls. Rick lay back on the worn couch dressed in an opened light-blue bathrobe, exposing his nude, hard body. His girlfriend, Darla, was on her knees in *auparishtaka*, her arms resting comfortably upon Rick's upper thighs, gloriously sucking on his thick, eight-inch penis; *eating the mango.*

Banner, exhausted from the long trip, froze at once, surprised. "Well what the hell," he said loudly. Rick sure looked as if he were suffering in shock from Lazarus' accident. He did indeed look somewhat discombobulated.

"Shut the door, mon, it's a little bit drafty in here," Rick told him, looking up with shining eyes and grinning widely at him. "Go on in the kitchen and grab yaself a beer. Sit down, relax, and take a load off your feet. How ya been, Jackson?"

"Oh, just fine, just fine," Banner answered, becoming embarrassed, but then realizing he was getting turned on by watching Darla, who ignored Banner completely. Banner shook his head out of reverie from watching them, then walked into the small cramped kitchen. He could hear Darla slurping a few feet away as he rummaged through the nearly empty refrigerator.

Beer and bread.

Christ what a communal combination, he thought.

"How was the trip on out here?" Rick asked him.

"Oh great, just wonderful," Banner answered, trying to keep the tremble out of his voice. "I didn't expect to see the climax of my trip topped off by watching you get a blowjob. With Lazarus near death as it is, my Gawd," and Rick just laughed. Banner stared into the interior of the refrigerator. "How's Phil doin'?" he asked.

"Ooh girl, what a mouth," he heard Rick whisper. "Phil'll be all right, mon," Rick said loudly. "The doctor . . . uh . . . the doctor said he'd run tests on him later on when he comes out of it, Ah guess . . . ooh. . . . Shit! He might have more nerve damage to his legs, I dunno."

"Oh yeah?" Banner asked.

"Yeah," Rick grunted.

Banner, thinking about how it must have felt—the accident, not glorious *auparishtaka*—grabbed a Dr. Pepper out of the refrigerator, walked back into the living room, and sat in an overstuffed chair to the left of them.

Darla was going for it all, but Banner thought she was only showing off for his benefit. Every once in a while, she glanced sideways at him, and did something obscene with her tongue, wrinkled her nose at him, smiled at him, or gently planted little kisses on Rick's swollen penis. Banner began to feel hot for her himself.

Jesus.

She performed the act of polishing for nearly a minute before suddenly absorbing Rick wholly into her mouth. Banner watched her do it again, shook his head at the spectacle, and took a long pull on the Dr. Pepper.

Darla was only barely 18—from what he had heard—but she acted a lot older than her age. She looked as if she really knew what she was doing.

When she brought Rick near the edge of orgasm, she held him tightly in both small white hands, her eyes smokily boring into his brightened, lust-filled ones, and whispered to him, her mouth just hovering over the head, "I want you to come in my mouth." She then sucked deeply. She pulled away from him again, looked into Rick's glazed eyes, and whispered, "I want you to come all over my face." She then really worked on him, all the while gazing sluttishly at him.

"Ah shit, baby," Rick suddenly gritted. 'Ah can't he'p it, darlin', Ah'm comin'! Jesus!" He held her head in his huge hands, locking them together behind her head, pushing his hips into her face as she absorbed him. She began pumping him rapidly with light strokes, her open, surrounding mouth barely touching him. He couldn't hold back any longer—she was Delilah—and finally ejaculated into her mouth.

She pulled him out and let him ejaculate on her face. Then she sucked Rick again, long and slow, her cheeks hollowing. Her mouth, lips, nose, chin, and cheeks were covered with shining sperm and saliva. She had him begging her to stop as she kept it up. When she finally did stop her ministrations, she lay back against the couch, licking her lips slowly and peering with half-closed eyes at Banner as she slowly sucked on her fingers too.

Banner sat silently for a moment as he pulled at the Dr. Pepper and looked at a half-conscious Rick lying wiped out on the couch, like a soul-sucked Samson, then looked back at Darla. "You little bitch," he told her softly, grinning. She laughed lightly; her eyes sparkled. "Cigarette?" He offered her one of his; she took it demurely with long slim fingers.

"Thank you," she murmured as he lit the cigarette with his lighter.

Banner shook his head. Poor Lazarus, if he had only known. "Christ,

I don't know. I've come to bail these guys out again. I'll never see the end of it."

He helped Rick finish the Ponca City job, saw Lazarus a couple of times in the hospital, then flew back to Ohio when the job was finished. Rick was with Darla every night, and the old trailer swayed at night from their sexual acrobatics in the master bedroom.

3.

Now, two years later, he was here again. It was ten minutes to midnight. The lights that glowed from the refinery at night could be seen miles away. Up close, the lights were very powerful, revealing everything in stark grays, whites, and cutting blacks. Banner had to squint to see. The wind still blew freezing air that came from the unseen snow-covered Rocky Mountains. It cut through Banner even with all his clothes stuffed by the long underwear. He was also riding a tremendous chemical high from the oil refinery's hissing and whining operations.

Lazarus came back to work a month ago, the day after Thanksgiving. His arms and legs suffered from ataxia after the accident, but only his right leg was still stiff, and he now walked with a cane. The therapists had told him to exercise it whenever he could; Lazarus walked for the exercise. He was still in remarkably good shape: wiry, taut, and fair-skinned, but he was a little more introspective, not outgoing as he was before. Though he was only 24, the accident had aged him. He took his time and didn't rush through things. He was now always careful about being around the high voltage electricity. Banner was here to do all the heavy work, but Phil wanted to get right back into it. Banner watched over Lazarus and made sure he stayed away from the high voltage. It was now a standard procedure rigorously enforced by Archwood when someone worked with Lazarus: Archwood wanted someone with Lazarus at all times to make sure it didn't happen again.

"Hey, we only got 20 gallons of 10-c left, right?" Banner asked him.

"Ten-four," Lazarus said.

"What time is it?"

Lazarus looked at his watch. "Almost midnight," he answered.

"What say we call it a night and start over fresh tomorrow."

'"We'll be behind."

"We already are. The hell with it, it doesn't matter. I don't give a damn what Parker or B.S. thinks. Let's get back to the motel, this car just ain't warmin' me up." Banner finished the rest of his coffee.

"Okay. Lemme go out and shut down the equipment." Lazarus opened the door and stepped out of the car. Cold came blasting in even more.

Banner turned down the volume on the radio. "You want me to shut off the valves, Phil?" he asked loudly.

Lazarus shook his head. "Nah, stay here. I'll take care of it."

Banner watched Lazarus walk with his cane as he maneuvered into the rig. From inside, the whine of machinery slowly died down, until nothing ran except the furnace, and it was the last thing Lazarus shut off. The sudden silence squeezed itself into Banner's ears. Lazarus walked to the transformer and closed the top and bottom one-inch valves. Everything was secured. They had put on a new gasket and reattached the port-lid later after the transformer was filled to the normal level. Banner was tired, and he saw the pinched expression on Lazarus' face when he climbed back into the car.

"You ready?" Banner asked.

"Yeah yeah," Lazarus mumbled. "Christ it's cold. Let's go."

"Okay." Banner gunned the Monza and it rumbled into life, twin headers running along underneath the two doors and vibrating softly through the car. He reversed it, stopped, then turned and drove out of the refinery at a slow crawl.

"When's Rick comin' back?" Banner asked in the darkness. He lit one of Lazarus' cigarettes from the Monza's lighter, watching the red glow of the burning end.

"Tomorrow."

"You think he's finally over it?"

"I fuckin' doubt it," Lazarus said, and laughed. "Man, he wanted to marry her."

"Yeah, I know," Banner said.

Rick and Darla had begun fighting for nearly a year and two weeks ago they separated. Darla, Rick's cute little 19-year-old cocksucker, ran off and married, Banner heard as Rick had screamed through the telephone two weeks ago into his ear: "Some a'coholic, Ubangi-faced, bongo-lipped, nappy-headed, vine-swingin', African *tree-hoppa*! Can you at all fuckin' *buhlieve* it?" and it didn't go down well for the young white buck from Arkansas.

Racial hatreds still die hard.

Darla eloped with the Negro the same night after she and Rick had walked out on each other. When Rick found out the next day what had happened, he drunkenly telephoned B.S., told him he was coming home for two weeks to get smashed even more, and to send someone down to replace him.

Lazarus said Rick was very drunk the day he left. By the time the jet took off from Wichita, Banner was getting ready to leave from Cleveland. The same routine. Go bail this one out. The company had drafted him for the work. This was Banner's third time in this part of America. And now he was out here near the beginning of a new year. A little over two years ago he was still in college.

Mercy, how time does go by, Banner thought.

The disk jockey on the radio said, "It's now two minutes to midnight, y'all. Let's have a listen live at Times Square in New Yawk City."

The cold Oklahoma night engulfed the car in its thick darkness and the pinprick lights of a million stars. The hissing oil refinery was the only sound alive amid the quietly sleeping town.

Cigarettes and Coffee
Part III

1.

Jackson Banner could now clearly see Dellasandro in the cab as he looked into the side-view mirrors trying to maneuver the tractor-trailer rig in through the entrance of the substation, the mounted citizens' band aerials on both mirrors whipping frantically back and forth. A cigarette was tightly held between the center of his lips as he turned the steering wheel. Banner saw his long, black bushy hair flying back and forth as he turned his frowning head, the white cigarette clearly outlined in the midst of his equally long black beard which covered half his dark face. Dellasandro drove the truck straight on in, looking at Banner and Rick, squinching his cold blue steely eyes and smiling sweetly at them. He gave them both the finger as he geed and shifted the rig to a lower gear toward the transformer nearest the shed, braked, mysteriously blasted the air horns in two long loud bursts, left the big rig idling, then hopped out of the cab and rapidly walked toward the second truck as it began maneuvering into the entrance. Ignoring them, Dellasandro jumped up to the driver's door of the suddenly stopped truck, opened it, and pulled Leroy Chessan out of the seat without even giving Leroy time to grab his hardhat and jacket. He hopped into the seat, ground through the gears and spun the tires deliberately—the fucking show-off—as he drove the truck around behind the middle transformer.

Banner didn't move from the doorway of the shed, but stood with his arms folded across his chest, gazing at Dellasandro. To say that he didn't like Dellasandro wouldn't be strong enough; memories die hard, and he never forgot.

Banner married the Bee a week before Christmas over two years ago, and he told Archwood that he was taking a week off from work. He had been the only one in the whole outfit who hadn't taken any vacation (he had been on the road most of those months, and been getting really jumpy). The company was still backed up in the work log.

"Can you be back here the 26ᵗʰ? I gotta easy local job for ya to do when you get back," Archwood said to him.

"Yeah," Banner answered.

"Don't wanta overtax ya," Archwood said, deadpanned, but there was a mocking grin on his face.

"Uh-huh," Banner archly replied.

The next late Sunday evening they returned home from their initial three-day honeymoon and found one of the company's oil tankers and the large oil rerefining rig parked on the side of the dark and quiet street, idling with only their parking lights glowing in the night, reflecting off the slowly falling, thick snow. As Banner and the Bee climbed out of the Jeep and gathered their suitcases, Banner saw the glows of unseen lit cigarettes in the cab of the tractor-trailer rig. Banner knew then that it was the Fryman brothers—twin Navajos originally from Arizona—and he knew something was up, and he just wasn't in the mood for it. He felt tired looking at the trucks.

Banner saw Dellasandro as he and the Bee came to the outside wooden steps that led up to their house. He had cleaned off the snow on the three bottom steps and was leaning back against them, smoking a cigarette and gazing with his mocking eyes at the newly married couple standing warily before him.

"What do *you* want?" Banner asked.

"Time to go to work, college boy," Dellasandro said, looking the Bee over as he would a tasty prime rib dinner.

"B.S. told me to come back to work tomorrow morning. I'm still on vacation."

"But we need ya now. We gotta job in North Carolina to do and we're leavin' tonight. So pack your gear and let's get a move on."

"I'm not goin' anywhere with you, guy," Banner told him flatly. "Archwood's got somethin' else lined up for me to do. Somethin' local here."

"Well . . . ain't . . . this . . . somethin' . . . now. Ain't even gonna follow orders. Ya know," Dellasandro said loudly, flicking his cigarette into the snow at Banner's feet without taking his eyes off Banner, "a man sure acts differ'nt when he finally gets his first piece of *ass*."

Banner heard his wife's surprised gasp. The foul remark made Banner hot immediately. All the anger he had carried with him from just being around Dellasandro while working with him welled up at once. "You son-of-a-bitch!" he shouted in the silence, the only words that came out of his mouth, the only thing he thought of that moment in his sudden rage. He punched a smiling, mocking Dellasandro on the nose as Dellasandro began to stand. Banner hurt his hand immediately, feeling Dellasandro's nose snap loudly and flatten beneath his fist.

Dellasandro, taken by complete surprise, bellowed like a wounded bear, holding his face between bloodied fingers as the blood spurted out, and slipped backwards on the steps. When he stood again to pounce on Banner, Banner punched him harder on what was left of his nose, and Dellasandro slipped again in screaming rage. Banner wouldn't let him get up. Each time he tried, Banner hit him in the face.

He would have continued punishing Dellasandro were it not for the fact that the next thing he knew four hands grabbed him from behind, pulling him away from the injured man. Tommy Fryman held Banner's shoulder with one huge paw while his brother Jimmy stepped in between Banner and Dellasandro. Both brothers were huge, lumbering, quiet and intense fellows who stood well over six feet, with long straight black hair worn in braided ponytails down their large backs. Jimmy kept staring at Dellasandro and Banner, then shook his head stoically. The silence was unnatural; the neighborhood still and desolate.

"Personally, I think you slipped and fell on some ice, Kemosabe,"
Jimmy quietly told Dellasandro, grinning mirthlessly into his face. "Leave
'em both be. It looks like Banner here is ready to bring ya down, tie ya
up, brand ya, and cut off your balls for the sheer pleasure of it, Sammy.
We all got enough problems without another stinkin' fight to parley to."
He turned to Banner, who stood with Tommy's paw still holding his
shoulder. Banner was still intent, a stonily cold expression upon his face,
ready to assault Dellasandro again. He was opening and closing his right
hand, his eyes fixed on Dellasandro.

"Settle down there, cowboy, gawddamn me I never knew ya had it
in ya to fight like that, heh heh heh," Jimmy said. "This was supposed to
be a little joke anyway. Sammy wanted to stop here and harass ya for a
little while. It's just him an' us goin' to Carolina country."

He turned back to Dellasandro. "Come on, Kemosabe, we gotta
make a stop at emergency, get that nose fixed," and he roughly pulled a
somewhat subdued, but glaring Dellasandro to the rig. His blood covered
the front of his jacket and the snow at his feet.

"I'b godda ged you for dis, Badder!" Dellasandro shouted, wincing in
pain even more. "You're by beat!" and shook his fist at him. Jimmy held
Dellasandro's arm in a steel grip while pushing him to the rig.

Banner stood still, held by Tommy. He just shook his head and said
flatly, "You ain't gonna do *shit* to me. The next time I come at ya with a
hammer or a fuckin' pipe wrench. Get the hell outta here, ya make me
sick. Motherfucker."

They glared at each other for another minute, as if ready to start
throwing more punches, but Jimmy opened the passenger door of the
Kenworth and shoved Dellasandro unceremoniously inside. He turned
to Banner and looked at him once from head to toe. "Go on inside and
enjoy your last night of vacation, cowboy. Christ, man, ya deserve it 'fore
hittin' the road again." Banner just shrugged. He suddenly felt drained of

all inner rage and energy. Tommy let go of his shoulder, and Banner was startled to see the large man quietly slide an evil-looking bayonet back into a sheath in the inside of his boot. The Bee stood behind Banner, watching in silent horror, her brown eyes wide and pupils dilated. Jimmy nodded to his twin brother, then went around and climbed into the rig. Tommy silently disappeared into the Kenworth oil tanker. A moment later, the trucks were zooming away into the snowing darkness.

Banner wanted to puke.

The next morning after Banner had driven to the shop, he was surprised to see Archwood already sitting behind his large scarred wooden desk, smoking a cigarette. "G'morning," Archwood said, "how was your vacation?"

"Not long enough," Banner answered, waiting for it.

"Uh-huh. I gotta call last night from Jimmy Fryman. He said that Sammy had slipped on some ice and busted his nose. He said he did it at your place."

"Yeah," Banner said flatly.

"What the hell was he doing there at your place that time of night? He shoulda been on the road, headin' south."

"Said he wanted me to go along. Said that you wanted me to go with them. I said no I wasn't going. That's when he got up off some steps that lead to our house . . . and broke his nose."

"Mm-huh," Archwood said. He took another drag on the cigarette, frowning.

"Is he all right?"

"Who?"

"Sammy."

"Oh yeah. Yeah, he's all right. He's all bandaged up. I guess he's got one hell of a swollen nose and two big shiners," Archwood said. "He sure musta fell hard."

"Yeah."

"What'd you do to your hand?" Archwood asked, pointing with his cigarette at Banner's own swollen and red right hand.

"I slipped on some ice, too," Banner answered evenly "Last night as a matter-of-fact."

"Uh-huh," Archwood said, smiling thinly, nodding. "Well, shit, I can see that I'm gonna have to keep you two guys apart for a while. It won't happen again, do ya *hear?*" Archwood asked, somewhat sharply, giving Banner a silent but knowing look. "Understand?"

"Yeah," Banner answered.

"Good. I don't need my men fightin' when they have to work in the substations. No doubt whatever he did last night he deserved what he got. There been times when I wanted to punch the guy myself, but I need his ass out there in the field. And yours. You're beginnin' to be one of the best guys I ever had workin' in the subs, and I don't want to lose you either. Jasper won't get wind of this, or your ass would be out on the streets right now. So there ain't no use involvin' him in it. Now you ready to come back to work?"

"Yeah."

"Good. I'll make sure that Sammy gets the word. No more of this shit with you, he's gonna leave you alone. I really don't care about your lives when you're off the jobs, but when you're in the subs, we need all the co-operation we can get. 'Cause there ain't gonna be anyone else out there to save your ass except yourself, you got it?"

"Yeah."

"Good," Archwood said, smiling and stubbing out his cigarette. "Now let's go over these data sheets. You're gonna go on over to American Steel and take their six-month oil samples again. That should give ya an easy eight hours today, huh?"

"Yeah," Banner answered, grateful to Archwood for closing the subject, for he was already sick and frustrated at what had happened, but felt that Dellasandro had gone too far—especially in front of his wife, who had to listen to it. Everyone else was afraid of Dellasandro, except the Fryman brothers, who didn't take any crap from anybody.

He went over the data sheets with Archwood.

2.

Leroy Chessan ran over to the shed and shelter, dripping wet and slapping his wet and dirty boots. "How you doin', Leroy?" Banner asked, letting him inside.

"Oh, mighty fine, Jackson, mighty fine," Leroy answered in a high soft voice, looking happy, smiling broadly and stroking his wet blonde goatee. His eyes were wide and always seemed to be focused at something not immediately in front of him.

"Nice trip?" Banner asked.

"Oh yeah," Leroy answered breezily.

"How's Dellasandro?"

"Same as usual. Meaner than ten junkyard dogs with bad cases of rabies." Leroy laughed softly.

"Any problems?"

"Nah," Leroy said, shaking his head. "After we ate at that '76 truck stop, you know, by Lodi? B.S. was in such a hurry to get here that he got pulled over by the state troopers for doing 75 in a 55 mile-an-hour zone." He shook his head.

"You oughta heard Sammy though. He thought it was funnier than hell. He made us pull over and wait for B.S. only a quarter mile from where the cops was writin' the ticket. Sammy was goin' on an' on about the whole situation over the c.b., real sarcastic like, you know how he is," and Leroy shrugged.

"Anyway, the cops musta had one of their radios on in their cars, or they heard it over B.S.'s radio, 'cause the next thing I know, after the cops wrote B.S. the ticket, they came up roarin' to Sammy's rig and proceeded to chew his butt 'bout the illegal use of the c.b. Man, I could hear 'em yellin' and screamin' at Sammy even from where I was at, and I was behind his rig. Anyway, they let him go with a warnin', and B.S. just zoomed on by us and he was givin' it to Sammy jus' like Sammy had given it to him. Lord it was hilarious."

"Jesus," Banner said, shaking his head. "How much for the ticket?"

"B.S. said over 80 dollars."

"Holy Christ."

"Amen, brother," Leroy said, and laughed again. "You oughta heard him goin' on an' on about it all the way here. Jesus have mercy on me a po' sinner, but I sure have connected up with a funny bunch of people. Lord, Lord," Leroy said, and sighed, slowly shaking his head.

"So who's driving the tanker?" Banner asked.

"Lazarus."

"*Phil?*"

"Yeah."

"When'd he get back from Ponca City?"

"'Bout three days ago."

"No kidding?"

"How's he feeling?" Rick asked.

"Okay, I suppose."

"Great," Rick said enthusiastically. "Life is gonna be a little more pleasant around heah." He turned to Tower. "Tower," he drawled, "I sure hope like hell Archwood makes you work with Phil." Tower only shook his head sorrowfully. Ringo began laughing at Tower's self-induced misery.

"Anybody else come?" Banner asked Leroy.

"Yeah," Leroy answered. "A new kid named Buckingham. I think he's Phil's cousin."

"Where's he at?"

"He rode on up here with Dellasandro."

"Oh Christ, what a way to start a job."

"He looked pretty scared when we were eatin' breakfast."

"A raw recruit," Banner said, shaking his head. "What a way to go, especially with Sammy." They fell silent. Each one of them knew what it was like to work with Dellasandro for the first time, especially Tower.

Tower groaned again, sounding miserable.

3.

Dellasandro and his crew were in the City of Brotherly Love when two days later he called B.S. and told him: "I need three more men on this transformer we're on!"

Archwood said flatly, "Sure, no problem." He wanted the job done fast and didn't want to waste any more time on it because they were already two months behind in the work log.

He screamed from his cramped cubby-hole office: "Jackson!"

Banner, who happened to be analyzing transformer mineral oil and was tired and numb after eight straight hours in the laboratory, nearly dropped a full open bottle of oil on to his lap when Archwood hollered.

Now what?

When he reached the office, he was told to find Rick and the new trainee, Tower, and leave the shop at 1700 hours, to head over to the City of Brotherly Love and help out Dellasandro's crew.

It had almost been time to call it a day.

Cursing, Banner drove home and packed his clothes. He'd only been home two days himself. He left behind an aroma-rich kitchen, where the Bee had been broiling two thick ribeye steaks and preparing a salad. She was pouring homemade elderberry wine when he had entered the house. She had warm candlelight in the darkened oak dining room with a fire roaring in the hearth, and was looking forward to the final and exciting prospect of making love for dessert. After kissing his sobbing wife good-by, he raced back out the door.

Rick and Tower waited for him at the shop, both sitting in the ten-wheeled rig they were taking. Tower wore a dirty white sweatshirt and bib overalls. Rick always looked sleepy through hooded laughing eyes.

"Ready?" Rick drawled.

"You bet," Banner answered sourly. "All the friggin' time."

The further away they drove from the shop, heading east, Banner and Rick kept cursing about the job, because they knew what was coming. As they swapped stories back and forth about Dellasandro, Tower just shook his head and screamed: "Bullshit!" He had stopped at a liquor store before returning to work and brought three six-packs of beer with him into the truck. He sat on a narrow bench between and slightly behind them, split the packs with Rick on the interstate highway. Banner smoked as they drank. Here he was on the road again; no way out of this particular job, stuck with a drunken trainee and a hot woman at home.

Dellasandro and the Fryman brothers were at the downtown Holiday Inn waiting for them when they finally arrived in the City of Brotherly Love at midnight. Everyone went barhopping around the city that same night and got vilely, stinking, fighting drunk, especially Tower. He thought he was a real member of the group and felt great all night—*hey*, working for this company was going to be *his* cup of tea—and everyone kept howling with laughter whenever it was brought up how Tower had pissed on poor old Ben Franklin's grave that night.

They had a great time.

The next morning was shattered by the telephone. Banner answered his wake-up call, head pounding: "Good morning, sir," a delicious female voice purred. "It's five a.m."

"Oh yeah yeah," Banner mumbled, wishing it were his wife waking him and not some gawddamned desk clerk. He answered, "Thank you, sweetheart," kissed the mouthpiece, hung up, and sat blearily on the side of the cold bed.

He tried unsuccessfully to rouse a snoring, groaning, farting Tower. The room reeked of beer, beer sweat, beer piss, and stale air. Tower's clothes made a scattered trail from the door to his bed; Banner had fallen asleep with his still on. He nearly gagged: "Jesus Christ!" overwhelmed by the stench as he tried to wake Tower, already aggravated by a raw recruit. Gawd, he hadn't been like this when he first hired on. Tower was even worse.

"Time to get up, *turd*, let's get a move on," Banner croaked loudly next to Tower's ugly, hairy, exposed ear.

"Yeah yeah," Tower mumbled unintelligibly, and sank serenely back into his pillows.

Banner shook his head as he stared down at the lifeless hulk, then went into the bathroom and performed his morning ablutions. The shower revived him more than he thought. He dressed warmly, knowing it was going to be a bitch, and walked downstairs to breakfast. He made it a practice to warn trainees only once when working with Dellasandro.

Turds, Dellasandro called them. *Trainees under rigid discipline.* Dellasandro had loved the Marine Corps.

Tower snoozed on obliviously.

The other men were in the dining room, all stone-faced and barely awake, sitting in a silent communal stare around a large table, cups of steaming hot black coffee beneath their noses. They were miserable and nasty with pounding hangovers and hacking cigarette coughs and frustrated libidos. They looked like hell. With the Fryman brothers though, it was hard to tell: they sat unmoving; stoic; the revelry hadn't bothered them. Rick looked as if he felt the full impact of the night a few hours ago. Dellasandro, his bushy black beard exploding from his dark face, contemplated Banner with that mocking bright gaze of his, sitting back in his chair and smoking a cigarette. He looked as if he had a full eight hours' sleep. Banner felt oddly out of place in his oil- and dirt-stained work clothes, long hair pulled back into a tight bun at the base of his skull, *Varmer Joiles* beard framing his face.

They ordered breakfast.

The prospect of facing bleak, icy weather on the Delaware River and putting up with Norwegian rats as big as pussy cats who lurked and squealed in the corners of the drop forge foundry where the job was located wasn't too thrilling for the lot of them. This particular job was almost an impossible one to do: refitting and making up new gaskets for 15-foot-long tubed radiators on a high voltage transformer, replacing the gaskets on the side-mounted insulators, and replacing the pressure, oil and winding temperature gauges. They had to rerefine nearly 5,000 gallons of toxic askarel that had to be drained first before they could do any work on the transformer. The transformer stood nearly 20 feet high and 15 feet wide all around, located in the coldest and darkest part of the foundry. On top of it all, the company had subcontracted a crane operator at 100 dollars an hour to lift the radiators, and the man with the crane was always at the job site sharp at 0700 hours, eagerly ready to work even if the crew wasn't.

No wonder Dellasandro called for help.

No wonder they were all drunk, Banner thought.

When he had sat down, he asked loudly, "What time did we finally crawl back here?"

Stony looks greeted him in reply.

Rick croaked out: "'Bout three or so, mon," and almost took a nosedive into his coffee.

"Jesus," Banner said, managing a grin, shaking his head. "We're gonna be in great shape to hit it today."

"Where the hell's Tower?" Dellasandro barked flatly, looking mean and nasty. "Where the hell's our trainee? Where's my *turd*?"

"Oh, him," Banner said rather airily, waving his hand. "He's still in the sack. I cahn't get him up."

"Oh yeah? I'll fix that red-headed juicer, heh heh heh," Dellasandro said, smiling grimly. "Gimme your key after we eat. I'll get him up. Everyone else is here, ready to go. And since he seems to need so much of his fuckin' precious beauty sleep, he's gonna filter askarel today, heh heh heh. You can have Rick. I was gonna have him do it, but now I got me a better candidate."

"Great," Rick mumbled.

"Askarel," Banner muttered, and shuddered at the word.

When they finished breakfast and paid their bills, Dellasandro took Banner's room key and left them. Banner and the other men trudged outside like Dr. Zhivago into the freezing wind and started the cold trucks. Banner let the ten-wheeled rig warm up. Rick went with the stoic Fryman brothers.

Banner shook out his first cigarette of the day, lit it, and sat back and waited for Tower to show. He did not have to wait long.

Suddenly, as the lobby doors burst wide open, he saw Dellasandro and Tower stumble out of the hotel and down the front stone steps with Dellasandro close behind Tower. People scattered hastily out of their way as Dellasandro screamed apoplectically in Tower's ear, pushing him to Banner's truck. Tower piled into the passenger seat, breathing hard and looking green. He was hastily dressed.

Dellasandro glared at Tower, standing inside the open door. "You're my meat, ya son-of-a-bitch, when we get on the job site! You're stayin' and roomin' with *me* when I let Banner and Rick go inna couple days, and you're gonna be *swimmin'* in askarel every *gawddamned minute of every gawddamned day we're here!*" His mocking eyes flicked to Banner. "On the way over, get this crybaby some coffee." He flipped Banner's room key to him, then slammed the door, rattling the window, and stalked to his truck.

Banner had been leaning against the driver's door, his arm draped across the back of the seat, silently smoking and looking at a wretched, moaning Tower.

"Awake?" he asked mildly.

Tower shook his head slightly, turning even greener than he already appeared to be, and muttered, "That motherfucker put a *firecracker* in my bed." Miserably moaning he leaned against the door, opened it, and puked on the snow-covered ground.

Banner couldn't stop laughing.

Finally, Dellasandro's voice crackled over the citizen's band: "Let's roll, college boy, we gotta lotta work to do. Get that *turd* back in his seat."

"Ten-four," Banner answered, and laughed as Tower puked again. He'd been there too many times himself. "You ought not to drink. It's bad for your gizzard."

"Shut up," Tower said.

He wasn't worth a damn after that day; oh, yes, he received his catechismal baptism in handling askarel. Exhausted beyond belief and still hung over later that day, he sobbed and moaned because he had been sloppy working with the carcinogenic dielectric fluid, and got the chemical on his exposed skin. The hydrochloric vapors had burned into his pores, turning his skin redder than it naturally was. His eyes constantly teared and burned and looked bloodshot. He'd been warned twice by Dellasandro not to get the chemical on him during the hard day. Dellasandro had no sympathy for him.

So that night in the fine hotel room, Tower lay naked upon the bed like a crucified Christ, feeling as if he were on fire. The men knew what he was going through, because they had all been there themselves. Banner felt sorry for him.

Later that same night he went to his room and gave him two pairs of rubber gloves, skin barrier cream, and two gallons of castor oil to rub on his body in order to neutralize the chemical that burned invisibly in his skin. Taking a shower never helped, Banner told him, because the water only heightened the skin's burning sensation. So really the only protection one had, he said, was to stay fucking sober, and be gawddamned careful how you handled the chemical when around it.

4.

Banner turned and watched a shaking Tower trying unsuccessfully to half-way sober up drinking the foul coffee. After the City of Brotherly Love job, Tower was stuck working with the chemical. Half the time he stank of alcohol, castor oil, and askarel; it was only recently that he had been put with Banner and Rick so that he could have the chance to redeem himself. His wife was threatening to divorce him if he didn't straighten up.

Banner turned back and watched in silence as Lazarus drove the 40-foot oil tanker in through the gate, but saw him stopped by Dellasandro, who stood in front of the rig with his hands on his hips, rain pouring over him, glaring at Lazarus. "Get the fuck outta there!" Banner heard him scream, and watched Lazarus jump out of the cab and Dellasandro climb in after being nearly clobbered by Lazarus as he flailed his heavy wooden cane at him. Dellasandro drove the tanker straight in and parked it between the shed and the nearest transformer, blocking the other two trucks.

Meanwhile, the three rigs that carried the three huge transformers on the low-boy trailers idled in front of the switchyard. Banner saw that the two stoic Fryman brothers and Dick Lake—an independent trucker who was a friend of Archwood—stood by Archwood's pick-up truck. His truck sat on the side of the road, parked in front of the three rigs. He sat behind the wheel, conversing with the three men. A moment later, the three men went back into their rigs while Archwood peered through the side window at the switchyard, watching Dellasandro maneuver the last truck. He then pulled into the substation and parked his truck by Banner's and Ringo's.

Banner caught Lazarus's eye and they both greeted each other in silence. Banner saluted him with a finger to his hardhat. Lazarus grinned widely. Banner watched him walk still stiff-legged to the rig that Dellasandro first drove up in, using his cane very little, it looked like now; thank God. He saw Archwood and Dellasandro talk for a moment— "Phil looks okay," Rick said quietly: "Yeah," Banner answered—then watched Dellasandro head toward the rerefining rigs and Archwood over to the shed.

"We better go find a place to sit," Banner muttered to Rick and Leroy. They turned and sat on the last two chairs, while Leroy hitched himself on to one of the drums of ten-c oil and began munching on an apple that he held in his hand.

"Gawddamn rain," Archwood said flatly to no one in particular, stamping into the shed, frowning and looking at his men. He wore a bright yellow raincoat and white hardhat and yellow galoshes over his shoes. He was tall and skinny, raw-boned and intense, with eternally bloodshot green eyes from too much booze and not enough sleep, high hollowed cheekbones, and pale tight white skin. His blonde hair was plastered to his skull as he took off his hardhat and shook it over the floor.

"How you guys feel?" he asked, not enthusiastic at all.

"Tired," Banner answered, "but we're all here."

"Yeah, I see that."

Leroy crunched loudly on his apple.

"So what kind of mess did you get us into now?" Ringo asked. His eyes looked small and piggish behind the thick-lensed black horn-rimmed glasses he wore.

Archwood grinned wryly, almost a grimace, then shook his head. He glanced outside for a moment. "We gotta call two days ago from Wyandotte Power Electric Utility. It seems that the guys who work up here went on strike almost a month ago, and the power company threatened to fire 'em if they didn't go back to work."

"Why'd they go on strike?" Banner asked, glancing at Rick, who looked back at Banner with sudden realization in his eyes. It looked as if the strikers drained the transformers. If they did that, Banner thought, what else are they capable of doing? It looks like this is going to be a long, drawn-out affair.

A strike.

"These guys up here want to get their contract settled, something like that, and from what I get, management is being a hard-ass about it. They been workin' without a contract for almost a year now," Archwood said, shrugging.

"Oh great, that's just fuckin' *great!*" Rick suddenly shouted, sounding pissed off. "Mon, we're *non*-union, remember? What are they gonna do, mon, when they find out *we're* heah?"

Archwood shrugged again. "What can I say? Algis Jasper took the call and said yes, we'd do it, of course we'll do it, and he's gonna charge 'em an outrageous price for it. I gawddamn wish that I took that 'phone call, or we wouldn't be here, I don't want any part of it either. This smells like trouble. Anyway, I got L.A. Ross back at the shop trying to talk Algis into not chargin' 'em so much for the job here. If we come out of this all right, I'd like to get their business later on, but only until things cool way down. I just hope nothin' else happens while we're here."

"Great, that's still fuckin' great," Rick was muttering. He didn't like being stuck in these types of situations. None of them relished the idea.

"What happened here?" Banner asked, gesturing outside.

Archwood sighed, and was silent for a couple of minutes. The rain beat steadily down. The day was becoming gradually lighter. "From what I gather," Archwood suddenly said, looking at Banner with a tired and worn expression on his pale face, "two or three men who work for this power company opened up the bottom valves of the transformers. From what I been told, when the oil level came down to a certain point, the sudden pressure relay devices operated, tripping the circuit that feeds this substation, and knocked out that line. The relays isolated and killed the transformers when the o.c.b.s out there tripped. The transformers then just kept draining themselves out of oil. But the company up here is wondering if any damage was done to the units. Make sense?"

"Assholes," Banner muttered disgustedly. "What a stupid thing to do. If they really wanted to do any damage, they coulda just pulled the relays and blown the transformers. Is this the only sub affected?"

Archwood shook his head. "There are two more—"

"Two?" Rick yelled.

"—but they're smaller banks."

"Jesus, if this thing drags out, we could be up here a long time," Banner told Archwood.

Archwood only looked back at him inscrutably; his face was naturally drained of color.

"We got enough oil in that tanker?" Banner asked, gesturing outside again, already resigned to the fact that Archwood had him by his inflated balls and was pulling them.

There was, Banner saw, no way out of this particular job.

"We got 10,000 gallons in the tanker, and both of the filtering rigs are full and ready to go. If we need any more, the power company up here told us it'd be no problem getting 10-c oil. If those banks are blown, though, we got those transformers out there on the rigs ready to install. I told those guys out there to stay in the trucks until I find out what the hell we got up here." Archwood paused a moment. "If we need 'em, I got to get hold of a crane operator. I got a number here to call in case I need one. Gawd I hope we don't need 'em. This is gonna be a son-of-a-bitch one way or another, no doubt about it."

"Jesus," Banner said, lighting another cigarette.

Tower, Archwood, Leroy, Rick, and even Ringo, bumming from Banner, also lit up cigarettes, each knowing what a bust this was going to be.

"So how long do we have to do this job?" Banner asked, taking another drag and blowing the smoke out nervously.

"Faster we get it done, the faster we get out of here," Archwood told him, but speaking to them all. He looked outside. "I didn't figure on all this rain." He fell silent.

They listened to the falling rain as it pounded hellishly against the roof and the concrete apron. It started to get humid inside the shed. The cigarette smoke hung heavily in the room, blue and barely drifting. If the strikers weren't finished and there was no future settlement in sight, then they could be up here for an indefinite amount of time.

Jesus.

"Damn," Banner said into the silence. "So what do you want us to do?"

"We gotta ratio those transformers to see if there's been any internal damage. The fuckers drained 'em while they were still energized, and," here Archwood consulted some wrinkled and coffee-stained papers he pulled from beneath his raincoat, "and Elmer Boggs and two of his men drove on out here when they got word from their dispatch office. I guess they found the breakers already tripped open by the relays, so they went ahead and opened the disconnects in the substation. The oil had already gushed out of them. People were out of power for a while until they re-routed it over other lines." Archwood looked at them wryly. "So they called us up a couple days ago for help. Now we're here and gonna wait for Elmer Boggs."

"Another fine mess," Ringo piped up.

"You got that right!" Archwood said. "And you can thank Jasper for it." He shook his head wearily and gestured outside. "There's real trouble up here, I guess, so we got to be careful, and on our toes. Elmer says that he has only a skeleton crew helpin' him out, keeping an eye on the main substations they got around here. He doesn't know what the hell is going to happen if this thing keeps dragging out. Everybody's on edge. He was also tellin' me yesterday that the strikers're carrying guns and blowing out pole-top transformers and shooting at the insulators on the line towers all over the countryside."

A litany of groans and wails rose up.

"Oh Christ," Banner prayed.

"Great!" Rick screamed, cigarette falling out of his mouth. "What's the matter with that dumb son-of-a-bitch back at the shop? Ain't we makin' enough money for him that we gotta cross picket lines and probably get shot at? Jesus, mon, Ah'm a scab, Ah'm always a fuckin' scab. Ah had my belly full of this crap, crossin' picket lines and workin' under union people," Rick yelled in frustration.

Archwood shrugged wearily. "Well, try not to worry about it. Elmer says he's gonna have police protection for us. Sheriff is supposed to show up here sometime this mornin'."

"Uh-huh. They should be here *now*. Did they ever catch those jerks who sabotaged this place?"

"They have no idea who did it. There ain't no hard evidence. Nobody's talking about it. Everyone who works here has keys to all the substations. It's a crap shoot."

"Uh-huh," Rick said again. "This is fabulous, just fuckin' fabulous. We shoulda stayed in Florida." He turned to Banner, angry and sullen. "Why in the hell did you answer the gawddamned *'phone*, Jackson?"

"I was already up," Banner mumbled.

"Shut up, Rick," Archwood said flatly, frowning. "Just relax. All I want you guys to do is ratio these three transformers, then go with Elmer or whoever and ratio some others that Elmer wants done."

The tired young men's faces all lit up with undisguised joy at Archwood's gracious and startling announcement.

"That's it? That's all you want done?" Jackson Banner asked, incredulous, suddenly enthused, thinking, *we're going home! We're going home!* Home, hearth, and warm-loving wife. Suddenly, the day seemed to get brighter.

"Yeah," Archwood said, shaking another cigarette out of his pack, "that's it. *If* these banks are still good, and the other banks at the other substations are good, *then* you get to go home. I got other work for you back at the shop. But you get to leave here only if these banks are still good. I certainly hope the fuck they are. I don't feel like bustin' my ass up here anymore than you do," and he lit his cigarette.

Scabs

Prologue

They had finished the oil sampling job in the mountains of Harlan County in southeastern Kentucky, and headed to Philadelphia for the next one. They drove all night, each taking turns behind the wheel and driving through the winding valleys and steep mountains, then followed the course of the muddy, slow-moving Ohio River on the old West Virginia side. When they arrived in Philadelphia, the sun was just appearing over the horizon.

They ate breakfast in a busy truck stop first, then drove over to the steel mill.

1. Becker

It had taken them most of the autumn day to retrieve the twenty-four mineral oil samples from the large coal company's high voltage substations because the substations were scattered over four huge mountains that dominated the small town and the coal mine in the valley below.

An old rotting wooden sign nailed to two huge leafy trees had welcomed them to Kentucky as they drove over the winding, dusty, rutted, two-lane road that had been carved long ago through the mountains. Jackson Banner and Rick Pitts looked at each other in silent amusement as they passed the sign.

"Welcome to Harlan County," Rick told Banner. He shifted the ten-wheeled rig to a lower gear as they wound through the top of the road and around another blind, shaded curve, then slowed the truck's speed for the steep, straight, two-mile downhill ride.

They arrived in the small town that lay in the floor of the surrounding, autumn-colored mountains. The town itself looked old and weathered, with small ramshackle houses carved into the steep hills and hidden beneath a carpet of thick large trees. Several old gray wooden houses stood among the others, windowless and boarded up; abandoned. A tiny gasoline station, a general store that also doubled as the post office, and an old Baptist church made up the center of the town.

At the other end of the small town lay the gray-cindered entrance of the coal company. They saw coal-loaded conveyor belts come down from the mountains above them, and huge stockpiles of the grayish-black mineral behind four large tipples and attached old buildings—blackened from years of coal dust—that had already been mined from the bowels of the mountains.

The electrician who greeted them when they pulled into the mine's parking lot was tall and rangy, clean shaven, and had flinty blue eyes that stared right through a person. Weary crows' feet were etched around his eyes, and a deep vertical scar ran from his hairline to the start of his right eyebrow. Stuck to the side of his light blue battered hardhat a large decal said CHRIST IS THE ANSWER in huge black-blocked letters against a white background, and across the front was his last name: Becker.

He told Banner and Rick he had orders from the owners of the coal company to have the transformer oils taken to be analyzed for insurance purposes, especially after one of their transformers had blown up a week ago, nearly creating havoc in one of the mine shafts when a group of miners was trapped for nearly eight hours with no way out except up and a near lack of oxygen that they had to contend with after a while. He said he would personally show them where the substations were located so they could do their work. He also told them the other coal mine union electricians knew they would be here doing work, and that his electrical union brothers didn't particularly appreciate it either.

"When they found out you were all coming here," Becker said, his eyes piercing right through Banner, making Banner feel absolutely naked, "they immediately went and filed grievances and were ready to go on a wildcat, but I talked them out of it. I had to do a lot of fast talkin' to get you boys here. Everything's cool now, but you all better stay close by me so everyone here'll know that you're with me. They know you're non-union. We don't want any trouble here now, do we?"

"No, sir," Banner answered, Rick silently shaking his head, both agreeing stoically with Becker that they didn't need any trouble, none whatsoever, especially here in Harlan County, and so they stuck close to Becker.

They followed the dusty trail of Becker's old, battered Chevrolet pick-up truck over the back-mountain roads that were on the coal company's property. They wound over climbing horseshoe turns in the ten-wheeled vacuum-dehydration rig that protested about being taken over the carved-out trails. (They had just finished two transformers in a substation in a Bristol, Tennessee vacuum-cleaner manufacturing plant three days before.) The coalmine-operation's substations were located near the tops of the mountains, where they too had been carved into the sides, exposing rock and coal seams, on the inside of the dusty roads. The transmission lines came down over the mountains sharp and taut at very steep angles, entered the substations, and left at nearly the same angle down further into the valley, the flexible line towers standing in line, creating a bare, steep scar through the colored forests. Once Banner and Rick were inside the substations, it didn't take them long to retrieve the oil samples, inspect the electrical equipment, and record the nameplate information. What took so long was the traveling over the roads, especially when they had to pull over closer to the precipitous edge than they really wanted to be to let fast-moving loaded coal trucks move down the mountains, stopping to let the thick brown dust settle before they crawled up the road to the next substation.

But it was interesting, to say the least, both looking silently at one another in resigned wonder, that there happened to be two or three electricians either inside the substations too, pulling weeds, flaking old paint off the electrical equipment slowly with makeshift scrapers, or outside looking the substations over themselves whenever Banner, Rick, and Becker showed up. The electricians invariably kept working while Banner and Rick performed the tasks assigned to them by their own company, but they felt the others' eyes upon them nonetheless. While they were inside the substations with the ubiquitous electricians, none of them really hassled them, but they made their presence known, and Banner knew they were being watched closely. It made Banner uncomfortable, while Rick just seethed in silence, his jaw muscles working as he ground his molars. There was no way out of this one, Banner knew, Archwood having assigned him and Rick to the job after Bristol was finished, knowing they would be able to handle it if they kept their wits about them, and their mouths shut.

These electricians watched them out of the corner of their eyes, not saying anything, nothing to each other, or to Becker, or to Banner and Rick, but just silently watching the young men perform their tasks in a seeming unassuming manner, as if they felt unaffected by the whole situation. Becker never said a word either, not even acknowledging his fellow electrical union brothers, but just sat in his truck in zen. Banner felt that Becker had laid himself on the line for them to be here, and during the day began to feel a great deal of respect for the man, but he felt bad about the circumstances. He knew it was no one's fault, except perhaps the coal company's management personnel knowing full well what they were doing when they hired an outside contractor to do some work, especially a non-union one. There was still an air of unreality as he and Rick worked. All he wanted to do was get the job done and get out.

On top of one of the mountains they pulled up next to a particularly large substation filled with oil circuit breakers and transformers. A half-dozen men were already inside it, looking over a transformer that obviously was out of commission for good, because it was entirely blackened with a large gaping hole in the side, with the large tubed radiators twisted and bent and partially melted from an intense fire. Banner knew this was the transformer that Becker had talked about.

It sat near the high wire-meshed fence away from the other transformers, disconnected from the bus work. That part of the fence was in the process of being dismantled by burly sweating Negroes as they wielded picks and shovels along the perimeter. A crane sat silent near the fence with an operator sitting in the cab smoking a cigar. A large Peterbilt with a low-boy trailer was parked next to it, with more Negroes setting huge, blackened porcelain insulators from the useless transformer inside wooden crates in the front part of the trailer.

"A fucking mess," Rick said lowly to Banner.

"Yeah," Banner answered. He noticed that the end of the substation structure was partially blackened from the fire, and the transformer next to the damaged one was partially scorched on one side. A new transformer sat on another low-boy trailer nearby, its radiators and insulators still boxed in crates on the ground next to it. A large spool of copper cable lay next to the crates. Banner thought about the picture in Jasper's office.

The electricians inside the substation warily watched Banner and Rick take the oil samples out of the live electrical equipment. They stood next to Becker as they watched the two men work. When they finished, Banner told Becker they were going to take an oil sample out of the burned-up transformer for their own analysis, knowing full well that it would be highly carboned and full of other debris and chemicals. A ladder leaned against the side with the hole in it, and Rick climbed it without permission and peered inside with a flashlight. Banner looked into it too a moment later, finding about three feet of oil sitting in the tank and the windings all fried and melted together.

"What caused it?" he asked Becker.

"Don't know," Becker answered.

The other electricians just watched them as Banner and Rick looked at the transformer. Rick took the oil sample: it was, as Banner figured, blackened and smelled bad.

"Acetylene," he told Rick.

"Water caused it," Rick said. "Wanta bet?"

The electricians just looked at them curiously as Banner and Rick talked to each other out of earshot from them, then followed them out of the substation and looked at the oil rerefining rig, parked next to the gate.

Suddenly, at first startling Banner, one of them asked Banner what the rig was for, and Banner said that this was one of the trucks the company used to filter transformer oil.

"Oh yeah? What's it do?"

He told them that most of the work they performed was done while the electrical equipment was still on-line. This was what the company he worked for had based its reputation upon, and ever since its men had begun performing such feats—working around the live high voltages, always watching what they were doing, monitoring the equipment, staying alert in the face of hazards—their track record so far had been almost one hundred percent, except for Phil Lazarus, who, Banner solemnly stated, had nearly died when thousands of volts had jolted him through his skull and blew out his elbow and leg.

The electricians' attitudes changed immediately after Banner told them that. Silent looks passed between them; Banner saw them physically shift toward a friendlier stance. It was as if he were watching a silent ballet being performed. Even Becker started to relax, as if he, too, had seen the wary tension disappear. There was a different light in their eyes as they heard Banner explain to them that they worked in live high voltage substations nearly all the time.

They understood him, well enough, because they too, knew what danger was, especially being inside a coal mine tunnel where almost anything could happen: that eerie groan in a seamed ceiling above the miners; that first faint smell of gas; that first small spark from a tool to ignite the coal dust; somebody fucking up around an operating piece of machinery; a transformer blowing up. They empathized with the young men, and knew then they worked hard and long and were as familiar with danger and hardship as any one of them.

Word traveled quickly throughout the area, for afterwards Banner and Rick were treated like comrades. There were no electricians waiting for them in the rest of the substations to watch what they were doing, so the oil sampling and inspections went on in relative peace and quiet. Even Rick loosened up a bit. He didn't like unions very much—"That's why Ah joined this heah organization," he told Banner—and kept quiet most of the morning, and let Banner do all the talking.

At first, he thought Banner had given away too much about what kind of work they did, and had talked too much about the oil rerefining rig, but Banner said the electricians would probably never operate this type of equipment because it wouldn't be cost-effective for them to use, like Becker had said, and that they'd never filter oil in the energized transformers anyway. From what they had seen, the mine couldn't shut down the transformers because it looked as if each one was needed to keep the mine running at full speed.

The substation which contained the damaged transformer didn't have a redundant double-bus, double-breaker system in which they could isolate each piece of equipment and work on them effectively. They had to de-energize the entire substation to fight the fire, and that had stopped the mine's operations for quite a while until everything could be returned to normal.

Becker later had told Banner and Rick that it was almost like a

Chinese fire-drill after the transformer blew up, with the electricians scrambling and de-energizing everything in sight. So, they found out, much to the chagrin of management, that it would be cheaper in the long run to have an outside contractor come in and do the work of drawing oil samples and installing new transformers when needed, because they would already know how to do it, get it done, and get out as soon as they were finished. The coal mine electricians apparently had had enough of being around higher voltages than 480.

"Sound about right?" Banner asked.

"Yeah," Rick answered, but he still didn't sound convinced. He didn't trust union electricians. This was just his nature after being through some hair-raising experiences of his own: crossing picket lines, enduring threats and curses as he worked on electrical emergencies inside industrial plants that had to have power (due to perhaps a mysterious pipe-bombing of a main substation transformer after the personnel there went out on strike), or having rocks hurled at the vehicles as he had driven through manned gates, or caltrops thrown on the highways leading into the plants, or any of a variety of other things that angry, frustrated men could think of to harass others, who, like themselves, were only trying to make a living.

"Everybody has to eat," Rick always said stoically, "but all Ah ever want is to be left the fuck alone."

The rest of the working day they continued drawing oil samples out of the transformers and oil circuit breakers in the scattered substations. When they were nearly finished, Becker took them on a ride down a coal shaft elevator and gave them a walking tour of the mine's operations. Neither Banner or Rick liked being inside the black bowels of the mountains, but they finally saw how coal was extracted out of the earth, taken outside and down the mountains to be piled and processed out. Becker even asked them seriously if they would like jobs here as electricians—the other union electricians had concurred with Becker about it—but he was turned down, not because of the wages, which were damned good and generous—hell, it was a lot more than what Banner was earning at the time—but because they would be beneath the ground most of the time working on the electrical equipment which had to be continually maintained, and making sure that the miners had enough light so they could see what they were doing, enough fresh air being pumped into the tunnels they could breathe, and checking that the conveyor belts were still in good shape, along with all the little, but important, things that always needed tended to, like making up extension cords and wiring electrical boxes and rewiring motors.

Banner thanked Becker for the offer, but told him that the area was too isolated for him to earn a living; he wouldn't be happy here; he liked being closer to civilization.

"Yes, but civilization starts right here," Becker told him, holding his arms high above him. "Without coal, this country wouldn't be where it is today," and Banner agreed with him, but still turned down the job offer.

He liked it much better where he was at, thank you, even though the money wasn't that great. At least, he was always on the open road and saw America and found how other men earned their living. It made him appreciate the job he had, because it was a real eye-opening experience for him to see how others lived, and he often wondered how these men did it, day after day after day, all tied to the same job in the same place in silent busy pain and laughter, nothing really changing in the work or the land they lived in. There were no more territories now to carve out and claim as one's own; they had all been laid out and settled long ago.

Everyone's freedom to do what they wanted seemed gone now.

But there was always the living, he found: the joking, the camaraderie, the drinking, the fighting, the arguing and bitching; and the tears of rage at injustice caused by accidents when one of their own came to a grievous end or a very grave injury, leaving one horribly crippled for life; and the tears of joy when one of them became a husband, a father for the first time, a Christian, or, by saving a life or serving his country; a hero. This was all that was left. Their faces, Banner saw, were etched in rugged, earthy experience: formal education wasn't necessary when common sense did so much more. But he often wondered what made men do the same work every day over and over again. Yet, he knew that he, too, did the same work over and over, but he was always on the move, traveling from one place to another, at times feeling as if he were a technical gypsy.

While standing inside the last substation to be finished, he realized that all men's jobs were tied together by electricity: the miners digging the coal to produce it, "symbols of a grim, strange war . . . being waged in the sunless depths of the earth," as Crane had written, sometimes dying for it, awakening others to their cause; the roustabouts in the fields drilling for oil and natural gas out of the ground; the Navajos mining the uranium to get it to the nuclear power plants. It was these men, he knew, who gave America the fuel in their silent, dangerous war to keep everything going.

The power generating plants produced the electricity that went out over the high voltage transmission lines, threading the landscape delicately like a spider's web, giving life to the whole country. There were men who watched over this machinery, who watched over the electrical power grids, always making sure that everything kept running so the masses could live their lives in unassuming freedom. They were society's unacknowledged vanguards, and knew they always would be; unsung.

The last high voltage substation, containing three large, 69,000-volt primary McGraw-Edison transformers was located at the very top of one of the mountains. It stood next to the dusty road on the edge of a small, rocky cliff, the transmission lines running steeply up the side of the mountain to the rust-colored, galvanized steel structure glowing dully against the violently bright autumn forest. Banner and Rick piled out of the truck, stretching and admiring the view. All around them thick forested mountains filled the blue sky with bright colors until they faded smokily in the distant horizon.

"Beautiful sight," Banner said.

"God's country," Becker answered, standing beside Banner. "See why I don't leave?"

"Yeah."

When Banner and Rick opened the bottom valve of the first transformer to retrieve oil, they were surprised to find five gallons of water pouring out.

"Shit," Rick said.

"Son-of-a-bitch," Banner said at the same time.

"Run or stay?"

"Fuck it. Stay. Get ready to run."

Each of the liquid level gauges in the other two transformers read "High" also, like the first one; then, when the needle bounced to the "Normal" mark, the oil started to flow. Becker had been surprised too as he witnessed what had happened. He told Banner that he would get the transformers inspected and repaired as soon as possible, or the coal mine would end up with a burned-out transformer like the one they had seen earlier.

After securing the equipment inside the rig, glad to be alive, they stood outside, ready to go; Becker to his job, Banner and Rick on the road. Becker kept staring at the two humming transformers inside the old substation, as if trying to figure them out, how the water got inside the main tanks.

It was becoming cool on top of the mountain, the wind rustling through the trees. Banner felt chilled. The sun was casting long shadows over the mountains. He and Rick still had a long way to go; to be in Philadelphia in the morning.

"Well listen," Becker said, shaking hands with them both. "I appreciate what you did down here. I'm gonna get on this right away and see what I c'n come up with."

"Get 'em fixed as soon as you can. You got a bad leak in all three of those transformers, probably coming from those insulators," Banner said.

"I'll do that."

Banner and Rick were silent for a while as they drove down the mountain and reached the coal company entrance and finally worked themselves through the rutted two-lane road out of the small town.

"Only one thing I can say about this friggin' place," Rick said, looking around.

"What's that?" Banner asked.

"It's a good thing that you an' me were workin' here rather than you an' Gordon, or me an' Gordon."

"Yeah," Banner agreed, and shook his head at the sudden mention of Gordon Short. He sat back in the seat and lit a cigarette, the first of many.

"Yeah," Banner said again. "I guess we oughta be thankful for small favors."

"You bet," Rick said.

2. Gordon Short

Gordon Short tested air circuit breakers and various relays in double-ended substations and other switchgear panels inside industrial plants. He drove his own truck that the company had purchased and redesigned to fit the specifications he needed to test the switchgear equipment. He was hardly ever seen in the shop because he preferred staying out on the road, moving from town to town across America, telephoning in to Archwood whenever he completed a job to find out where the next one was located. He lived strictly on his weekly expense account and had all his paychecks deposited directly into the bank. Whenever he needed assistance on a job, he called Archwood and let him know he would pick up his fellow worker at one of the metropolitan airports that dotted the country, and that he would take care of everything else. Some of the men didn't like working with Gordon because they thought he was a little crazy.

The first time Banner met Gordon was in the shop. That day Banner had been analyzing mineral oil in the laboratory, and was outside dumping the tested oil into a 55-gallon drum when a huge black and tan dog that he recognized as a Rottweiler ran through the open sliding door at full speed right at him, coming out of nowhere—a true nightmarish hellhound—barking and snarling madly, its eyes seeming red with fury, large mouth baring sharp fangs and slavering heavily.

Banner stood in silent shock and horror, nowhere to run, thinking at the moment that he was going to be devoured alive. The Rottweiler buried its nose deep into his crotch, snuffling madly and growling. Banner was afraid to move for fear of being bitten and deprived forever of his vital organs. He stood there with the five-gallon can of tested dielectric oil still poised in the air. When he shifted slightly, feeling the dog's nose wet and its hot breath soaking into his pants, the large dog growled louder and bared its teeth even more, still looking at him.

"Oh shit," Banner mumbled. "This is it. Good dog, good dog, easy does it. I ain't gonna hurt ya."

Then Gordon Short walked into the shop, saw what had happened, and began laughing harshly. Banner was surprised to see that the man was small and wiry, and so different than what he had pictured him to be from all the stories he had heard about him. Gordon had curly, shoulder-length black hair and a scraggly black beard. He wore a black leather jacket, black pants, and shiny, pointed-toed cowboy boots. A World War II Luftwaffe air force hat completed his outfit.

"I wouldn't move there, guy," Gordon shouted, laughing, across the deserted shop, "or you just might end up singin' soprano, and we'd have to send you over to Russia with those other castrated bastards who run that fuckin' country."

He whistled once, sharply. "Come here, Rocky. Let the guy be, he's on our side. He's an amigo," and the dog, thank Gawd, went charging back to his master, where it sat by Gordon's feet, still alert, its reddish eyes still fixed upon Banner.

He found out one day that Gordon Short didn't like union electricians. Banner had to go to a western Pennsylvania steel mill located on the Monongahela River to repair a pinhole leak in a large askarel-filled autotransformer near the steel mill's generating plant. Gordon happened to be working at another steel mill about ten miles away and was asked by Archwood to help Banner complete the job. The leak was seeping out of one of the autotransformer's tubed radiators.

The steel mill electricians had discovered the leak and dutifully reported it to their foreman, who in turn reported it to his superiors, who in turn told the foreman to get his own men to fix it, who, when they heard what the foreman told them what his superiors had said, whipped out their Memorandums of Understanding and told him to go fuck himself, because they didn't want to be near any toxic chemical that would mess up their reproductive organs, *gawddamn no*, not us. So, as a last resort, B.S. Archwood was contacted, even though it went against everything the union men stood for, and Archwood wearily sent Banner on his way to do the job. Banner met Gordon by the entrance gate to the steel mill. Gordon left his truck parked outside with his snarling dog inside it for protection, and rode inside the complex in Banner's truck.

To repair the leak, the autotransformer had to be de-energized first. The union electricians took their sweet time in going about it, acting as if they did not know how, poring over electrical schematic prints and arguing among themselves as to what switches to use. They walked over to the old gray switchgear panels inside the bright generating plant and pointed and shined their flashlights at the enclosed air circuit breaker cubicles and relays on each cubicle. Then they walked back to the table where the prints were and pored over them again. This went on for nearly an hour-and-a-half, until it became time for the men to take their designated, m.o.u.-guaranteed, morning coffee break. They stood by the schematics, lighting up cigarettes, pouring coffee out of thermoses, munching on snacks, farting loudly, scratching themselves, picking noses, telling dirty jokes, completely ignoring the two young men who had come to repair the radiator.

Banner and Gordon had sat in the foreman's cramped, paper-littered office all this time, smoking cigarette after cigarette until the air became blue and hazy. They silently seethed because they knew they were being fucked over. All they wanted to do was get the job done and get out: Banner wanted to go home to be with the Bee; Gordon had an unopened bottle of Jack Daniels in the cab of his truck and a whore waiting for him in his motel room.

Finally, after the union electricians went on their break, Gordon got fed up. He crushed out his cigarette, told Banner to follow him, then went out to where the electricians were. He grabbed the large electrical schematics, flipped through a couple of the prints to find what he wanted, then studied them for a full minute to the sudden silence of the group. He then unceremoniously threw them back upon the table.

Banner held his breath; he wanted no part of it, but he stood in the midst of it anyway, no way out.

"I can de-energize that fucker inna half uh minute," Gordon said loudly, and looked intently at his watch.

The electricians stared hostilely at Gordon, then at Banner, then looked at their foreman. The foreman—a big, beefy red-faced man with Mislowski stenciled on his hardhat—looked grimly at Gordon, too, who still looked at his watch. He glanced at his men, then jerked his head to the switchgear panels, and three of the electricians walked away from the group. No one said a word.

"Motherfuckers," Gordon muttered, lighting another cigarette, and lighting Banner's.

"Really," Banner said.

Gordon looked at Banner wryly. "Listen, Banner, meanin' no disrespect, I like you an' all, but I don't think I wanta work with you anymore. It's bad luck every time I work with someone. Especially in places like this where you're always being spied on. I'm a loner, an' I like it better that way. That's why Archwood sends me out by myself. Ya know what I mean?"

"Yeah," Banner said.

But—alas—there had been a second time they worked together. It wasn't too long after the Pennsylvania steel mill job, and it happened to be local, about ten miles away from the shop. Archwood received a telephone call from the local roller bearing mill that oil circuit breakers had just been installed in a substation under construction, and would he send somebody over to put oil inside the breakers? Archwood told Banner, who was ready to leave for another job in West Virginia, to go to the new substation.

Banner loaded the oil filtering rig with the equipment he needed: five boxes of dry-pack and Fuller's earth cartridges, extension cords, oil hoses, and fittings. The mineral oil was already in 55-gallon drums at the substation. All he had to do was filter the oil into the breakers, then put one pass on each one of them. Gordon Short burst into the office trailer at that particular moment and Archwood decided then and there to send Gordon with Banner.

"Oh shit," Gordon said.

It was supposed to be a relatively simple job. When they drove over to the substation, they found it was to supply electrical power to the roller bearing mill's new water treatment plant. They had turned off the main highway and entered the long property through a large chained-linked main gate. The substation and treatment plant were swarming with hard hatted men.

Gordon began cursing. "Unions," he said. "Christ why me?" He turned to Banner; his face wooden. "Banner, you bring me bad luck."

"Amen," Banner said, and laughed once.

Nearly a dozen office trailers sat side by side, next to a building under construction. Across the dusty road that led to the water treatment plant, against some trees left standing among the great many that had been unceremoniously chopped down, old cars and pick-up trucks sat near them, parked haphazardly. Banner felt suddenly self-conscious, as if everyone knew they were coming. He parked the rig as near as he could to the substation. There were electricians everywhere, all of them looking busy, and working fast.

The whole day was a hassle from beginning to end. The substation was built on a small steep hill. The four oil circuit breakers stood on small individual concrete foundations in a large square, the insulators jutting brightly out of the tops. The graveled foundation hadn't even been poured yet. The column foundations were set into the still hard and heavily rutted ground. Banner and Gordon saw a dozen oil drums a hundred feet away, lying below the substation, and surrounded on three sides by bricks, wood, iron rods, and electrical equipment. The only way to get the mineral oil into the breakers was to roll those full drums up the rutted hill. They didn't have hoses long enough and knew that even if they did, it would be harder than hell to get the rig down there.

"Son-of-a-bitch," Gordon said.

"You said it," Banner answered.

Gordon wanted to move the materials away from the drums, but was stopped when three or four men up on top of the hill shouted at them not to move any of their fucking equipment. Gordon was ready to give them the finger when Banner grabbed him and said: "Hey, come on. Let's just get the son-of-a-bitch done so we can get out of here."

It took them nearly two hours to roll and heave each drum up the hill, being warned all that time by bricklayers, carpenters, and ironworkers not to touch any of their stuff either, and being jeered at by the electricians who wouldn't get out of their path if they were standing between the oil circuit breakers. They were watched as they laid the oil hoses out ("Hey, git that hose off mah brick!") and were taunted when they grabbed pipe wrenches out of their tool boxes: "Hey, Ah didn't know we had plumbers workin' here too!" and everyone laughed, except Banner and Gordon. They continued working, hurrying through it as best they could, but, as usual, it took a while to get things set up. By the time they were ready to start filtering the oil into the breakers, the union men had already taken their union-guaranteed, morning coffee break, and were looking forward to their union-guaranteed lunch.

The two young men continued working through lunch, first filtering the oil into each of the new breakers before putting a pass on each one of them. The other union workers, especially the electricians, jeered and laughed as they ate their lunches by the trees. The bricklayers, carpenters, and ironworkers ate too, apart from each other and the electricians, watching the young men work in the substation. Banner saw during the day that the four union groups were pushing each other as well, each trying to keep ahead of the others, with the electricians behind them all. There was no co-operation between the four groups either, but when the two scabs showed up, they all seemed to silently co-operate and needle the work that Banner and Gordon were doing.

"If it ain't us, it'll be somebody else," Banner told Gordon.

"It's always us," Gordon answered.

When lunchtime was over, they had just started on the first oil circuit breaker. Each of them held 150 gallons of mineral oil, but the oil had a dielectric of 20 kilovolts. Filtering through the dry-packs and heaters didn't raise the oil to a higher rate. So they constantly changed the filters every twenty minutes, testing the oil with each change. It was a long and tedious process, and after an hour the dielectric had risen to thirty.

"Archwood wants forty," Banner said.

"Just my luck," Gordon answered disgustedly.

They were on the third oil circuit breaker when 4:30 came around. The work activity ceased suddenly. All the union men stopped whatever they were doing, gathered toolboxes, prints, and equipment, and hurriedly stored them away in the office trailers. As one, they all seemed to get into their vehicles at the same time, some two and three in one car or truck, and roared off the site, dust raised high and drifting in the air as they left. In less than five minutes, everyone was gone.

"Well, *damn*, that was quick," Banner said.

"Yeah," Gordon said.

The only sounds heard were the generator and heater as they filtered the third oil circuit breaker. It was quiet otherwise, the stillness overwhelming from the buzzing, heckling activity of minutes before. Banner and Gordon were the only ones left in the entire work site. It gave Banner the willies, but at least he felt better with the others gone. Now they would be able to finish the work in peace. The last breaker they finally finished after dark. November's days were becoming shorter, the breath of winter hinting in the air, the sun setting just before six.

After they finished, they rolled all the drums down the hill again, leaving them the same way they had found them. They loaded the equipment back into the truck: oil hoses, pipe fittings, and their tools; then climbed back into the truck, exhausted and famished and out of cigarettes.

Banner started the truck and they drove slowly away from the substation, glad that the work was finally finished. All he wanted then was a hot shower and some of the Bee's home cooking. But the large entrance gate was closed, a huge padlock hanging in the center of the huge chain wrapped around the two posts where the gate swung open on both. At first, Banner was astounded, not actually believing that they were locked inside.

"Oh no," Gordon said.

"Oh fucking yes," Banner replied, staring at the closed gate.

"Shit," Gordon said. "Gawddamn it all! Those motherfuckers! I knew you couldn't trust those bastards! No wonder they left so fast! They knew we were still here! Son-of-a-bitch! I'll bet you right now they're laughing at us in some gawddamned bar someplace!"

"Yeah," Banner resignedly said. "But how do we get out of here?"

They drove back to the substation, got out, and tried every office trailer to see if any of them had a telephone. But all the trailers were locked up tight. Gordon started cursing again after they had checked half the trailers. The situation looked hopeless. *Now what?* Banner thought. Suddenly, Gordon found a huge sledgehammer lying beneath one of the trailers. He grabbed it and ran down to the drums. Banner watched him go through the material and saw him pick up a short thick iron bar and climb back up the hill.

"Let's go to the gate," Gordon said, grinning, piling into the passenger seat.

The truck's headlights shined brightly on the padlock as Gordon pounded on it, Banner holding the iron bar against the handle and body of the lock, hoping Gordon wouldn't miss in his anger as he pounded and cursed the lock. After ten minutes, the padlock smashed open. Gordon laughed, almost maniacally. They swung the gate open and drove through, then shut the gate. They put the heavy chain links through the padlock. Gordon pounded the bottom part of the lock as Banner gingerly held the handles against the center posts. When it clicked shut, they stopped and looked at each other.

"I'm gonna fix those sons-of-bitches," Gordon said. "You gotta portable welder here in the truck. Was that for the other job you were gonna do this mornin'? Get the generator started, I'm gonna weld this lock shut, and then I'm gonna weld the fucking hinges on this gate. And the chains too. We'll see who gets the last fucking laugh. You bet. And I'm keeping this sledge."

It didn't take long for the helmeted Gordon to weld the padlock and the chains and the gate's large hinges. Banner stood by the back of the truck, listening to Gordon laugh gleefully as he welded and averting his eyes when the bright blue arc-weld lit the ground. "That oughta do it," Gordon said, finishing and rubbing his bony hands together. "Let 'em try to get in here tomorrow. Gawddamn, I wish I could be here to see it, heh heh heh." Banner grinned, then helped Gordon place the small welder into the truck.

They never did find out what happened, but only imagined what the union men thought as they saw the welded gate the next day. The two men told Archwood the next morning what had happened. Archwood solemnly listened, then burst out laughing when Gordon told him what he did. Nothing was ever said: the roller bearing mill paid for the services rendered as agreed upon, and no mention was made about the gate. Archwood thought the unions didn't want to say anything, just wanting it to lie and be forgotten. How could they explain it to the mill's people? After all, they needed to work as much as anyone else, maybe even worse, and it would look bad for them if word got out. "Yes," he said, laughing again, "I think they'll keep their mouths shut, if they're smart. It was good poetic justice," he told them. "So don't worry about it. You did all right."

After that, Banner never had the opportunity to team up with Gordon. That day, Gordon left the shop with his dog, heading for Nebraska, while Banner and Tower headed east to New Jersey. Whenever he thought about Gordon, he always remembered him welding that gate and padlock shut. Gordon's name on the magnetic tile always seemed to shift from city to city on the large green job board, usually far away from Banner's jobs. Yet he continually heard stories about Gordon's adventures on the road from the other men who happened to work with him, and Banner noticed that Gordon's attitude remained the same with union workers.

Entr'acte

"Well," Banner said, lighting another cigarette, turning to Rick. "I'm sure glad Gordon is on our side, and not theirs."

"Who's?" Rick asked, peering out into the darkness, scanning the twisting highway ahead.

"Unions."

"Yeah," Rick agreed "He'd be a son-of-a-bitch if he were a union man, wouldn't he?" and laughed, because he too had worked with Gordon many times.

They drove the rest of that evening and the nighttime, too, through the southern Kentucky mountains, stopping only to get fuel, to eat, and to answer the call of nature. They each took turns behind the wheel driving through the winding valleys and steep mountains, finally coming up on the muddy, slow-moving Ohio River on the old mountainous West Virginia side. They followed the course of the river to Pittsburgh, then drove slowly towards Philadelphia.

Banner found the lights of the small cities and towns along the river lonely against the hilly darkness and the winding course of the large river. As he drove and passed through the small river towns, he pondered what the people living by the river did with their lives, how they made it through life each day. He wondered if they were scabs like him, ". . . working long hours, getting next-to-nothing for wages," as Jack London had written, picking and performing work no one else wanted to do, just making it paycheck to paycheck each week.

Around 0500 hours, Banner pulled into an old grimy busy truck stop, woke Rick, and told him that he was getting breakfast. Rick said, "Yeah, that sounds good," and sleepily joined Banner. "We in Philadelphia?"

"Sure are," Banner answered. "Can't you smell it?"

"Lovely place."

"Paradise."

"How far away are we from the mill?" Rick asked.

"About five miles. B.S. told me it was just down the road from this place."

"You ready then?"

"As I'll ever be."

"Well then, let's go."

3. Dutch

Dutch, the steel mill electrician whom Banner and Rick met at the entrance gate, was old and weathered, with one day's growth of white stubble sprouting through a rough, leathery face, a mouth squashed together from the lack of dentures, and a thick wad of tobacco bulging in his cheek. He stood by the gate with large, hairy thumbs hooked into his old leathered electrician's belt, the belt strapped low and looping around his grimy, scuffed blue jeans. He had on dirty, cracked, steel-toed motorcycle boots, a blue work shirt, and wore a battered yellow hardhat.

He stood silently next to Banner in this same position as Banner and Rick, both ignoring Dutch, busily worked to prepare a de-energized sixty-nine thousand-volt-primary transformer for oil rerefining: to raise the dielectric by heated vacuum-dehydration. This particular transformer was a borderline case, but the steel mill's electrical supervisor had wanted it done anyway, and B.S. Archwood reluctantly agreed.

Dutch himself de-energized the steel mill's main substation: an old dark spooky structure with three 69,000-volt transformers and old primary and secondary oil circuit breakers. When the circuit breakers were opened, the entire steel mill went instantly black. The silence of the mill seemed stark amid the contrast of the hooting barges on the river, the trains roaring by, and the traffic making a constant thrumming din. The electrical supervisor, Dutch's boss, who also hated Dutch's very existence for some mysterious reason which Banner couldn't fathom, assisted Dutch in de-energizing the oil circuit breakers inside the building, behind the brick wall of the main substation where the switchgear panel was located. The other electrical union brothers stood somewhat nervously inside the substation, next to the opened iron-meshed gate, as the oil circuit breakers were switched out of service, watched as Dutch and the supervisor returned. Dutch started with the secondary switch rack, opening the line and bus disconnects in slow, deliberate moves, then walked to the primary switch rack where the three large oil circuit breakers stood beneath the structure. After opening all three line disconnects from each circuit breaker, Dutch then swung the bus side ground-operated air-break switches in slow 180-degree arcs. The bright, thin, arc-weld of the sharp blue crackle of 69,000-volt electricity danced and sizzled loudly between the opening clips of the disconnect blades for a couple of seconds before it quit and disappeared.

"Yeah," one of the electricians said quietly as they watched Dutch break the connections. There was some sniggering from the rest. Dutch looked and squinted at his fellow workers in silence. Then, somehow nobly, he spat a wad of thick tobacco juice at the base of the galvanized beam where the air-break handle was attached. After that, he and the electrical supervisor walked a quarter-mile toward the entrance gate and watched the local power utility operators open the line side disconnects of a large oil circuit breaker that fed the main substation's primary bus, thus isolating the entire substation. This way Dutch and the supervisor would be able to ground the incoming line. Rick had gone with them to watch the utility operators.

Meanwhile, as this was going on, Banner stood and watched the electrical union brothers snicker and guffaw about the high voltage electricity. One of the men with an unlit cigarette stuck in his lips walked over to the ground-operated air-break switch that Dutch had just used. He began swinging the switch nonchalantly back and forth in slow motion, the switch's linkage meshing to also swing the disconnect blades. The disconnect blades above them buzzed and arced intermittently, the bright blue 69,000 volts of electricity dancing crazily between the clips and the blades. Banner wondered if the man knew what he was doing.

"Why don't you all go on up there and light your cigarette, Frenchy?" one of the blue-shirted electricians said loudly, laughing once.

"Fuck you," Frenchy answered, just as loud, shaking his head and grinning.

"Hey, guy, don't you know your men are doin' some more switchin' down at the gate?" Banner asked quietly.

Frenchy just looked at him, hard. "Fuck you, too," he answered, but he put the air-break switch back into the open position. He dug a pack of matches out of his pants pocket, lit his cigarette one-handedly, blew the fire out of the match, then tossed it at Banner's feet. Banner didn't move. His arms were folded across his chest. He looked at the disconnect blades and saw they were pointed away from the bus work. There was air between the clips and the blades. This was the only thing that concerned him.

Fuck these union people.

Five minutes later, Rick, Dutch, and the electrical supervisor came back, Rick nodding to Banner that everything went okay. The supervisor told the men that the incoming power lines were dead. He then said that Dutch was going to ground the substation for their safety.

Even with the substation de-energized and isolated, it still gave one a creepy feeling, knowing that one was going to crawl up into the structure amid all the conductors: the bus work, the stand-off insulators, the transformers, the potential transformers, and the oil circuit breakers. After all, this was the main substation that fed raw power into the mill to give life to the gigantic blast furnaces, the rolling mills, the forging presses, the drop hammers, the huge overhead cranes, and the conveyor lines that the melted steel would flash red-hot at incredible speed—but now everything was dead, and they knew they had to go up into the structure and do work they normally wouldn't want to do. The silent steel mill seemed to arouse a primordial fear in the electricians; they were not used to having their place of occupation totally shut down at any one time.

"Let's go and close the ground switch, Dutch," the electrical supervisor said, and pointed a finger to a red-painted air-break switch handle, like the other line and bus disconnect switches Dutch had used to open and isolate the equipment. It was locked in the open position when the other disconnect switches were closed into the electrical grid. Dutch looked at where the man's finger was pointing, then spat accurately at the base of the red ground switch's galvanized beam.

He stepped next to the ground disconnect switch located at the end of the primary bus, just below three metering potential transformers. He unlocked the cross bar that prevented the ground switch to suddenly fall and close itself upon the three-phase bus. He then grabbed the red-painted handle, let his squinting eyes roam over the ground switch's linkage up the side of the structure, and unceremoniously closed the switch, the disconnect blades sliding with a loud snap into the three-phased clips of the primary bus.

"Primary line's grounded," the supervisor said aloud to the men. "Let's get to work." He turned to Banner, pointing his finger at him. "I suppose you all know what to do. You're on your own. You got eight hours to do it," and then walked away.

Dutch flipped the man the finger behind his back, then looked at Banner and spat another wad of thick brown juice at the base of the column. When he relocked the ground switch, it was then that the men grabbed the cans of wax and rags and began climbing the substation structure, grumbling lowly among themselves.

There was really no lunch break through the day's long work. Dutch stuck to Banner closely through the rerefining process, watched him and Rick change the Fuller's earth tanks using the gawddamned knucklebusting chain hoist, and watched them measure the voltage breakdown of the rerefined mineral oil, check the specific gravity, the acid level, the interfacial tension, even calculate how long it would take to filter the mineral oil completely to raise the dielectric ten thousand more volts.

The electrical union brothers paced themselves to keep up with Banner and Rick, who continually monitored the rig and transformer, chainsmoking cigarettes at the same time, taking only brief moments to sip at their lukewarm coffee when they could. The electrical union brothers could only take theirs at the designated m.o.u.-guaranteed hours, and they sure took advantage of them, taking their slow sweet time in climbing down off the structure, in slurping coffee and munching on sandwiches, telling dirty stories, smoking cigarettes, and then slowly climbing up into the structure to get back to work again.

They didn't like being up in the air—hell, all they knew what to do was change light bulbs and pull wires through conduit—and there were stories floating above about filing grievances because of scab labor, so to speak, all eyes looking at an exhausted Banner and an exhausted Rick, who only tried to ignore them during the course of the day and keep working.

Then Banner had to step away from a falling glob of huge wax that spattered wetly and thick near him: "Oh, 'scuse me, boy, I musta got too much uh this heah gunk on this heah insuhlator," the other men sniggering and looking knowingly at one another, hard grins on their faces. Banner mentally shook his head.

He knew these poor laughing sons-of-bitches two, three years from now would be out of work because the eastern steel mills were slowly shutting down. He had seen it from steel mill to steel mill in the northeast: things were slowing down, dying out. There was cheaper labor overseas, and no unions either: the trilateralists knew what they were doing. *What would the unions do then?* he thought. *Let 'em have their fun. At least I'll be working.*

Then the wax fell with regular rhythm. Banner and Rick had to get out of the way a lot as the wax fell around them. They had been told many times never to arouse animosity toward electrical union workers: just do what you were supposed to do and then get the hell out. It was the territorial imperative, right out of Anthropology 101. Banner smiled inwardly, knowing what the situation was all about, really feeling for the electricians, but wanting to know why they felt so threatened.

The electricians looked and acted like alpha monkeys up in the structure, slinging shit, no different than if they were in a group of trees. Have we really changed at all? He silently cursed Archwood for getting them into this, and at the same time was doubly glad that Gordon Short wasn't here. He saw Rick's jaws tighten whenever he stepped out of the rig to check on the transformer. After he checked it the third time, he stayed inside the rig, watching the system there.

"Fuck 'em," Rick told Banner, and lit a cigarette.

The wax stopped falling suddenly when they saw Dutch walk away from the rig and leisurely up to the ground disconnect switch again and unlock the closed handle.

"Hey, Dutch, heh heh heh, you old son-of-a-bitch, what inna hell you gonna do?" one of them called.

Dutch just spat and looked up at the man, holding the red ground handle in a large, leathery hand. No one *ever* touched switching handles while men were up in the bones of the substation structure, and no one ever would have the idea of deliberately putting a key in the lock, unlock the ground disconnect handle and be ready to remove the ground from the substation. Even though the oil circuit breaker near the entrance gate was opened and the line disconnects opened, it made all the electrical union brothers suddenly nervous and unsure as to what Dutch was up to. Banner thought that Dutch would actually go out and close the line disconnects himself; the old man looked that determined.

Dutch pointed to all the splattered wax on the graveled foundation, then with the same pointing finger, drew it silently across his throat.

"Yeah, right," the same man who had yelled.

"Whatever you say."

The crazy son-of-a-bitch, Banner thought, he was mean enough to go ahead and re-energize the entire substation with all the men still in the structure. The man had no sense of humor. Banner was impressed though at how well the men hurriedly went back to work with this mere gesture on Dutch's part. Dutch leisurely relocked the ground disconnect switch, then walked back to Banner, who stood and watched the whole incident happen, and saw Dutch take his usual stance with his thumbs hooked into his electrician's belt.

The work became more pleasant to do after that, with no wax to contend with, and the electricians on subdued and grumbling behavior. Banner and Rick were nearly through with filtering the transformer anyway: they found they wouldn't have to change filters again.

"Good," Rick said. "After we're through here Ah'm gonna call B.S., tell him we're ready to come home."

The dielectric had greatly improved. Banner wrote some numbers on the back of a transformer data sheet, figuring out the time it would take to finish the transformer. Dutch watched Banner perform the calculations.

"You all seem to be pretty good with them figgers, boy," Dutch said to Banner, standing close to him, watching him scribble on the paper. His thumbs were still hooked into his belt and he had that contemplative squashed look upon his face.

"Yeah," Banner answered. "I went through school for four years. But I didn't graduate."

Dutch whistled, sounding sarcastic, then broke into a squashed grin. "Is that right? What'd you study?"

"Math."

"Oh yeah? You mean you like studied calculus?"

"Yeah, I studied calculus. And the higher order stuff."

"Is that right?" Dutch asked again. "So, you're pretty good at jugglin' them figgers then. Diff'rentation and integration and all that other stuff."

Banner stopped writing at that moment and stared at Dutch. Silent, Dutch squinted back at him, his leathery, brown face impassive like an Indian's, his left cheek swollen with tobacco.

"Yeah, that's right," Banner said.

"Well then," Dutch said, nodding as if he understood, and spat another wad of brown juice at one of the bay columns. "Well then, that's just fine. Look, I got somethin' for ya then if ya think ya can use it." He stared at Banner. "You all gonna graduate soon? Become a schoolteacher or somethin'? You ain't gonna be doin' this shit the rest of ya life, are ya?"

Banner shrugged, not wanting to think about it. "I'm still studying differential equations. When I take the test and pass, then I'll get my degree. I don't know 'bout teaching."

"Oh yeah?" Dutch asked. "Well then, I just have somethin' for ya that y'all could probably use."

"What is it?"

"I gotta slide rule in my locker, been keepin' it there now for nigh on to 20 years. Some engineer who worked here 25 years ago left it on his desk when he quit. I'd just joined this here chickenshit outfit, saw it, kept eyeballin' it for a few days, figgerin' the guy 'ould come back and git it, but he never showed back up. So I picked it up and kept the gawddamned thing in my locker for near 20 years now. Never had any use for it though. If you all think you can use it, then I'll go git it and give it to ya. D'ya want it or not?" Dutch leaned away from Banner, folding his arms across his scrawny chest and looking at the young man.

"Sure, I'll take it," Banner answered, enthused. "Is it the big one with all the scales?"

"Hell, I don't know, boy, I ain't never studied the thing," Dutch said, somewhat disgustedly, then jerked his head at the building behind them. "You'll have to look at it yaself. Come with me and I'll give it to ya."

Banner followed Dutch through the old red-brick building, passing through old make-shift hallways and cramped offices and finally through a small part of the steel mill itself, where huge thick steel ingots lay stacked and numbered, ready to be moved on to the rolling mill or the forging presses. At one end of the dark building, they came to a large concrete-walled bathroom with a long row of lockers against two of the walls. Dutch walked up to one of them, his fist holding a ring of keys.

The slide rule had all the scales, like Banner figured it had. The tool seemed to be in mint condition, with an old, but clean leather case with a red felt interior that housed the slide rule itself. Banner was impressed with it. He had always wanted one. He began sliding the cursor and runner immediately.

"Are you sure I can keep this thing?"

Dutch nodded: "Long as you can find some use for it. Far as I'm concerned, it's yours. S'keep it. I'm gettin' ready to retire mahself and I don't use the son-of-a-bitch."

"Well, thank you."

"*Shee*-it," Dutch said.

When they returned from the restroom to the substation, Rick was already dismantling the hoses from the transformer, wanting to go. He had already talked to B.S., he told Banner. The electrical union brothers were standing near the oil rerefining rig, talking among themselves, watching Rick closely. Banner put the slide rule on the motor mount inside the truck's cab, then helped Rick with the equipment. Dutch stood next to the ground switch and silently bided his time.

Finally, the electrical supervisor appeared and went up to Banner. "What kind of dielectric did you all get?" he asked, and Banner pointed to Rick.

"42," Rick answered.

"42, eh?" the supervisor asked. "Okay," nodding. "You all through here?"

"Yeah, we're through," Banner answered. "But I'd wait a couple of hours before re-energizing that transformer because of the air bubbles floating inside there now. Let 'em dissipate first."

The supervisor nodded again as Banner talked; then, when Banner finished, said, "That's all good to know, but I need these units back on the line."

"Whatever," Banner told the man. "They're your transformers. But I'm telling you anyway."

"That's right, they're my transformers," the man answered dismissively. "We're gonna re-energize."

Banner and Rick decided to leave before the substation was put back on the line. Just as they were ready to pull out—Rick in the driver's seat, gunning the engine, grinning mysteriously—Banner went up to Dutch, who stood, still silent and immobile, by the closed ground disconnect switch, and told him: "Well, Dutch, I guess I oughta thank you for the slide rule you said I could have," and offered Dutch his hand.

"Yeah?" Dutch asked, squinting at Banner, a myriad of deep tired wrinkles appearing on his face.

"Well yeah. Don't you think I should?"

"Beats hell outta me, guy."

"Yeah, right," Banner said, smiling but now embarrassed, suddenly realizing that Dutch wasn't going to shake his hand. He lowered it, self-conscious. "Well, we gotta go. We'll be goin' home for a few days."

"That a fact," Dutch said, and spat a thick wad at the base of the column.

"Yeah," Banner said. "So I guess I'll see ya later, huh?"

Dutch squinted at Banner, slowly looking at the young man once from head to toe, then back again. "Well," he drawled loudly, snorting, "I kind of fuckin' doubt it," then abruptly walked away from him.

Epilogue

Banner stared at Dutch, startled, then laughed once. He was different from other working men he had met. He tipped his forefinger to the old man's back in a silent salute, then hopped into the passenger seat of the rig. Rick drove silently through the plant's driveway, out the gate passing the local utility operators, and on to the main highway. Banner kept staring at the slide rule, running his fingers over the raised black markings, wondering about the old man.

"I fuckin' doubt it, too, Dutch," he said to himself.

"What say?" Rick asked.

"Nothing," Banner said, shaking his head. "Let's go home."

"Can't." Rick had a big grin on his face.

"What?" Banner asked, eyebrows raised. "Why not?"

"We gotta head back down to Becker."

"What?"

"It looks like ol' Becker called B.S., told him what we found, and wants us to do the work. B.S. said okay, and told me to head on back down."

"But, but, we don't have any more *filters*."

"It's bein' taken care of as we speak, mon. Somebody's gonna meet us down there. In fact, he's headin' down there now, with a full load of filters jus' for us."

Rick was still grinning.

"Who?" Jackson Banner asked suspiciously.

"Gordon."

"Oh no."

"Oh yes," Rick grinned, enjoying it.

"Oh *shit*."

Rick laughed, shifted gears, and continued laughing all the way back to Harlan County.

Cigarettes and Coffee
Part IV

1.

There was a sudden shock of recognition of who stood in the doorway. Water dripped on to the floor from his battered hardhat. A lit cigarette was stuck in his mouth, blue eyes mocking and intense and fixed on Tower's suddenly whitened face as if he were a two-pound steak. Dellasandro stood with his hands in his jacket pockets, black hair and beard wet and curly and bushily exploding from his leathered brown face—dressed in brown like most of the other men, all his clothes drenched and dripping—looking meaner than hell and not smiling at all.

"I want Tower's candy ass," Dellasandro snarled, his loud voice booming into the small shed.

Tower spilled coffee over himself, grimacing in agony and let loose a loud, fast, uncontrollable juicy beer fart.

"You gonna give me Tower, Archwood?" Dellasandro rumbled without looking at Archwood, who stood looking back at him as if he were puzzled, mulling it over.

"I wa'n't plannin' on it, Sammy," Archwood said, almost defensively. "These guys're pretty tired."

"From what? Their candy ass job in Florida?" Dellasandro sneered.

"Fuck you, you son-of-a-bitch," Jackson Banner said plaintively, quiet-voiced; angered. They had worked 16- and 18-hour days for weeks on end, busting ass each and every day.

Dellasandro shifted his hostile gaze to Banner. Banner stared back. Neither man forgot what happened nearly two-and-a-half years ago. "You talkin' to me, college boy?" he asked, mocking and intense, blue eyes mocking Banner even more.

"Ya gawddamned right I am," Banner answered, his voice mocking too. "You all leave Tower be. We're all tired enough as it is. We got here as fast as we could."

Dellasandro smiled mirthlessly; his mocking expression never left his face. "Tsk, tsk, college boy, can't take it anymore? I heard about you blowin' up that transformer. No," and he shook his head. "I want Tower. I just been through you guys' trucks. I know a fuckin' lush when I see one. I get Tower. *Ah'm* gonna work his ass off. *Ah'm* gonna make him earn his three measly gawddamned dollars an hour in this pourin' fuckin' rain."

He shifted his gaze back to Archwood. "An' I don't know why you hired that fuckin' kid cousin uh Lazarus. Jesus Christ. He stinks, like he ain't bathed in a week, and sides that he farted all the way up here. I think he even shit his pants. He's gonna be worthless up here too, I just know it. Just like Tower here. He's so fuckin' green he probably still shits like a gawddamned rug rat."

He threw his cigarette on the floor and crushed it viciously beneath his boot. "I'm gonna start the generators and set up the tarp over the transformers and start reeling out hoses. That all right with you?"

Archwood shrugged. "Go ahead. But no filtering 'til I get the word from Elmer."

"Screw Elmer," Dellasandro said, his cold blue eyes smiling at Archwood. "He'll probably get lost just like you did."

"*No filtering!*"

"Well, I'm gonna set things up. These *girls* gonna help?"

"Take Tower with you," Archwood said resignedly, seemingly tired, not caring, and waving his hand in a final limp-wristed fashion.

Tower's eyes pleaded with Archwood and Banner as they roamed between them, looking as if he were going to his own execution, staring down into a freshly-dug grave that he himself had excavated.

The shed was silent.

Dellasandro smiled widely, pearly white teeth shining in his black beard. "Come with me, Tower. We're gonna make a fuckin' *man* outta ya." The last mile. They all watched silently as Tower slowly stood, muffling a sob, and shuffled slowly up to Dellasandro, who was still smiling. When Tower got to the doorway, Dellasandro, his face darkening in de Sade pleasure, suddenly shouted, "Let's *MOVE!*" and grabbed Tower by the back collar of his jacket and rapidly hustled him out into the rain, Tower hanging on to his hardhat. *"Let's go, let's go, let's go, let's move your candy ass!"* Banner heard Dellasandro exultantly scream, and he sighed, "Yeah, Jesus," rubbing his eyes with forefingers and thumb, tired of it all, tired of Dellasandro, tired of being tired. He wanted to go home, to rest a while, to get away from the high voltage substations; but he was stuck here. There seemed to be a collective silent sigh of relief in the shed.

"Why the hell do you keep putting up with him?" Banner asked Archwood, who now sat down wearily in Tower's abandoned chair and sniffed the air.

"Jesus Christ Tower's rank," Archwood said, his nose wrinkling. "What'd he do? Drink all the way up here?" He shook his head disgustedly. He didn't mind the men drinking off-duty, but when on duty he expected everyone to work and be alert, especially around the high voltage electricity, hung over or not from a previous night's bacchanalia.

"Why do I put up with him?" Archwood asked Banner. "You know why. 'Cause whatever else you might say, Sammy's a damn good worker, and Tower'll stay alive with Sammy on his ass, plus Sammy knows substations."

Rick snorted. Ringo was gagging from Tower's fart, tears welling in his eyes. Dellasandro appeared in the doorway again, deliberately pointing his middle finger at Leroy. "Come on, Preacher Jesus, we got work to do."

"Amen," Leroy shouted enthusiastically, slapping his thighs and jumping off the drum. "See you all later, Jackson. The massah awaits," he said, laughing and winking, and he walked out with Dellasandro moving behind him, breathing down his neck. Leroy never lost his cool.

"Well," Archwood sighed, looking at the three young men who weren't even 25 years old yet, "how was Florida?"

"A lot nicer than Attica, Ohio," Ringo grumbled, gesturing outside, grinning sickly behind his blonde walrus mustache.

"Yeah, I'll bet," Archwood said. "It's been rainin' like this for three days now. Cold too. I wish this friggin' winter would get over with."

"So how're things back in the shop?" Banner asked. "Anything new?"

"Well, Gordon's workin' in Buffalo at that brass and copper company there, testin' breakers and relays. He's been there a week now. And we got L.A. Ross goin' to T.V.A. Leavin' today. While he's there, he'll be takin' over a thousand oil samples. I'll be needin' somebody in the lab for a while, it looks like."

"T.V.A., huh?" Banner asked, shaking his head, feeling a twinge of jealousy course through him because he wasn't there to look at that huge electrical power company that was spread over several southern states through the Appalachians.

"So how soon will we be down there?"

Archwood shrugged. "Hell, I don't know. There's a lotta people down there biddin' on it. We just gotta wait and see. So don't hold your breath. We gotta lotta work to do around here, enough as it is."

"Yeah. So what else has been goin' on?"

"There're about 500 oil samples to be done in the lab. Ain't nobody been there long enough to test 'em. We all been busier than hell lately and can't keep up."

"Jesus."

"So what happened down there at the cape?" Archwood asked. "How'd you blow up that transformer?"

While Banner told him the story, he saw Archwood's face become wrinkled in thought. He listened carefully and asked a few questions for more details. "Jesus," he said finally when Banner finished. "How do you feel now about working around high voltage?"

Banner shrugged. "I dunno. It left me pretty shook up. I think about it all the time now. I don't know. It's scarier now."

"No shit. It's always been a scary thing."

"Well, I'm thinkin' about maybe puttin' in the rest of the summer, then see if I can teach school or something."

"You wanta do that?"

"Yeah. I don't think I can take it anymore."

"Hm," Archwood said. "Well, I'd sure as hell hate losin' you, I could use you in the lab, but if you think you'd be better off. . . ."

"Well, I got to discuss it with the Bee, think about it for a couple weeks or so. Then I'll let you know."

"Okay."

"So," Banner said, sighing. "What'd you bring to test the transformers with? We don't have any test equipment."

"I got the T.T.R. in the back of my truck. I got some sample bottles too in case you guys didn't have any more." Archwood shook out another cigarette from his pack, lit it with a match. "My Gawd what a day," he mumbled, and tossed the match to the floor. "Thank Gawd there ain't no lightning, or we wouldn't be doing this at all."

"We shouldn't be working in this rain anyway," Banner told him. "Remember that July 4th when we were up near Cleveland?"

Archwood gave Banner a sideways glance. "You're tellin' *me*. But these guys wanted us up here to get these units back on-the-line a.s.a.p."

"This is gonna be a lot worse than the time we worked that one Labor Day weekend couple years ago," Banner said.

"Yeah," Archwood said, "and I'm afraid we're gonna be here longer. That job was only one transformer."

Banner now looked at Archwood, who stared out into the rain, taking a drag on his cigarette. He knew that working in this type of weather wasn't going to be easy—he remembered last July 4ᵗʰ—and that everyone would probably be bone-tired before the day was out. He was already tired from the drive north, but there was nothing that could be done about that either; he just hoped they could get this job done fast and get out. No one wanted to be here when there were striking workers roaming the countryside.

No wonder Archwood called the men: he needed all the help he could get, and made plans to do the work the day before while waiting for Banner, Rick, Tower, and Ringo to arrive from Florida.

"A guerilla operation," he had called it.

"So how're you going to work this?" Banner asked. "Are we going to work in shifts?"

Archwood took another drag on the cigarette. "Well," he said, "there's Dellasandro, Lazarus, Buckingham, and Leroy. Sammy wants Tower, so he stays. The Fryman boys are strictly here to off-load and reload the transformers on their trucks if any of these are blown. If none of 'em are, they'll head back to the shop to reload and drive another truck to meet us here." Archwood looked at Rick, who stared back at him. "I don't know whether to leave you here or Ringo," Archwood told him.

"I don't want to stay," Rick said flatly, shaking his head. "Not with that degenerate motherfuckin' Ahtalian cawksuckah."

Ringo was squirming in his seat. "Why not Jackson?" he blurted out, sweat breaking out on his round pale face. Banner looked at Ringo woodenly.

Archwood shook his head. "No, I need Jackson on another job."

"Another one?" Banner asked, surprised.

Oh Gawd, no rest for the weary, as Thomas Wolfe might have written.

"Yeah, another one," Archwood said.

"Where?"

"Just below Zanesville."

"What is it this time?"

"You remember that cement factory down there? There's another askarel transformer that needs repaired. One of the radiators is leaking. Axel Zimmerman called two days ago screamin' and yellin' about it. He's afraid of the E.P.A. comin' and findin' it. From what I gather it's one of those small pinhole leaks. You're gonna have to drain it to just below the leak, pull a vacuum, epoxy it, fill it up again, and filter it, like you did in Monesson. Only this time don't get it all over the place. And don't blow it up," Archwood said dryly.

"Yeah, yeah," Banner said. "Jesus, don't remind me of it, but another askarel transformer," grimacing and feeling suddenly lousy about it. "I thought we were getting out of those jobs. It's poison, mon, poison."

"There's nothing we can do about it. I told Axel I'd have a man there in a couple of days."

"There was nobody else?"

"Who do you want to do it?" Archwood asked, his voice suddenly shrill and sarcastic. "Jasper?"

"Yeah, yeah," Banner muttered, contrite.

Archwood stared at Banner for another moment, then shrugged, sucking a last deep drag on his cigarette and flicking it outside. Nerves. It was only nerves. Nerves and being tired; there was no end to it.

We render unto Caesar, Banner thought.

"I was gonna have Sammy go but we were tied up in Youngstown. Then I got the call from Jasper telling me that this one had just come up, top priority, so now I need you to go. Everyone else is gonna be here for a while."

"It seems I'm always going on askarel jobs."

"You're the best we have."

"I know. But still."

173

"Ah," Archwood said, waving his hand in the air, grinning. "You'll like working with Axel. He's a good man, but harder than hell to bullshit him. He knows what's going on. Don't piss him off or you'll be out of there before you know it."

"Didn't you and Sammy go down there one time, and he—"

"Yeah, yeah," Archwood said, interrupting Banner, giving him that look. "Axel and I didn't get along too well."

"So now it's all up to me."

"Yeah. Go down there and charm the birds out of the trees. You got broad shoulders. We need to get back into his good graces."

"Thanks. When do I go?"

Archwood shrugged. "I'd like for you to go tomorrow, but go Saturday. Friday you come in and just load your truck and spend the rest of the day testing some of those oil samples, then go home. No overtime. Just work your straight eight. You guys are probably tired enough, *Christ* we all are, so don't go busting your ass too much. Leave early Saturday, say five o'clock, get the job done, and have Sunday off. I'll be back Monday, see you at the shop."

"Thanks," Banner said, sighing. "Who goes with me?" He dreaded the prospect of working on another askarel job.

"Take Rick with you," Archwood said, rapping his knuckles against the table. Ringo groaned and began weeping boo-hoo-hoo: no Naomi tonight. Rick was clearly happy, tossing his hardhat playfully in the air.

"Ringo," Archwood said cheerfully and decisively, "you gotta stay here with Sammy. It'll be a couple days or a couple weeks maybe."

"Oh man," Ringo whined, "what about my wife and kids?"

"Don't worry, we check on 'em every once in a while, and I see her when she comes in and picks up your paycheck," Archwood said. Rick looked at Banner. Banner was thinking, Hm, he had heard rumors that

Naomi and B.S. were seeing each other all right, but so far it had been only a rumor. Rick slightly grinned.

"Oh man," Ringo moaned, sweat shining on his round face. "I don't wanta work with Dellasandro. I'm always workin' with him. This has been the first chance I've been away from him, and now I got him again. There ain't no justice. I'm tired of working with him. I always get stuck with him. Why?"

"Sammy loves you," Archwood said, pursing his lips.

Like hell, Banner thought. *Keep the man on the road with Sammy while Naomi goes out to play with the boys.*

"What's that?" Dellasandro asked, suddenly looming in the doorway again, nearly blocking out what light there was in the shed. "Who the fuck do I love?"

"Ringo," Archwood said.

"Oh yeah?"

"Yeah. He's stayin' here with you to work on these banks. Put him on whatever shift you want," and Ringo put his pudgy hands in his face.

Dellasandro looked at Ringo, then at Rick and Banner. He shook his head and snapped his fingers disgustedly. "You two bastards luck out again," he said.

Rick gave him the finger.

"Jackson and Rick are gonna ratio the transformers out here, put personal grounds on each of 'em, leave, and go do that askarel job Saturday."

"Piece of fucking fruit cake," Dellasandro said, eyes fixed on Rick, wanting his piece of meat. "Askarel's nothin'."

"I hear ya," Banner said flatly.

Dellasandro stared at Banner, but said nothing. He jerked his thumb toward the door. "Your buddy Elmer just pulled up with a couple of men.

You better go see him. We got the hoses out and the tarps're ready to be put on two uh the transformers."

"Just hold off 'til I talk to Elmer," Archwood said.

"Anything you say."

"Where's Phil and his cousin?" Archwood asked, standing and putting his papers beneath his raincoat.

"They're out in the rig gettin' the generator ready. Chessan's with 'em helpin'. Tower's in the other one. I got him changing out the Fuller's earth tanks. He's barely fuckin' alive." Dellasandro looked at Ringo. "C'mon, Pillsbury. Let's get some of that excess fat offa ya. Be fit and *strawng* like me," and he slapped his abdomen, hard. He suddenly glanced at Rick. "You I deal with later," he said flatly, pointing at Rick.

"*Shee*-it," Rick said.

Dellasandro laughed harshly and stalked out of the shed.

"Well," Archwood said, ignoring the diatribe that had taken place, "I want you boys to come with me. Ringo, you go with Sammy." Ringo began boo-hooing again.

2.

They stood and filed out of the shed following Archwood.

Jesus Gawd, it was still raining; there was no let-up. Banner zipped his jacket tight and tried to hunch inside it. The rain lashed furiously against the earth. Large puddles formed in the low spots of the graveled foundation. The sky was dark and gray and violently purple. The rain came down too fast for the work they had to do.

Three men in yellow raincoats and yellow hardhats stood side by side next to a bright yellow bucket truck. They were looking at the men and equipment inside and outside the switchyard. Archwood, Rick, and Banner walked up to them while Ringo headed forlornly toward

Dellasandro. Dellasandro stood inside the 40-foot rig by the two large Fuller's earth tanks, smoking a cigarette, watching Archwood. The rain pressing in on him, Banner already felt detached by the work coming up.

"You Elmer Boggs?" Archwood asked a grizzled old man who wore wire-rimmed spectacles and was in dire need of a shave. He was shorter than Banner: his face was lined and leathered; iron gray hair showed wet beneath his hardhat.

"Yes, sir," he answered, shaking hands with Archwood, "I'm Boggs. This is Tiny Lewis," who was not tiny at all, but a huge man with rosy cheeks and a big mean grin plastered on his face. He stood well over six feet and weighed nearly 300 pounds. "And this over here is Charlie Marshall," who was Banner's height and more ordinary. He wore the same *Varmer Joiles* beard that Banner shared, and they stared silently at one another; very few men wore it anymore, except the Amish. Boggs gestured to his men, who both nodded silently in return to their introduction. "You Archwood?"

"Yeah," Archwood said. "This is Jackson Banner and Rick Pitts. So, what do we have here? What's going on? What's the story?"

"What do we have? Well," Boggs said slowly, drawling the words out, a flicker of laughter behind his glasses, "we want you to put oil in these transformers so we can fire 'em back up again."

Banner started laughing.

"It may be a week or two, Elmer," Archwood said, squinting at Banner. "You know, the weather and all. Those transformers been opened and drained, or they could be blown."

"Take your time, take your time," Boggs drawled. "There ain't no hurry now. We got the power rerouted over other lines and I got some men patrolling the power lines and some standing by in the other switching stations to protect 'em and let the sheriff know if there's any sign of trouble."

"Well, what's the situation up here?"

"Well," Boggs said, "it ain't good. I don't know what's got into these young bucks' heads aroun' here," suddenly launching into a diatribe, his eyes flashing behind his glasses, "this utility's been doin' fine for years with the electrical union we got . . . now all of a sudden management doesn't wanta deal with the union 'cause they said they're already makin' too much money as it is. Well, they been negotiating nearly a year now and now they're all riled after management said no on the final offer, so they went on a wildcat and this is one of the results."

"They catch 'em?"

Boggs shook his head. "No, but we gotta idea who did it, yes, sir, by Gawd."

"They ain't gonna bother us here, are they? I mean, how many of 'em are there you're contending with?"

Boggs shook his head again. "A dozen, we think. Everyone has keys to the substations and the switchgear cabinets. We notified the sheriff that we had you guys come up here, some help, so he's gonna send a couple uh his deputies out here to watch out for you guys to make sure nothin' happens. Gawddamn I hope nothin' goes on today. It was a spooky son-of-a-bitch lemme tell ya a couple days ago when the alarms lit up in the dispatch center. Jesus Christ, it was shittin' and gittin' for a while there. We almost lost the whole gawddamned *control area* for Christ's sakes! Breakers were opening up for free like mad for 20 minutes until we got out to the subs and made sure nobody was there. Since then we've had our men who decided to stay on the job stay in the subs. Everything's quieted down somewhat. No one knows the next move. Christ sake, you'da thought we were in gawddamned coal minin' country."

Banner and Rick looked at each other.

"Jesus," Banner said. He didn't want to hear any more. "We'll go get the T.T.R., B.S.," he told Archwood.

Wildcat strikers are the worst, Banner thought.

He had been in and seen similar situations, but this one sounded bad. He wanted to get the job done and go home; he didn't want to waste any more time here than necessary. The upcoming askarel job Saturday looked pretty good to him now.

"Wait a minute," Archwood said.

Banner hunched his shoulders, wishing they were talking inside the shed instead of in the rain. It wasn't letting up at all, there were no signs of it as such, and he was soaked, nearly water-logged. Rick and Archwood looked just as worn but stoic, enduring the weather. His throat felt raw.

"So how you want to go about this, Elmer?" Archwood asked.

"I want your men to isolate those transformers. We got all the disconnects open, both primaries and secondaries on the oil circuit breakers over there, and we got the secondary pot switches open too. We've grounded the secondary bus. But what I want is those primary and secondary cables detached from those bushings up there. And remember that the main lines coming into this station are still hot, so that whole primary bus there is energized, hot up to just above those open set of primary disconnect clips. I know you won't go near it, no need to, but I just want to remind you all of it. You all do that and then I can give you a clearance on the transformers only. If you want personal grounds put on either side of the transformers that'll be up to you. But I'd recommend doing it."

"We'll do it," Archwood said. "I'll make sure I'll tell the other men. You guys got this? That bus is hot?"

"Ten-four," Banner said.

"Hell, ya can hear it buzzin' all through that switch rack there," Rick said.

"Yeah." Archwood turned back to Boggs. "What's in that building over there?" he asked, gesturing to the building behind the secondary switch rack.

"That's where the switchgear is. We had it on emergency battery power for a while. We'll be bringin' in a generator though to put it back on a.c. Can't leave it on d.c. forever you know."

"Can we use it to stay out of this friggin' weather?"

"Sure. There's a bathroom in there too if you need to use it, and it's mighty warm in there too. No use pissing in the rain, don't you see. Enjoy every little convenience we got."

"Great." Archwood turned to a grinning Banner and a grinning Rick, and then grinned himself. "You guys go get the T.T.R. I'll tell Sammy to start removing cables." He turned back to Boggs, now serious. "If they turn out okay on the winding ratios, we're gonna drape 'em with tarps to protect 'em from the rain. I don't know how good the results are gonna be when we're through here. I figure our megger readings are gonna be screwy when we're done, and our oil tests are gonna come out with low dielectric what with this weather and all."

"I expect that. I don't rightly care," Boggs answered. "I need this station back on-the-line as soon as possible. You all get started, then I'll give you the go-ahead clearance."

"Ten-four. Okay, Jackson, let's get started."

"Oh, yeah," Banner said. This was it.

Rick and Banner hurriedly walked over to Archwood's truck. Rick opened the back door of the small camper shell and Banner followed him inside.

"I like the guy."

"Who?"

"Boggs."

"Yeah."

"Man, I'm tired. I want to go home," Banner said, squatting on his haunches. He took off his glasses and wiped them with a snot-dried bandana. "I'm soaked and I think I'm catching a cold. And I ain't ashamed to say I don't want to work, and not here. You know?"

"Uh-huh," Rick said noncommittally, opening the transformer-turns-ratio case and checking the leads, the test set itself, and then snapping it shut. "I don't want to work either," he said, turning to Banner, then stared out into the rain. He looked like a wiry drowned rat. "It's only eight o'clock and it's still raining like a son-of-a-bitch. And this job is gonna *be* a son-of-a-bitch too. Ah just know it."

"Tell me about it. But at least we'll be going home today."

"Uh-huh, and askarel Saturday, heh heh heh."

Banner looked out into the switchyard and saw Dellasandro point to the top of the silent transformers with Leroy and Tower looking too.

"Where's a ladder?" Banner heard Tower ask.

"You don't need no fuckin' ladder, Tower!" Dellasandro yelled. "Get your ass up there! Go on! Get! Climb them fuckin' radiators, *you ain't no old man!*"

"You ready?" Banner asked.

"Just wait 'til they're done up there. I don't wanta get any wetter than Ah already am now. Christ sakes, we're all gonna die here because of this fuckin' weather."

"Remember what the voltage was?"

"Yeah," Rick said. "115 primary, 34 secondary."

Banner nodded, dividing the numbers in his head. "Yeah. What kind of ratio is that? Three point four?"

"Somethin' like that. Delta delta zero degrees angular displacement. It's gonna be smooth. Just A to B, B to C, C to A. Piece of cake."

"I wonder how many taps B.S. wants done?"

"We'll ask him."

They watched as Tower struggled to climb on to the first

transformer—Chessan nimbly the middle—Tower drawing his heavy body up the side, hanging on to the radiators in seeming desperation, wedging his feet in between the tubes, and then sprawling like a floundering walrus on the top.

"Let's get moving!" Dellasandro was shouting. "Hurry it up!"

"Give me a 5/8ths socket and wrench," Tower shouted weakly down at him. Dellasandro none-too-gently threw the tools to Tower, who caught them one-handed against his belly; then had to stand *relevé* and reach above him to start unscrewing the nuts and bolts with shaking hands.

"Let's go," Rick said.

"I'm gonna get the ladder from the truck."

"Sammy's gonna ride your ass."

"Fuck Sammy. I ain't married to him. I don't see his name on my friggin' paycheck."

They climbed out of the truck and walked over to the dark blue one, raised the rear door, and pulled out the ladder that lay on top of the other equipment. They met Archwood by the first transformer, who was looking at the bottom drain valve.

"How many taps you want covered?" Rick asked him.

"Do the one it's on now," Archwood said. "Then switch to the next primary tap up, and ratio it again. Don't be slow about it, but don't fuck up. No use in being out here longer than you need. Just be careful up there."

"Always," Rick said.

Banner was shocked to see dark circles forming underneath Archwood's eyes already; he knew what he was feeling. Banner felt the same way upon discovering that the transformers had been drained and left open.

"You have ground cables in your truck, B.S.?" Rick asked.

"Yeah. And there should be a set in one of the rerefining rigs. Get to work." Archwood headed toward the shed.

They leaned the ladder against the transformer and extended it all the way to the top. Banner checked the nameplate again, noted the configuration of the internal phasing of the transformer, then slowly climbed up the ladder. When he got to the top, he took the heavy transformer-turns-ratio set from Rick as Rick climbed the ladder. It was slippery and treacherous, but there was nearly fifty square feet to move around on.

"How ya feelin', Tower?" Rick asked laconically.

"Like hell," Tower grumbled, putting nuts, bolts, and flat washers into his jacket pockets as he worked. The rain poured off his hardhat, soaking his face and clothes. "That bastard Dellasandro is a pain in the arse." He tried to fart, but couldn't.

Rick laughed, grabbed on to the primary A-phase insulator, which towered two feet above him. "Who knows? Maybe you'll get to room with him."

"They wouldn't do that to me," Tower wailed, looking up into the raining sky, and Rick laughed again.

"Ah, well, thank Gawd we're goin' home today," he said slyly as Banner busily unraveled the leads with large alligator clips on the ends.

"What?" Tower asked, turning and facing him, looking shocked and surprised.

"We got an askarel job to do Saturday."

"Good luck."

"Wanta trade?"

"I'll swim in fuckin' askarel to get away from that Italian son-of-a-bitch."

"Well, it's too late, I already got dibs on the job. You're stuck here."

"You and who else?"

"Jackson here."

"You two are always lucky bastards."

"Really?" Banner asked, more to himself.

"That's what happens when you a live a clean, Godly, Christian life. You luck out."

"Bullshit," Tower said, shaking his head, then reached for another connection.

"What's this fucking ladder doing up here?" Dellasandro suddenly shouted from below. He was staring up at Rick and Banner, the rain lashing his face. He didn't even blink, just stared at the two men angrily.

"Say what?" Rick asked innocently, looking down at him.

"What's the matter? You fuckers lazy? Is that it? You girls too good to climb a transformer?" Dellasandro asked, grabbing the ladder.

"You take that ladder and I'll piss on your face, bitch!" Rick suddenly yelled.

"You ain't *man* enough, Pitts!"

"Just watch me!" Rick angrily stepped to the side of the huge transformer, unzipped his pants, pulled out his penis that Darla had once loved so well, and urinated over the side, deliberately aiming at Dellasandro. Dellasandro's eyes popped open in sudden surprise and he almost fell backing away from the ladder, the streaming urine barely missing him. Shaking his fist, almost turning purple with rage, Dellasandro screamed, "You cocksuckers just get it done and get the fuck offa there!" and he turned and walked rapidly to the forty-foot rig, where Banner, Rick, and Tower heard Dellasandro inside screaming insanely at the other men.

Rick finished and zipped back up, rubbing his hands together. "Well, that takes care of that," he said, laughing loudly. "The man's a pussy. C'mon, Jackson, let's get it over with."

Banner had watched the episode in stoic silence. He shook his head as he listened to Dellasandro raging in the truck. He was too tired to fight it anymore.

World's full of assholes, he thought. *Nobody ever said life was fair.*

"Jesus, you guys got balls," Tower said, looking at them almost in awe, shaking his head. "That was funnier than hell, you pissin' on his face, hee hee. Gawddamn I liked that, hee hee."

It was miserable working on top of the transformer. Tower finished disconnecting the cables and threading white cloth tape through the top part of the draw-lead type cable where it snaked down the center of the insulator and tying it off to the eye bolts on the lid so that the cables wouldn't slip through to the interior of the transformer. He climbed down the ladder and headed for the third transformer, grunting and sweating, terror and sickness pasted on his face.

Rick and Banner set up the transformer-turns-ratio test set, short-circuited the phases and rapidly ratioed the transformer, going from A to B, B to C, C to A, on the primary and secondary sides. The transformer seemed to be in still good condition. Banner kept making mental mathematical calculations as they went through the procedure. He cursed the weather, because he couldn't write the results on paper. The rain interfered with everything.

"I hope we don't ruin the set in this rain," Banner said, screwing and unscrewing the C-clamps from the insulators rapidly as they went through the procedure.

"Fuck it," Rick screamed, laughing, drenched and giddy.

They then repeated the testing after switching a tap on the primary side, recording a slightly different ratio, but still within five-tenths of one per cent of the standard tolerances. When they finished with the ratio, Rick put the tap switch where it was originally and locked it. Banner climbed down the slippery ladder, where he almost lost his footing and smashed his nose against one of the rungs.

Jesus Christ! Thank you, God.

The first transformer was like the second. Banner cursed the rain again, the transformer-turns-ratio set, and the men who sabotaged the substation a few days ago. He waited on top watching Leroy and Tower finish disconnecting the cables and tying them off on the last transformer. He suddenly felt strange standing on top of the transformer, amid the tall porcelain insulators that loomed over him.

Here is where it all starts, he thought.

"You ready?" Rick asked.

"Yeah. Let's do this one."

All three transformers were in good condition according to the ratio readings. Leroy had told Banner that the combustible gas fault testing came up with nothing out of the ordinary—no acetylene either—and the oil that was left in the transformers had a low 12,000-volt dielectric. That meant vacuum-dehydration while filtering new oil through the transformers.

Rick gathered the personal ground cables, laid them out on the gravel and attached one end of each ground cable to each transformer ground. Banner, after tracing the incoming primary lines to the opened disconnects on the primary oil circuit breakers, applied them on each of the phases on the primary side between the transformer and the opened line side primary disconnect switches, lifting the switching hot stick high in the air to clamp the ground disconnect on to the isolated power lines. He proceeded to ground the cables by calling out each phase he worked on and at a slow pace. Dellasandro waited by the first transformer with a heavy black tarpaulin lying polyhedral on the gravel at his spread feet. Archwood and the three electrical co-operative men had disappeared into the shed. Banner too wished he were out of the rain.

"I'm awful tired, Rick, how 'bout you?" Banner asked, his arms aching from the unbalanced lifting.

"Ten-four, mon," Rick answered; his face was drained and looked pasty. "Ah'm soaked all the way through to my *unduh*weah, imagine *that*, why don't ya?"

Banner laughed, despite himself. He felt the same way. He could only imagine what the others felt like. Dellasandro, Tower, and Leroy had two of the tarpaulins draped over the first and middle transformers, hanging over the insulators, shielding the tops, and down over the sides. Tower looked beat, drained of every ounce of muster he had within him; sweat poured off him even in the rain. Everyone looked soaked to their bones.

"You girls finally through?" Dellasandro asked them in his mocking and intense voice. He looked at them with hands on hips; through hooded eyes.

"They're all yours," Rick said coldly.

"What you gonna do?"

"Go see Archwood."

"Don't think you're gonna be let off easy. We're gonna need your ass."

"Bullshit."

"Heh heh, we'll see."

"Uh-huh," Rick said, and he and Banner headed toward the shed. Banner had nothing to say to Dellasandro. They hardly ever talked to one another since the incident, and Archwood kept them separated by making them crew leaders.

When they stepped inside the shed, Banner suddenly sneezed, almost knocking his hardhat off his head. Archwood, Boggs, and the other two co-op men sat around the table, Archwood frowning and intently smoking and Boggs futilely lighting a battered briar. Banner took out his soaked bandana and noisily blew his nose.

"Gawddamn it," he said.

"Everything check out?" Archwood asked.

"Yeah, everything's fine," Banner said, glancing at Boggs. "We ratioed them on the tap they were on, then switched to the next primary tap settings and ratioed 'em again. They're all within the tolerances. Did you hear Leroy say that the gas fault testing came out okay?"

"Yeah," Archwood said. "And the oil's low. Maybe we oughta run a Doble test on it."

"You got one here?"

"Yeah. I'll get Leroy and Ringo to do 'em just before we get started."

"Sammy's already got the tarps up."

"They'll work under 'em."

"You sure you don't want Rick and me to do it?"

"No," Archwood said. "I want you to go to the other sub."

"All right." Banner glanced at Rick, who stood by the doorway, listening in silence.

Rick grinned at Archwood's pronouncement.

"So you say everything's fine with those banks out there?" Boggs asked.

"Yeah. Far as I can see, they look all right."

"Good," Boggs said, nodding vigorously. "At least the sudden pressure relays worked and tripped open the breakers. The fuckers didn't succeed in doing any damage."

"Well wasn't that polite of 'em?" Rick asked.

"How fast do the relays operate?" Banner asked.

"'Bout 15 cycles after the new circuit is made up."

"Wow."

"So we knew about it when it happened, 'cause the whole gawddamned dispatch center went crazy. You ain't never seen so much scramblin' when those alarms came in."

"I can only imagine. You get many outages here?"

"Nah." Boggs grinned mischievously. "The only time anything goes on is when we have tornadoes and killer snowstorms when the power lines go down. But shit, this is one of the worst things I ever ran across in 20 years of workin' here."

"Jesus," Banner said. He suddenly felt depressed.

"Well, you all ready to go to the other sub?" Archwood asked, his voice somewhat cracking as he listened to Boggs.

"Yeah, I suppose so," Banner said. "We can't get any wetter. I'm already soaked, and I think I'm catching a cold."

"You'll live. Well, Elmer," Archwood said to Boggs, "can you take these guys to the other sub?"

"I'll," puff puff *suck* puff, "have Tiny and Charlie take 'em over," Boggs answered, successfully lighting his briar, smoke billowing out of his mouth and pipe like a smokestack, "it's only 15 miles away," *suck suck puff* and it went out again. "Gawddamn pipe."

"I suppose it's raining over there too, huh?" Banner asked sourly.

"My boy," Boggs said loudly and humorously, looking at Banner through tired smiling eyes, "it's friggin' rainin' everywhere, where you been?"

"Florida, *the Sunshine State.*"

"Uh-huh." Boggs looked long at Banner with his smiling eyes, then turned to his men and said, "Why don't you take these boys on over to Belltower Substation. When they finish there move 'em on over to Brokensword."

"All righty," Tiny boomed, grinning from ear to ear, his round cherubic face glowing rosy red. "We'll just go do that."

"You want us to come back here, B.S.?" Rick asked wearily.

"Uh-huh," Archwood said, nodding. "You just go out there and ratio and then while you're at it, you may as well disconnect those cables. You got tools and tape?"

"Plenty. Are they cables?" he asked Boggs.

"Yeah," Boggs said. "But they're smaller units."

"All right," Rick said. "We'll follow you over."

"What about the cops?" Banner suddenly asked.

"They should be here any time now," Boggs answered, looking at his watch. "But you should be all right with Tiny and Charlie escortin' ya over."

Banner blew his nose again. There was no time to think anymore, just hurry up and get the damn job done and be on the road heading for home. He could feel the tug of impatience coursing through his body: almost three months of constant work away from home and hearth and warm-loving wife and it was rushing through him like an amphetamine-laced acid trip.

And now it felt like he was catching a cold.

"You boys think you could find your way back here without any trouble?" Boggs asked. "I gotta have Tiny and Charlie back here as soon as possible. We gotta couple more subs to check out, and then we'll be back here with ya to take ya over to the other sub."

"We'll be able to find our way," Banner told him. "Just show us how to get there."

"Make sure you guys come *back* here," Archwood said, a finger pointing on the table. "Don't ya go taking off without me knowin' about it."

"No problem," Rick said.

"We'll be back," Jackson Banner said, saluting him with a tip of his finger, and followed Boggs' men out of the shed, Rick behind him carrying the portable transformer-turns-ratio set.

Electric America
July 4, 1976

1.

Lightning skittered across the sky.

Jackson Banner sat huddled in the passenger seat of the huge Kenworth cabover rig, silently holding a lit cigarette in the fingers of his left hand while palming his white-bandaged right wrist which now steadily throbbed, vibrating in beat to the rig's powerful roaring engine.

Rick Pitts drove the truck with 10,000 gallons of transformer mineral oil in the tanker attached behind the rig, not saying anything, but peering out into the raining darkness and watching the heavy fast-moving southbound interstate traffic ahead of him, the red taillights and interior dashboard lights reflecting on to his sallow pinched face. An open bottle of beer lay wedged between his legs. Occasionally he took a huge swallow without taking his eyes off the speeding traffic around him, then wedged the bottle between his legs again. He was on his third bottle. The first two bottles he had thrown out the window, not caring about the traffic behind him. Above the din of the truck's engine the windshield wipers whined in the loud volume of the Channel 19 traffic in rhythmic staccato, always in the background of the lyrical chatter that flowed through the citizen's band.

Banner stared out the side window.

Lightning streaked across the sky.

It rolled in slow majestic sheets through the scudding nighttime clouds, branching off into arthritic fingers hundreds and thousands of feet long, stretching through the rain and striking the earth in fat, brilliant arc-welds of light. It was enough to put the fear of God into one—the lightning stroboscopic, sheathing the land in bright light blue flashes—to see it streak in jagged lines overhead, not knowing where it would strike next.

Banner took another drag on the cigarette, not really tasting the smoke, but wanting only to relieve the tiredness he felt and the numbness of his wrist and mind. Sitting silently in the passenger seat, he felt like a spectator or a member of an audience watching an ongoing movie. He was too tired to think, not wanting to anyway, but just wanting to go home after such a long day. It was cold inside the rig. Banner's seat vibrated with every hole, bump, and crack in the pavement, and the vibration made him shiver, making him feel colder than he really was.

He wondered idly what the Bee was going to think when she'd see him walk through the front door.

Lightning flashed across the sky.

It was raining hard.

The windshield wipers ran at full speed, just barely keeping the windshield clear to see ahead of them. The traffic moved too fast for the amount of rainfall that bombarded the land. Rick kept the rig at 55 for the moment, mere inches from the rear of a Cadillac with Michigan license plates that kept the same speed. He seemed to drive almost nonchalantly. He took another swallow of the beer, then put the bottle back between his legs. He had hardly said two words to Banner or to anyone since leaving the job site. Banner knew why; he took another drag on the cigarette. His wrist throbbed in rhythm, the medicinal numbness wearing off, the stitches holding.

Rick grabbed a greasy brown paper sack off the dashboard in front of him and offered it to Banner without looking at him.

"Mountain oyster?" he asked.

"No thanks," Banner answered, nearly queasy at the thought. "Ain't hungry."

"You don't know what you're missin' out on," Rick said, popping one into his mouth and taking another swallow of beer.

"I know," Banner told him, crushed out his cigarette, then lit another.

The accident should never have happened, just like all accidents should never happen, but with the work schedule they'd been on, it was considered nearly miraculous that no one else had been injured on any of the other jobs which had been completed this past week and weekend. Now he was heading home: "Take a week off and let that wrist heal," the doctor who had stitched the deep gash had told him.

While stitching his wrist, Banner—oily and dirt-stained from the day's long jobs, stinking of sweat and mineral oil, and filthy from crawling around and working inside old high voltage substations—had fallen asleep on the table not two minutes after being told to relax. The doctor had to wake him. By then he had finished, and asked Banner how he cut his wrist. Banner told him and saw the look in the doctor's eyes, and figured the doctor must have thought him crazy for working in the high voltage electrical field.

Maybe Banner was, maybe they all were, but it was the only thing he knew how to do.

2.

The week before, Banner and Tower had finished an oil sampling job in Maryland and West Virginia, working in five plants, each plant different in set-up and what it manufactured, with each of their substations in various design and characteristics, none of them easy to work in, with all the transformers and oil circuit breakers still on-the-line; energized. All of them were old and hot and thick with years of industrial grime on the primary and secondary sheathed copper cables and the electrical equipment themselves. After taking the drawn oil samples—labeling each bottle and marking the nameplate information and location on the data sheets—they found the oil in the electrical equipment was in poor condition and knew there'd be plenty of work for the company to do if they received the contract to perform the large task.

Finishing in both states, another oil sampling and rerefining job was performed in Steubenville, Ohio. After Steubenville was completed, they drove further west to Lancaster, on the edge of the Appalachian foothills, and performed a variety of electrical tests upon two new huge transformers already on the concrete foundations in a substation still under construction.

From Lancaster they drove to a Newark aluminum plant and performed a transformer-turns-ratio test upon a 69,000-volt primary transformer that would have been reinstalled a day before Banner and Tower were to get there, if they had stayed on schedule.

The pressure was really on them to get the entire work completed in the two southern states and in Steubenville and Lancaster just so they could be in Newark to test the transformer there to get it back on the line and run the plant.

That Friday evening after driving from the completed Newark job, Banner and Tower arrived back at the shop.

All the other workers were there, with B.S. Archwood in charge and rechecking loaded equipment in the trucks and rigs. B.S. as usual looked harried, with papers stuffed and crushed in one hand, soggy paper cup of coffee in the other, and cigarette dangling from his thin chapped lips.

"Where the hell ha' you two been?" he immediately whined, completely forgetting that it was he himself who had sent both Banner and Tower down south in the first place. His eyes were reddened and crusted from lack of sleep, and he was flapping around like a chicken while he talked, not standing still for an instant. "You guys shoulda been here two hours ago."

"Why? What's going on?" Banner asked wearily.

"We gotta lotta work to do the next four days," Archwood said. "Let's git your truck unloaded an' repack it fulla filters, bottles, hoses, an' drums. An' don't forget *ya gawddamned toolboxes with some gawddamned pipe wrenches in 'em!* It's now," and here Archwood looked at his watch, damn near spilling his—*ack*—sweetened, cream-colored coffee, "eighteen-thirty, and we gotta be back here at 0200 sharp."

Tower groaned: "Oh, Christ."

"Fine," Banner said aloud, grinning cheerfully and not meaning it, already tired and frazzled from the long drive.

"Papers're on my desk," Archwood told him. "Right now I'm so fuckin' busy I don't even know what the fuck I'm doin'. I ain't even got time to pee. S'let's git a move on." Archwood grinned sharply, and walked hurriedly away, passing the 40-foot tanker, where Rick Pitts filtered new transformer mineral oil into the compartments.

"How ya doin', Jackson?" Rick called out, grinning. He held a long six-inch diameter hose between his spread legs, as if he were urinating, the oil flowing slowly out of the hose rich and yellow into the rear compartment of the tanker. He held one hand on his hip. "Ya wanna ride with me on the way?"

"Sure," Banner yelled back, grinning at the sight of Rick. "Just lemme get some things together first. I got some paperwork to do and got to load the truck yet."

These were the busiest times that Archwood and his crews faced, when the dying steel mills, automobile manufacturing plants, oil and chemical refineries, drop-forge foundries, and other various industrial concerns large and small throughout America shut down to perform preventive maintenance upon the electrical power systems and the. machinery inside the plants. After the plants were literally blacked out— no electricity flowing through them at all—the men worked hard, long and fast, and kept themselves going with nothing but cigarettes and coffee.

Even though there was a large backlog of other work to be completed elsewhere, the sudden shutdowns during the major holidays (or even major layoffs) opened up even more new work for them. They were paid a lot more during these times, and no one could get out of them. The new ones always took priority.

Archwood, Banner, and the rest of the crews were already exhausted from a regular 60- to 80-hour work week anyway, and Banner knew he wouldn't be able to sneak away for the whole weekend to spend some time at home with the Bee but would only catch a few hours' sleep there before going back on the road again. It always left the Bee in a daze, because he showed up so seldom anyway, and usually when he did, it was always unannounced.

After Banner and Tower parked the rerefining rig inside the shop, they immediately began unloading everything out of it. They cleaned out the back of the ten-wheeled rig, then reloaded it with the equipment that Archwood had on his list. Stacked and coiled equipment lay in neat cramped rows: three boxes of two dozen glass jars, each with lids; many bottles of Gerin solution and 10 gallons of distilled water, both used to test transformer mineral oil; the small portable equipment that was used to measure out the proper oil levels; potassium hydroxide, burettes, magnets, 50- and 100-millimeter beakers; a Bunsen burner with extra lengths of hose and five extra bottles of propane; the dielectric machine to measure the voltage breakdown of the mineral or askarel oils to be taken, with two cups, one for each type of oil; eight empty 55-gallon drums, one full drum of newly refined mineral oil from Texaco; two boxes of rags; an extra nitrogen bottle, checked full, with proper fittings, gauges, and hoses for the apparatus.

They drained the two large Fuller's earth tanks of oil—the rolling stone of Sisyphus, always and forever—dumped the used Fuller's earth, refilled the tanks with the fresh mineral, then reloaded the refining system with fresh oil and put new oil in the two large holding tanks attached beneath the belly of the truck.

Tower's toolbox was put back inside the rig, Banner's to go into the side compartment of the Kenworth tanker. They checked again for oil hoses and pipe fittings and plenty of rope and extra 18- and 36-inch pipe wrenches.

Then, after they were through, Tower cleaned the cab's interior and made sure the citizen's band radio, the stereo deck, and the A.M.F.M. radio still worked, and that there were extra batteries for the flashlights and emergency kits and road flares for use in case they were needed. The two pairs of hot gloves were replaced with newly tested ones.

Banner sat inside the office trailer with an exhausted Ringo sitting across from him behind Archwood's desk, writing the technical report for the last job completed in Newark he and Tower performed. He remembered not to forget their time cards, individual expense reports and receipts that had to be turned in.

"Any idea where we goin' first?" Banner asked Ringo while still writing.

Ringo only stared at him piggishly behind his thick-lensed black glasses, then tossed him a small pile of Archwood's papers. "Who knows?" Ringo wearily asked. "All I know is that I'm gonna be on the friggin' road again, boo hoo hoo. I been on the road now for four gawddamned months and I ain't even been home. Tonight I get to go home for a couple of hours, ain't it wonderful? Then on the road again. *Christ* I hope my kids recognize me."

Banner laughed. "Where've you been lately?" he asked.

Ringo groaned, then farted. "Ah Jesus, I been needin' to do that for an hour now," he said, waving a pudgy hand in the air. "Gawddamn truck stop food." He took off his glasses and pressed his fingers against his closed eyeballs. "I been with Dellasandro for a solid month in New Jersey, Gawd what a place. I *hate* that friggin' state!"

"You got Dellasandro again, heh?"

"Yeah, gawddamnit," Ringo said with the same piggish expression on his face. "There ain't a gawddamned thing I can do about it. I'm just a poor old workin' man who's locked in, just bein' grabbed by my poor balls that ain't lettin' go. Unca Sam loves me. I'm doomed forever, I just know it. The karmic wheel keeps me spinnin' on its spokes. I gotta get outta this work. Whaddaya think I should do?" he asked, seeming almost desperate, but knowing, yes, he was locked in, there was nowhere else he could go; there was really no way out. He had to stay in this job.

There were three mouths to feed and a fourth one on the way, his maybe; there was no way to tell anymore: one night of hot fast sex and then on the road for a few weeks, leaving his wife Naomi at home alone with two young children to tend to at night. She says the child is theirs, and only theirs, but now he has doubts like he has never had before, and something inside him which Banner could see in the man's forlorn nearsighted eyes was already withering slowly away. He just couldn't quit now. He had accepted his wife's pregnancy as if he were the father, and she never denied that he was, but the little niggling doubt had now wormed inside Ringo's depressed mood.

Banner had to admit to himself that Naomi was a hot-looking woman, with full features, full wet lips, a cute nose, and full cheeks with large dark brown bedroom eyes and long heavy lashes. He had seen Naomi's eyes bore smokily into his one wintry Sunday night when dropping Ringo off home and watched her slowly lick her lips mere inches from his own as he squeezed by her on the back door landing, helping Ringo carry one of his suitcases into the house. He felt the natural smothering sexual heat of her which seemed to engulf him, and it was then he really wondered about her and then about his own wife; *nah*, she wouldn't do anything like that, would she? He remembered all he had seen and all the stories he had heard while on the road. He thought about Naomi as he sat there listening to Ringo relate his tale of misery and woe. He had an erection.

Is anyone chaste? Banner thought, looking at Ringo, who, like the Kaaba of Mecca, sat still and squat while he wept.

It took him an hour-and-a-half to finish writing the technical report that was to be typed and filed later, to fill out his and Tower's time cards and weekly expense accounts, and pick up the extra cash in the mail slot which the secretary had left before going home from her nine-to-five job. After saying good-bye to a subdued Ringo, he rechecked the loaded rig a third time with Tower and then told Tower to take it easy while driving later that night, because of the two full live nitrogen bottles that lay on the floor jammed amid the heavier equipment.

He told Tower about an accident that occurred not too long ago when a nitrogen bottle had exploded at another industrial plant. A man, on the last day of his job before going into retirement, had accidentally knocked the top off a full pressurized nitrogen bottle and was instantly killed when it ripped his head off his shoulders and sent instant flames in a 200-foot radius around him after the bottle smashed into a hydrogen-filled tank.

Banner clapped Tower's shoulder, then left the shop with a few of the men still hanging around telling dirty stories and laughing at the foibles of someone's lyrical description of what had happened to him the day before yesterday.

Archwood yelled at him from somewhere: "You be back here at two o'clock sharp, Jackson!"

Banner just waved to the voice.

He left Tower staring warily into the back of the rig at the nitrogen bottles.

3.

Most of the time now he felt like one of those wandering 13th century Carmina Burana monks: always on the move, drinking in experience as he traveled from place to place; entering the religious altars of the energized high voltage substations; not wanting yet to be tied down to the chained vows of a real nine-to-five job at one place all the time, knowing it may not be that secure. He saw how it was everywhere he went, and he wanted no part of it. He wanted to be right in the center of it all—the Ark of the Covenant—within the electrical power grid system where modern American life now originated—"the strongholds of enlightenment," as V. I. Lenin had stated—overshadowing others' work, on the front lines at the edge of society, ahead of everyone else's electrical education.

There was no one home when Banner arrived. The Bee still worked temporarily at the hair salon. At the time he and the Bee lived in her brother's house and took care of the property and the small single apartments that were next door. He was hardly ever home and he really didn't give a damn about the house or the apartments or his brother-in-law. They had known each other since they were twelve years of age, and they married ten years later. They felt their life together was only beginning, but as soon as they were married, he had hardly ever been home. She still attended university classes at the time, working hard to finish her student teaching and other course work. She was nearly done now, and had been in school seven years, while also working part-time as a cosmetologist. Her advisors told her she had only 18 hours of work to do to get her Master's degree in education. Banner thought it was good for him to be away, so she could finish.

But the Bee gave him an anchor to come back to, a berth for him to rest from his working life. She was happy to see him walk through the open door still alive. When he did come home now, they spent their time with each other as much as possible. The loneliness she felt was still there when he wasn't around—her family constantly asking her why she insisted staying married to a man who was never home, and *Lord* only knows what he's *doing* out there!—but when he was home, she did not feel as if she were alone anymore. He always told her about how hard or easy the work was he and the others had been engaged in, the sights that could be seen from the open road, the places where he stayed, the antics and travails of the men he worked with. There was also in his face, she always saw, that picture of regret of being away from her for so long, the strong longing of wanting to be with her more than anything else in the world, but aware with the full knowledge that he was now finally in the working world.

Because she knew: this was his work and she knew he liked it from the time he first hired on. She knew he enjoyed the traveling and seeing what the rest of America looked like as he drove the highways. He was fascinated by how other men made their living. She knew how much he liked being in the states in the different industrial zones: the coal mines, the steel mills, the refineries, the diverse manufacturing plants; the rubber tire factories, the drop forges, the dusty steel foundries, the cement and paper mills, the underground substations in cities and towns, the fossil-fueled and hydroelectric power plants, busy railroad yards, and huge airports. All of them had their own high voltage substations which gave them artificial life, pouring electricity through to power the machinery that shaped raw materials into finished products, shaped by the hands and machinery of men.

She knew what he went through as he described when he stood next to live high voltage cables in an old substation that hadn't been inspected for twenty years, and what he thought when he stared into an exposed cast-iron transformer's iron core and copper windings, seeing the old mineral oil and smelling strong of oxidized acids and paraffin, listening to the exposed transformer still humming, the electricity flowing through, stepped-down to light the inside of a factory, wondering how long a transformer could last in these particular conditions; he found it miraculous.

She knew he took a lot of chances just by stepping inside the substations, no matter what he was going inside for. There'd been a lot of near misses, some heavy-going times; she could always tell by the pensive look on his face when he came home. He would hold her for hours, make intense love to her.

He seemed addicted to the work. Even though most of it was heavily physical, the mental burden was even more so. He always had to be aware of the live high voltages surging and oscillating, alternating 60 times a second under tremendous pressures and heat; invisible but truly alive, only seeking paths of least resistance. He made sure he didn't become a path for the electricity when he was around it, and stayed away from it, though knowing it was there, transformers humming in 60-cycle-per-second harmonics. The insulators and cables appeared benevolent to the eye, giving no outward sign that they were conducting high voltage electricity, giving life to mechanical systems. He had to be mentally alert, filled with situational awareness on top of all the physical labor.

And at the end of the working day—many hours later; staying on a job until it was done, or until utterly bone-tired from working—he was drained of everything; sometimes, he thought, even his soul. At times it seemed incredible to him: he felt as if he were in the very heart of life itself, helping to keep America and his Israelite countrymen living.

The house was silent, dark, and hugely empty.

He lay lengthwise on the old green couch, staring at the high beige ceiling while the television glowed silently into the large living room. Outside the Friday night traffic swished by, the sound muted by the closed double storm windows. He was only going to have about four hours here: to shower, to sleep, to be on the road again. He wondered, briefly, whether if it was worth it. It had been a strange long day today, he thought, now knowing he wouldn't have the time to wait up for the Bee when she'd come home, but now only time for a shower and then bed. He was already very tired.

The shower had felt good and hot and steamy and stepping into the cool air of the dark bedroom after he was through made him shiver. The nightstand next to the bed was bare except for a small reading lamp and alarm clock radio. He fumbled with the tuner, found a heavy metal rock music station, knowing full well had he tuned into the classical music station he preferred he'd never get up at 0100 hours to go to work. Classical music relaxed him, but he opted for the rock station.

The next thing he knew the alarm went off, the loud guitar-laden rock music going straight through him. He awoke with a "Shit," on his lips, his glazed eyeballs barely making out the time. He reached an arm out and lowered the volume, finding it by the dim light the alarm clock radio gave off. He felt the Bee's warm body cuddled next to him, resting in the crook of his arm, one of her legs thrown over both of his, her left hand grasping his hard cock, her right arm across his chest. The bedroom was absolutely dark. The walls were painted dark blue; the heavy drapes made the room feel almost like a warm cave.

"Time to get up," he said gently into her hair. She stirred slowly, groaning. She was still asleep. "Hey," he said quietly, shaking her, "I got to get to work."

"It's not fair," she mumbled, squeezing his cock gently for a moment. "You've only been here a couple of hours."

"I'll be back tonight," he whispered.

"Exhausted." She was suddenly awake.

"But I'll be home."

"Good," she said, and kissed his right nipple, her tongue slowly circling it.

"We don't have the time," Banner said, his skin shivering with her touch. He had not been home at all the last week. He only had a day off before that. He had been out-of-state during May and part of June. Sudden arousal welled within him, and he inhaled deeply, once, then slowly exhaled. He realized they really did not have the time.

"I know," she said, suddenly stretching her body taut against him, letting out her breath, too, then lying limp and warm. Her hand touched his cock again, then began stroking him. "But you're not getting out of this bed until you fill me up with all that hot, white sperm of yours, darling," she whispered lowly into his ear. "You've been gone too long, and I need you inside me."

Banner only grunted, giving in—*fuck it*—suddenly delirious, then slowly settled on top of her. He was surprised to find her so wet when she guided him inside with her fingers. He slid slowly all the way in, burying himself deep inside her. She sighed and wrapped her long legs around him, clutched him tightly, and hotly kissed him.

"Feels good," he mumbled.

"Yes," she murmured.

In the darkness, abandoning all thought of getting up right away, they slowly started the chanting, pulsating rhythm of lovemaking when the telephone in the kitchen rudely interrupted them.

The Bee suddenly said, "No, don't move," and squeezed him tightly within her. Banner, groaning and not wanting to get up, stayed still, deep and luxuriating, and he felt her move beneath him.

He groaned, "But I got to answer it, you think it's going to stop?"

She hugged him tight to her; he could feel her heart beating fast.

The damned telephone kept up its incessant ringing.

"Let it ring," the Bee said. "Fuck me. Give me your sperm. I need you." She whimpered as they continued making love completely buried under the quilt blanket, and the telephone never stopped ringing. There was no time as they made love in the dark, just the feel of bare skin and oneness with each other, and finally, inevitably, they both climaxed, Banner groaning, "God, you feel so good."

The telephone kept ringing.

Finally, Banner slowly—achingly—climbed out of bed, his body shivering from the cold floor and being away from her. He felt her fingertips trace a path down from his spine through the crack of his ass to his testicles as he slowly stood, groping for the night lamp. He found it, turned it on, dazzling his eyes, forcing them shut while the Bee suddenly buried herself under all the blankets.

"You didn't have to do that," she cried.

He stumbled into the kitchen and grabbed the telephone. After he lifted it, before he could say hello, a voice on the other end said, "It's about time you pulled your dick out of your wife's ass, college boy. Ah'm just makin' sure you're up. Ah ain't gonna put up with a bunch uh crybabies." It was Dellasandro, and Banner laughed.

Jesus, he couldn't believe it.

"Fuck you," Banner answered, eyes closed, hand to his brow. "I'll be there at 0200 just like everyone else. You just be ready."

"Fuck you," Dellasandro snarled, and then hung up loudly in Banner's ear.

Banner sighed, awake now, and felt the start of a dull headache. He replaced the receiver, then looked around in the dark kitchen.

The Bee had turned on the bathroom light, and the light streamed in behind her as she stood in the doorway. She had put on an old flannel robe and was leaning against the wall. "Who was that?" the Bee asked.

"Dellasandro. Two a.m. wake up call."

"What did he want this time?"

"To tell me to be there at the shop on time. Can you believe it?"

The Bee just shook her head, then smiled wistfully. "Well," she said, "you two never did get along too well. Why don't you all get dressed, and I'll get your things ready." She looked at him solemnly. She wanted it all, but it would have to wait: *sphutma bandha*; *jrimbhita asana*; *lata asana*; *suhapadna asana*, and *vaidhurit asana*, her favorite. She liked the *Kama Sutra* and the *Japanese Pillow Book*. The way she leaned against the wall made Banner want to scoop her into his arms and take her back to bed and make love to her again. When he walked up to her, he stopped when she reached out and touched his erection, slowly stroking him. "I'll wait up for you tonight when you come home," she said softly as he stroked a finger through the sleek wetness between her legs. "You can do anything you want to me when you come home, all right?"

"Mm-huh," Banner answered, suddenly aroused by her invitation. He just held her close to him, lazily enjoying her ministrations and closeness and smell. They were both horny and wanted each other; he saw it in her flushed face and glazed look in her eyes. They kissed deeply.

Suddenly she dropped to her knees and deeply fellated him, looking into his eyes, and he filled her mouth with his sperm within a minute from her intensity, and she coughed and gagged, but wouldn't let him go.

"Damn, woman," Banner told her. "You're too good to me."

There were tears in her eyes as she slowly stood. "I love you," the Bee said. "I would do anything for you." He nodded and they kissed passionately again. "You better get dressed, love, we can't keep everyone waiting," she told him, and he smiled at her. They stood for a moment, staring hungrily at each other in the darkness. They kissed again, lightly.

Then, sighing, "I'm drained, I need my vitamins," Banner left her to her laughter and kitchen noises and began mechanically to find some work clothes to wear. He made sure he had an extra pair of clothes to take with him in case he needed a change. He got dressed and washed his face and smelled coffee brewing and heard eggs frying on the stove. He suddenly didn't care if he was late for work.

He finished getting ready: red bandana in right rear pocket of brown corduroys; wallet with extra expense money, gasoline credit cards, American Express in his and the company's name, telephone credit card, and black comb in left rear pocket; three dollars and odd cents in change in left front pocket; small ring of keys in right front pants pocket with Zippo lighter resting in the fob; in the long-sleeved brown shirt pocket Cross pen and pencil, an open full pack of Old Gold cigarettes with matches between the cellophane and the pack itself; and unzipped brown, quilt-lined jacket with leather mechanics' gloves stuffed within the pockets. He walked out to the cluttered kitchen, sat at the table, and watched the Bee finish cooking a breakfast for him. He ate in silence the eggs, the steak, the hashed browns, toast, and her home-made strawberry preserves.

The Bee sat next to him, her long blonde hair pulled into a ponytail on one side of her head, the flannel robe loose and flowing around her body. They were virtually still newlyweds; they were still getting slowly used to one another even though they had known each other many years. He told her the breakfast was very good; she kept her eyes on him as he ate. She traced her fingertips over his hand as he sipped the coffee. "What time will you be coming home, Jackson?" the Bee asked. "Where will you be going today?"

He looked at her and said: "Somebody said somethin' about going down around the Cambridge, Zanesville area today. Maybe Cleveland, I don't know. I really didn't look at B.S.'s papers. I was just too tired. All I wanted to do was come home. It's gonna be a hell of a long day anyway." He shrugged as he pushed himself away from the table.

The Bee moved on to his lap, putting her arms around his neck, her legs spread wide over his large thighs. He buried his face in the valley between her breasts, liking her smell and flesh. He wetly kissed and licked her body just below the middle of her breasts only once. She sighed, wrapped closer to him, then relaxed just as suddenly.

"You feel good," he said to her. "*Damn* good. I hope you been takin' care of yourself while I'm not here."

"Oh yes," the Bee answered. "There's mother and dad to see, and I'm in the last of my student teaching. I'm just keeping busy this way, hoping you're okay out there." She fell silent for a moment, then said, "I just want you to be careful. I want you to come home to me safe and sound."

"Yes, I know," Banner said, then kissed her throat and her open mouth and leaned back and looked at her. "Well, I'll be careful. I'll be here every night at least for a week. Maybe things'll slow down. I don't know, at least we'll be sleeping together." He grinned at her.

"Mm-hm," the Bee answered, then slowly slid off his lap and stood next to him. "Well," she said. "It looks like you should be on your way." She looked at the small clock by the back door. "It's now twenty to two. You've got to go."

"Yeah," Banner said. "I got to go. I only wonder how much longer."

The Bee shrugged: "Until you get worn out or get tired of the traveling, I guess."

"Maybe. What else can I do?" Banner said and shrugged. He poured the hot water out of his thermos before he filled it with the hot, black coffee, then screwed the lid on tight and placed the red plastic cup on the top of it. He picked up the thermos and in the other hand held the hanger of clothes he would wear on the road. "Well, I guess that's everything, huh?" he asked. He looked at her.

"Yes, I suppose so," the Bee answered, not really looking at him, but flitting near him, her hands roving lightly over his pockets, brushing away imaginary dust and lint. Banner knew she was feeling down because he was leaving again. She hugged him close to her again; her body was always so warm and fresh and alive. She was a strong young woman.

When he kissed her good-bye on the back porch, she interrupted their kiss by pulling back away from him, her eyes suddenly bright. "I just remembered something," she told Banner. "You received something in the mail that just came today, yesterday, I mean. Wait here a minute," and she left him and walked out of the kitchen. He stood in the open doorway of the back porch waiting for her, silent and patient because he knew how she was with things like these. She reappeared in the kitchen, this time carrying a large, brown stapled package that was surprisingly heavy when Banner took hold of it. He knew right away the books he had had the Bee send a money order for arrived. He suddenly felt a thrill go through his body.

"You want me to open it here?" Banner asked her.

"No." The Bee shook her head, her brow slightly knitted. Banner saw that she wanted to see him open the package right then and there, but knew there was no time. She told him: "Open it on the road when you have some time to yourself. I'll look through it later." She closed her eyes and tilted her face up to him for a kiss. "You have to go. I'll be here tonight when you come home, my love."

Banner leaned over and kissed her again; her lips pliant, tongue sweet and velvet, hands soft. She held on to his jacket, her fingers clenching tightly around the material. "Just be safe," she told him under his lips. She knew this weekend for her husband was going to be long and grueling; it showed in his weary face and eyes.

"I'll be all right," he told her.

"Just for me."

"Don't worry. I'll be all right. You just try to get some sleep. I'll be traveling the rest of tonight anyway," Banner said, letting go, and climbed down the steps and walked over to the car. The Bee remained by the opened back screen door. "I'll see you tonight, okay?" Banner called out in the darkness to her, putting the items inside the car. There were crickets calling close by.

"All right," she said. "Just be careful. I love you."

"I love you, too," he answered, starting the car. "You go back to bed."

4.

When he arrived at the shop five minutes before the appointed hour, the trucks and vans and even the old converted fire truck oil pumper were idling in front of the huge, dark blue building. The yellow-painted sliding door was still raised, high above the graveled foundation. The other men's cars were parked to one side of the graveled drive. Beyond the cars, the silhouettes of large oil tanks and a few spare transformers loomed against the night. Banner parked his car on the end closest to the entrance of the property.

When he stepped out, the only sounds he heard were the running engines of the trucks and thousands of crickets chirping loudly in the night. The Kenworth with the oil tanker growled lowly compared to the rest of the parked vehicles. The Fryman brothers were in another Kenworth that hauled the new vacuum-dehydration and vacuum-filling rerefining system. The two brothers sat in large comfort inside the shining blue cabover rig. Banner saw they were smoking cigarettes. When he waved to them, he saw the red trail of a cigarette circling the air in silent response.

Banner carried his thermos with him inside the building, beneath the sign that said: **THROUGH THIS DOOR PASS THE WORLD'S FINEST CRAFTSMEN.** He'd take his other things with him when they got ready to go. Everyone else seemed to be inside the office trailer. His heels clicked loudly upon the concrete foundation.

There was standing room only inside the trailer.

The interior was stale with oil, sweat, and cigarette smoke. It also seemed humid inside, what with all the young men here tonight cramped into this little front office. The air conditioner, though continuously running twenty-four hours every day, never comfortably cooled the interior.

Archwood sat behind his desk, a lit cigarette dangling from his lips. He wore his old, striped railroad engineer's cap that flopped over his head. He looked like hell: his cheeks were hollower in the trailer's interior light. The cigarette smoke trailed upwards from the end of the cigarette to his eyes, and his eyes squinted from the rising smoke as he thumbed through the wrinkled papers, making his face appear drawn and haggard. Archwood looked as if he hadn't slept. His hands shook as he held the sheaf of papers. The other men sat or stood or leaned against the crowded walls as Archwood talked. Most of them were smoking and looking already tired and worn as much as Banner. Only Rick and Dellasandro looked as if they had eight hours of sleep.

"Well, I see you made it," Archwood said to Banner as he stepped into the trailer.

"Time to spare," Banner answered.

Dellasandro looked hard at Banner. He stood behind Archwood, arms crossed against his chest, lit cigarette mashed between his tight lips. Banner stared back at Dellasandro, then grinned mirthlessly at him. Rick, leaning against the opposite wall from the entrance with a haggard-looking Tower and Ringo, was paring his fingernails with a pair of clippers. His eyes flicked to Banner only once; then he went back to his fingernails. He wore an old blue short-sleeved sweatshirt turned inside-out, with a knitted brown cap on his head that covered his entire scalp, leaving his thick long braided hair and ears exposed beneath it. An old pair of blue jeans and black motorcycle boots completed the outfit.

"We gotta slight change of plans here this morning," Archwood told Banner, as Banner stood in the doorway, looking back at him.

"What is it?"

"Just after you left here last night, we gotta 'phone call from the Charleston area," Archwood said. "Some guy, name's here someplace," rummaging futilely through the papers, "says he's got some strange voltages coming out of his switchgear, that he can't run his machinery because of the voltage fluctuations. It's a cement plant down there in hilljack country. I want you, Rick, Tower, and Ringo to go down there and find out what's wrong. Take the fire truck with you. We put— How many gallons we put in there, Ringo?" Archwood asked, interrupting himself.

"2,000," Ringo answered dully. "The front compartment's empty."

"So," Archwood said, turning to Banner again. "I want you to go down there and find out why there's voltage fluctuations. My own feeling is to check the oil in the transformers, especially if they're free breathers. If that ain't it, then you'll have to look over the switchgear panels. Gawddamn," Archwood said, shaking his head. "I hope it's the oil. You get a sample of it, all right?" he asked, looking at Banner, then at Rick.

"Got it," Banner said.

"Yo," Rick said, tipping a finger to his forehead.

"If it's the oil, change 'em out, flush 'em, then filter new oil in 'em. Put one pass on each of 'em just to make sure, and get a high dielectric."

"That oil already gotta 42 k.v. dielectric," Dellasandro suddenly said, sarcastic.

"Put a pass on 'em anyway," Archwood said, ignoring Dellasandro. He went through his papers again. "After Charleston— Yeah, here it is." Archwood looked at Tower and Ringo. "Tower, Ringo, I want you two guys to go to Zanesville after that and on your way back stop in Cambridge. Two oil sampling jobs in Zanesville—"

"Piece of cake," Dellasandro growled lowly.

"—and a sampling and megger job in Cambridge. Can you two handle that?" Archwood asked.

"Yeah," Ringo said lowly. "We can handle that." His jacket and pants made him look like an overstuffed brown pillow. He looked worn and tired. *Being home a couple of hours or so seemed not to cheer him up any,* Banner thought to himself. Archwood laid the papers on the desk. Ringo scooped them up without looking at them. A hung-over Tower looked at the floor, cigarette burning uselessly in his fingers.

"After you're all done in Cambridge, I want you to come up to Cleveland and meet us at the coliseum up there, you know where it's at?"

"Yeah," Ringo said.

"Be there at 1400 hours," Archwood said. He looked at Banner and said, "You too. After this Charleston job I want you to go to Akron to this rubber company up there," handing over a sheet of scribbling to Banner, "and put a new bottom valve in a transformer they got up there in a vault. I been promising this guy for six months now that we'd be up there, and he called a couple days ago bitchin' and moanin' about his leaky valve again. Can you go up there from Charleston an' do this job?"

"Yeah," Banner said, Rick only nodding.

"See if you can get those electricians there to shut down the transformer for you. If you can, it'd be better. But if they can't, do it while it's still on-line. You ever done one of these before?" he asked Banner.

Banner shook his head. "Not that I can recall," he said.

"I know how to do it," Rick said, nodding at Banner. "I'll show ya how."

"It ain't too difficult," Archwood told Banner. "Just don't get any damned air bubbles goin' up through the oil. Christ, I'll never hear the end of it then," and he started laughing, a loud braying that ended in a salivating snigger. "I don't need no fucking dead men around here," and laughed again; once.

Banner and Rick stayed silent. They glanced at each other, then shrugged.

"After you're through with that valve, take oil samples outta the rest of their units. The company up there expects it, okay? Good. Then after you're through with that, meet us up at the coliseum," Archwood continued. "We're gonna need ya there. 1400 hours. That should give you guys plenty of time. The rest of us are gonna be up in Lorraine, Mansfield area. Sammy here and the Frymans'll be working there today to scope things out before hitting it tomorrow. After they're done lookin' things over, they're gonna be with me today at the coliseum. The other guys'll be left on their own. After we're done up there, we go our separate ways. You and Rick will be taking samples at American Steel in Alliance on the way home. That should keep you guys busy. They have a second shift, and they know you're comin'. Ringo, Tower, you're gonna be at the oil refinery here in town and do some repair work. Leaking bushings in four old Kuhlman transformers. I looked at 'em yesterday with the electrical foreman and told him we'd do it. Job'll be a piece of cake. De-energize the transformers. Use eighth-inch gasket material. They're just small 480 stuff. Okay then. And everybody be back here at 0100 hours tomorrow, hour earlier than now. Today'll be easy. Tomorrow's gonna be a bitch." Archwood suddenly belched. "Ah shit, I cheated my ass outta that one. Is everybody ready?"

Grunts and various retorts assaulted the staleness of the interior, and Banner found himself outside, standing on the concrete foundation and watching the men exit the trailer. Rick appeared in the doorway.

"Ready?" Banner asked.

"Yeah," Rick answered. "Let's go."

They were turning to walk out the building when a shout came from inside the trailer. "Rick!" Archwood called. Rick stopped; Banner stood as Archwood came out the door with an open grease-stained box in his hands. "Here's the gawddamn valve you're gonna need for the job. Christ I almost forgot all about it," and gave it to Rick, who held it away from his body as if he did not want to get dirty.

"What are we taking here, which truck?" Banner asked Rick.

"We'll take the blue one, how 'bout it?"

"Okay. What about my toolbox?"

"Leave it in the tanker. It'll be up there at the coliseum later. Sides that, we can use mine. They're in the van."

"Okay. I got to get a couple things out of my car," Banner said. "I'll be with you in a minute."

Rick sat in the driver's seat wiping his hands on a clean rag while Banner stowed his gear away: thermos lying flat on the cab's scratched metal floor, red plastic cup half-full of coffee upon the motor mount, hanger of work clothes directly behind his seat, and the brown package upon the dashboard. Rick had the engine idling and country and western music flowing quietly out the radio. He and Banner watched silently as the trucks began pulling out of the drive. The citizen's band hissed loudly in the dark. "Ready?" they heard Dellasandro ask over the radio.

"Ugh, white man," one of the Fryman brothers answered.

"Get a move on, college boy," Dellasandro suddenly said.

"Is he talkin' to me?" Banner asked Rick.

"Don't know," Rick said. "Fuck him anyway. I'm gonna follow Tower out."

Banner pulled the cigarette pack out of his shirt pocket, shook one out, lit it, then sat back and slowly French inhaled it. Tower was in the red fire truck, Ringo in one of the large white, six-wheeled trucks, behind Tower. They all waited for the Fryman brothers in the Kenworth rig and with Dellasandro following in the Kenworth oil tanker. As soon as they pulled out on to the road, Tower slowly eased the fire truck out. Rick hummed along with Willie Nelson over the radio. Banner wanted to go back to bed to his warm, loving woman, and not be out here going to work at two o'clock in the gawddamned morning.

5.

The trip down through the middle of dark Ohio was uneventful, the headlights piercing the night, the broken white center of the interstate highway flowing by in regular rhythm. Banner sipped his coffee most of the way, watching the night, listening to the static on the citizen's band; on the road once again, but not like Kerouac. Small silent scattered towns flickered ghostly by in the darkness, houses and buildings lit starkly by street lamps and lonely traffic signals glowing green over isolated highway intersections and those that crossed through the middle of the towns.

Banner knew they were in the farm lands. The interstate highway rolled up and down gently through the Ohio countryside: he could smell the rich odors of clover and land. Most of the houses were dark and silent as they drove by, the Amish shunning away from the electricity available to them, and the intrusion of modern-day life. He really didn't blame them; their lives were much simpler—reminiscent of early America—not like the pell-mell world that he had grown up in, with electricity pushing everyone forward, as if you were on a permanent acid trip, leaving behind the past to only distant, fragmented memory; nostalgia. The roar of the truck's engine and the static on the radio told him about the world he lived in; the scattered lights of quiet towns and the blazing reflection of lights into the nighttime sky of cities showing him that high voltage power lines spanned the landscape, bringing life and light to those who knew nothing different.

It was slightly over four hours when they arrived in Charleston, with the sun arriving through the surrounding old mountains. Banner was still tired when they arrived at the cement factory southeast of the city, a sprawling dusty complex located in the valley of two tall tree-filled mountains near the Kanawha River. Trucks roared in and out of the area, taking off on to the main highway destined for construction sites scattered over the state. Banner was surprised to find the factory still busy so early in the morning, and near a national holiday. Though the place was well-lit, he saw that the lights were flickering; jumping: the buildings seemed to move beneath the lights. It was highly surrealistic, making him feel giddy.

It took nearly four hours to complete the job, and they worked hard and fast to get the transformers drained, flushed, and filtered. Taking the secondary breakers out of service was no problem, except that the entire cement factory blacked-out, and the silence where once was *musique concrete* virtually screamed at them. It was as if all reality were in suspended animation, and they talked and worked in hushed tones; the machinery that once was alive was now stilled and dripping in silence, hanging over and around them like old cold temples of yore.

The main substation wasn't that large. The three single-phased transformers were yoked together to work as a single-phased unit, 7,200 volts pushing through the primary side to come out as 480 volts wye-connected to 277 volts, through the secondary bus and into the switchgear that fed the cement factory. They were old Kuhlman-built transformers, painted dark gray with tubed radiators coming out of the main tank six inches almost all the way around them. The high voltage insulators on the tops and sides of the transformers were short, squat, and thick with old cement dust that covered the porcelain. Banner could see that these transformers had never been inspected before. From the oil samples he had drawn—heavy, dark mixtures of oil and sludge thick as molasses—he wondered how they could still be operating.

After opening all the load circuit breakers and then the transformer main circuit breakers, Rick and Banner opened the low-profile primary disconnects that were in the substation itself. Rick checked the transformers dead, then put personal ground cables on the incoming power lines between the bus and the transformers and to a ground on the substation fence. Then Rick and Banner went into the dark building to the switchgear panel, Rick playing the flashlight over the metering gauges as Banner checked them and tagged the circuit breaker handles. It was dark, crackling silent, with only Rick's flashlight illuminating the interior. The silence overwhelmed Banner, the entire factory seeming in suspended terror as he stepped back outside to the crew.

"Let's do it," he said.

They worked hard and fast, cleaning the primary and secondary voltage insulators, draining the transformers, flushing them, and finally filtering the new oil from the tanker into each one. The cement factory creaked and groaned unnaturally, its noises echoing off into the morning. The generator in the truck continually roared and sputtered as they worked, adding to the surreal surroundings. None of the men could believe what the oil looked like as it drained out of the transformers. Trying to flush the units was nearly impossible, with hand-held lights behind their backs, the aroma of the old paraffin-based oil filling the senses. They ended up changing filters every 20 minutes for two hours until they were satisfied that the new oil had a low neutralization number and maintained a high dielectric of 42,000 volts. When the substation was re-energized, the lights seemed brighter and stable; machinery around them whined steadily. The plant's electrical maintenance foreman was a happy man. They were soaked in oil and dirt by the time they finished and were more tired than when they started. Banner wished he could go home after the job, but knew more loomed ahead of him, with a lot of traveling in between.

The four young men packed the hoses, fittings, tools, ground cables, hot stick, hot gloves, dielectric test equipment, soaked oil filters into the once empty 55-gallon drums they carried, and rags back into the vehicles. There was a lot more work to do before the day was out.

Banner thought of the Bee's offer to him before he left the house hours earlier. He wanted the day over with already so he could be home with his woman in erotic embrace. But he wasn't there, only here hours and miles from home and loving woman, earning his bread and butter. And the day had just started. No wonder he felt tired all the time. He had just come back from three other states and came upon the annual July 4th shutdown. He knew they were all going to work themselves to the bone. He saw it coming.

They ate at a roadside Mennonite diner that was already packed with Saturday laborers and weekend tourists. They had large breakfasts and drank lots of coffee. Banner had the waitress refill his thermos. They talked about what Tower and Ringo were going to do, then what Banner and Rick were going to do, then where they would meet when they got the other assignments done—in the first rest area above the Rubber City on the interstate highway later that day.

"I just want to go home. I don't want to go to Zanesville and Cambridge," Ringo groaned. They all wanted to go home, but there was no way out, except quit.

Banner and Rick watched the other two leave before they pulled on to the interstate highway. The morning sun was up behind scattered, gathering clouds: rain. There wasn't that much traffic on the new interstate highway heading north, and Rick pushed the truck as fast as it could go. The citizen's band radio squealed static and talk on Channel 19.

Banner lit another cigarette, his nth for the morning, tired and soaked from the job, belly now full of breakfast.

About five hours later, Banner could smell the old industrial city before he saw it. The raw industrial haze of rubber compounds permeated the area. With the low clouds hanging overhead and the threat of rain everywhere, the chemical odor was powerful, irritating one's lungs without mercy. Rick knew where the rubber tire company was located, on the southeast edge of the city. He had seen the leaking valve on the transformer and had told Archwood about it. Now they were here to replace it, and take oil samples afterwards.

The rubber factory was no different from the cement plant they had left in Charleston. Built of bricks and sheet metal, covered with the years of soot, dust, and grime, windows turned a yellowish-green from the years of industrial exposure, it sat as if from another era—which it was—old, but still carrying on the main processes that it had been built for. It had seen men come and operate the machinery that dwelled inside, churning out the products that the people used in America and abroad, and it had seen the men leave after working eight hours to their god, to be dormant and idling until the next morning, its great machinery silent and waiting. But it was always still alive, for there was a low murmurous steady hum that pervaded throughout, never stopping, just there, taken for granted by most; a sign that the building was still alive.

Banner and Rick found themselves in a dark, close, oily-smelling vault with blackened brick walls surrounding them, and two bare light bulbs glaring down from above. The floor was thick with a black oil and grease mixture. Long ago someone had covered it with cardboard and fine gravel, but now they were mixed in with the oil and grease. Wherever Banner stepped, he felt the cardboard spring up and down like a sponge, and saw the oily grease ooze up around his boots. It was also very slippery, and a couple times he almost took a spill on to the floor, which he really didn't want to do because the transformers surrounding him and the exposed copper bus work were very close, and he didn't want to come into contact with the equipment.

The transformers were old and covered with thick grime. Because Banner and Rick were in the small vault, the transformers seemed to hum louder than usual, and they were hot when Banner touched the sides. He felt the sharp heat through his hands, and had to let go only after a few seconds. The transformer that had the leaking bottom valve stood next to the wall. The valve was facing the rear wall. Banner and Rick both knew that this was going to be an impossible job to do. The electrical foreman had told them as soon as they arrived that there was no way he could de-energize the transformers.

"Shit," Rick said.

They were going to have to do it while the bank was still on-the-line; *just like B.S. had figured,* Banner thought. He took up position in between the middle transformer and the one that needed repair. The side-mounted secondary insulators had frayed greasy cables hanging ten inches above the valve and then back up before they disappeared into duct work to the outside of the building. It was a tight fit. He had just enough room to squeeze his upper torso through; he had only his left arm free to help Rick.

Rick was on the other side, sandwiched, like Banner, between the black grimy wall and the transformer. The valve and fourteen-inch pipe wrench lay in the box where he could reach it with his left hand. Banner felt claustrophobic. He checked where the hot frayed wires were, where the blackened insulators were, wanting to make sure he wouldn't fuck up and get himself killed or—worse—injured. It wasn't a comfortable position to say the least.

The transformers were hot to the touch, operating under heavy load, feeding electricity to large machinery, and Banner's skin burned beneath three layers of clothes. He could only adjust by pressing either the front or back part of his body against one of the transformers to relieve the burning from the other side.

"How we gonna do this?" he asked Rick.

"This way," Rick answered. "We just gotta make sure we don't get air bubbles up through this thing when we take the valve off. Ah jus' don't feel like wantin' to know what would happen if it did, ya know what Ah mean?" Rick asked, and grinned, though his eyes weren't laughing.

"Yeah," Banner said, envisioning the thought. It'd be nearly predictable as to what would occur: air bubbles up through the iron core and copper windings of the transformer while alternating 60-cycle-per-second high voltage electricity flowed through the circuitry would, in all probability, fail and blow up. Certainly he and Rick would be dead. The vault wasn't very big at all. "So how do we do this?" he asked Rick again.

"You loosen the bottom valve heah," and he handed the pipe wrench to Banner, after carefully lifting it up with his left hand, passing it up close to his body and dropping it near his freed right hand. "Just be careful you don't get near the cables."

"Yeah," Banner said. He took the pipe wrench, slapped it upside-down on the valve, the handle facing him, and stiffly, one-handedly opened the jaws enough to grip the valve, and pushed the handle toward Rick, watching where his arm and shoulder moved. His body twitched with the hot contact between the two burning transformers. It was silent and close inside the vault. He sweated profusely. Rick grabbed the handle as Banner pushed it toward him and completed the turn.

"Loose enough to do it by hand?" Banner asked.

"Not yet," Rick said. "One mo' time should do it."

Banner put the wrench back over the valve and pushed it toward Rick.

"Easy," Rick said, as Banner felt the valve start to loosen. Rick took the pipe wrench and put it back into the box. "Transformers are hot, ain't they?" Rick asked.

"Yeah," Banner answered.

"Wanna stop and smoke a minute, or get it done?"

"Let's get it done," Banner said. "Ain't no use in postponin' it. Faster we get it done, faster we get outta here. What's next?" There was nothing he could do about the hot transformers burning in through his clothes. The steady electrical chant of the transformers suddenly filled his head. He was aware of how dark and close everything was. He felt the grease-and-oil mixture beneath him soak into his clothes.

Rick looked at him. "Ready, mon?" he asked.

"Ready."

"Okay, Ah'm gonna unscrew the bottom valve. When Ah get it off, put your hand over the pipe and leave it there. When Ah get the other valve ready to put on, move your hand up and over it. Ah'll screw it on a few threads, then you'll put some of the pipe tape around the pipe. Got it?"

"Yeah," Banner said.

"It's gotta be done almost at the same time, ya know what I mean? We don't want air goin' up through this bitch. And from what I know about these bitches heah, Ah'll bet they're all pullin' a vacuum. Okay?"

"Yeah," Banner said again.

It didn't go as expected, of course, though both tried to run through the exchange without a hitch. They heard bubbles go up through to the surface of the hot mineral oil inside the transformer. Banner thought he counted five distinct ones, and, with left hand clamped over the open end of the pipe, waited for them to pass through the iron core and copper windings and detonate the transformer. He knew it came close: the steady electrical chant changed to a lower tone for just less than a second before resuming its frequency.

"Jesus," Banner said, gritting his teeth. "The son-of-a-bitch is hot," he yelled at Rick, the palm of his hand suddenly burning, wanting to get up and leave, move his hand, move his burning body, listening for any more bubbles rising through the transformer.

"Hold on," Rick shouted back at him, excited too, knowing that Banner wasn't yelling at Rick out of anger, but at the situation they were in, having to be careful of the high voltage cables hanging low. Suddenly he had the new valve behind Banner's hand, ready to twist it on to the threaded pipe.

"Go," Rick yelled, and Banner moved his hand over the top of the pipe as Rick lined up the valve. Air bubbles surged suddenly upwards through the mineral oil.

"Son-of-a-bitch," Rick screamed.

"Get it on," Banner told him, panicking, listening to the low rumbling the transformer made, waiting for it to go, wondering what it would feel like, wondering if he would see it explode before he died.

Rick twisted the valve quickly and the rumbling slid into a steady chant. Banner wanted to scream anyway, feeling an exaltation go through him, despite the burning heat. Sweat poured off his face; his glasses were perched on the end of his nose. "Air went up the side. Put the pipe tape on," Rick said. He was sweating too, but still had that controlled, stoic look upon his sallow face, not looking at Banner directly, but the flicker of a sardonic grin trying to crack through his features. He took the tape out of his shirt pocket with his left hand, unsnapped the lid, then one-handedly wrapped the tape around the pipe threads against the valve's edge. "That's good," Rick said. Banner pulled the tape, snapping it off. Rick silently handed him the pipe wrench. Tightening the valve took a long time because of the tape; they also kept listening to the transformer for any other signs of deviation.

When they finished, Banner slid out from between the transformers and stood in the center of the vault, the bare light bulbs glaring down at him from above. He unzipped his hot, soaked, greasy jacket. He was drenched in sweat, but his body was easing, cooling down from the burning heat.

"Man, I'm stiff," he said. He was glad this particular job was over. He didn't want to do to many of these.

Jesus.

6.

They found both Ringo and Tower sound asleep in their trucks at the roadside rest stop north of the city. Rick woke Tower up by holding a lit firecracker in his hand and kicking at the passenger door of the old fire truck where Tower was snoring. Tower jerked upright in his seat, his eyes bugging when he saw the firecracker. Shades of Dellasandro: "Gaaaaaahhhh!" he screamed, Rick laughing, and tossing the firecracker over his shoulder, where it loudly popped ten feet away. "You all ready?" he asked them, grinning. "You all ready to hit it?"

"Yeah yeah," Tower groaned, shaking. "You son-of-a-bitch, Pitts," he said. "Don't do that to me again, ya hear?"

Rick sniggered, then hopped back into the truck, where Banner sat, smoking, as he watched Tower and Ringo start their trucks.

"Now that you scared the shit outta them," Banner said.

"Yeah." Rick sniggered again, and they slid out on to the interstate.

It was 15 minutes before 1400 hours by the time they arrived at the sports arena. B.S. sat in his pick-up truck by the main entrance to the huge empty parking lot, Dellasandro in the seat next to him. The western sky was boiling with the threat of rain. Banner could feel the change in the weather: the wind picking up, the hot humid day dissipating, a low system moving in and to the east. He knew they were all going to work fast, and knew they'd be working in the rain if it came to that.

Which looked like the case, he thought.

Rick pulled the truck up next to Archwood's, and he and Dellasandro stared at each other. Dellasandro was smoking, looking at Rick with those hooded, mocking eyes. "'Bout time you girls made it up here," he jeered. Rick gave him the finger.

"You guys get all that work done down there?" B.S, called out, looking over Dellasandro's shoulder.

"Piece of cake," Rick told him. "Jus' like Sammy said it'd be." Dellasandro gave him the finger.

"What about that cement plant?"

"Sand in the oil." Banner silently gave the full sample jar to Rick, who gave it to Dellasandro. They looked at the oily sludge. B.S. shook his head, pursing his lips as he rubbed two fingers together after dipping them into the oil.

"Everything okay down there?" he asked.

"Couldn't be better," Rick told him. "Guy down there thinks we walk on water."

B.S. sniggered, shaking his head. "How'd that valve job go?"

"Nothin' to it. Little tight, hotter than hell, but we did it. We still alive."

"Okay. Good. Just follow us. We gotta lotta work here, and I want to get it at least started before this fuckin' rain starts." B.S. gunned the engine and took off across the parking lot without another word.

"Let's go," Rick said into the citizen's band microphone to Tower and Ringo, and followed the pick-up.

The sports arena was a huge, round building that glowed ferociously white against the asphalt parking lot that surrounded it. They drove around it to get to the substation. The high voltage lines came in on single column steel truss poles to the top of the substation structure. Three large oil circuit breakers sat underneath the bus work, with three large

Westinghouse-designed transformers behind the breakers. Secondary oil circuit breakers sat opposite the transformers beneath more of the structure, where the load cables ran straight into ducts beneath the ground and into the large building. The substation was beautifully designed, Banner thought, in perfect symmetry. The silver galvanized columns shined, the stand-off red porcelain insulators glowing, the transformer and circuit breaker foundations on clean concrete, the heavy gravel spread evenly all around, no weeds growing anywhere. He was impressed with the substation.

The Kenworth oil tanker and rerefining rig were parked outside the perimeter, near the main gate. A small crane sat next to the transformer closest to the trucks. The Fryman brothers stood in the rear of the rerefining trailer, watching the men pull up to the gate. Two other men stood by the open gate, watching them too, both dressed in blue coveralls, each one holding a walkie-talkie. Everyone stepped out of the trucks, stretching and looking around, greeting the Fryman brothers and the men by the gate. Archwood and Dellasandro walked up to them, with the others following.

"You the men in charge of switching out that transformer?" Archwood asked.

"Yes, sir," one of the men answered. "My name's Bell, Ron Bell. This here's Eugene Mange."

"Okay, Bell," Archwood said, looking through some papers he held. "We're supposed to change the radiator gaskets on this unit and the bushings, is that right?"

"Yes," Bell answered, nodding. "That's right. You wanta look at it?"

"Of course," Archwood said, squinting at him. Dellasandro spat on to the gravel. They walked into the energized substation, the gravel shifting loudly. The transformers hummed loudly and steadily. It got on Banner's nerves after a couple minutes, the electrical chant going through him like fingernails clawing down a blackboard. He saw what the problem was, all right: three radiators were leaking oil down the one side of the unit. They looked fresh: two weeks ago, he found out, Archwood and Dellasandro had been up here and thought by tightening the bolts the leaks would stop, but it didn't work. Now they were back again, this time to redo the work. De-energize the unit, drain the oil, take off the radiators, cut out new gaskets, remove the old ones, put the new ones on, reinstall the radiators, refill and filter the oil again inside the transformer. And at the same time, remove the top primary and secondary insulators and regasket them for good measure.

"Six hours," Archwood said aloud.

"If we bust ass," Dellasandro growled.

"We'll all bust ass."

"Ah shit," Rick muttered.

Banner sighed. Dellasandro was going to be in charge of this particular job, while Archwood would leave in a very short time. *Damn.* He heard Ringo mumbling to himself.

"What about the rain?" Ringo asked.

"Whatsa matter? You afraid of gettin' wet?" Dellasandro snarled, turning to him, already in his element. "You afraid you'll melt?"

"You bring the tarp?" Archwood asked.

"In the rig," Tommy Fryman boomed.

"I want the clear stuff if we got any."

"We got that too."

"Great. We'll use that." Archwood turned back to Bell and Mange. "You guys gonna switch this transformer out?"

"Yes, sir," Bell answered, looking at Mange. "We'll be doin' it, but—"

"Great. Sooner we get started, sooner we get done." Archwood looked at the sky, then shook his head. "It looks like we're gonna have one hell of a rainstorm, gawddamn it, but there ain't nothin' we can do about it.

Not unless you want to cancel and we can do it some other time," raising the other men's hopes, all looking at Bell.

But Bell shook his head. "No. The boss says we got to get it done. Insurance company says it has to be fixed. I guess because of the liability."

"Okay." Archwood nodded. "You get this unit de-energized. We'll throw our grounds on it and cover it up." He shook his head, eyebrows knitting. "Son-of-a-bitch, Sammy, if it rains, it's gonna be harder than hell to get those radiators and bushings lifted offa there."

"We'll do it, no problem," Dellasandro said, lighting another cigarette. "I'll get Banner and Pitts on top. They look like they need the exercise, heh heh heh." He looked at both men and Banner saw the evil triumphant smirk on his face.

"All right," Archwood said, lighting a cigarette, then turned to his men. "Here's how it is. When it's dead, Ringo, Tower, apply the grounds. Jackson, you and Rick get that clear sheeting up and over the transformer. Tommy, Jimmy, you all get the rig ready to pump the oil out into the tanker. Make sure you got everything covered in that tanker, I don't want any rain goin' into it, got it? Sammy's gonna operate that crane, get these radiators off. Those insulators are gonna come out too, and it's gonna be harder than hell to get 'em off. Rick, you got sneakers in your truck?"

"Always," Rick said.

"Okay. You might havta climb down inside there, makin' sure those cables don't slip down inside. Kill the nitrogen feedin' into this unit, let it air out before you go down there. And don't drop anything down there, I don't need to remind ya of that, right?"

"Right."

"Get those gaskets made up as soon as you can. Ringo and Tower will be up there too, helpin' ya and makin' up the gaskets. Everybody's gonna be busy. Especially in this rain that'll be here anytime. No breaks. No time for dinner. You'll all eat when you're done. No slacking off. I want this son-of-a-bitch done so we can do our other work tomorrow. I'm gonna leave here soon and check up on what we havta do tomorrow an' the rest uh the week. Tomorrow's gonna be a longer day. When you're all done here, head on back to the shop, reload, and go home. Jackson, you and Rick gotta go to American Steel after here. Paperwork'll be on my desk. Everybody's gonna be at the shop sharp at 0100 hours. Sammy an' the Fryman boys'll be on the lake tomorrow. The rest uh you guys, we gotta four-hour ride to the job site and a four-hour ride back. So this job has got to be done today." He stopped and thought for a moment. "We got those lights still in the rig?" asking Dellasandro.

"Yeah," Dellasandro said. "Enough that we can light up the whole gawddamned area and hold a rock concert." All the while Archwood talked, Dellasandro had been pacing like a caged tiger, just waiting for Archwood to give him the word to begin.

"All right," Archwood said. He turned back to Bell and Mange. "I'm gonna send Sammy with whoever's gonna kill these breakers."

"That'll be Mange," Bell said.

"Okay, Mange then." Archwood turned to Dellasandro again. "You go with this guy just to double check him. I got some danger tags in my truck so you can— Oh," he said, nodding as Dellasandro pulled them out of his back pants pocket. "Okay, you got 'em." He turned back to Bell. "You all ready, then? We ready to go?"

Bell nodded, somewhat tentatively. "Yes, sir," he said. "Understand we ain't never switched anything like this before, so you gotta bear with us."

Archwood nodded. "We'll stand by. Just let's hurry it up before the gawddamned rain starts pourin' down all over us."

"Yes, sir. You ready, Eugene?"

Mange just nodded.

"Sammy, you go with Mange here," Archwood said, jerking a thumb at the man.

"Whatever you say," Dellasandro said.

"Okay. Sammy, take off. You other guys, get ready."

All of a sudden there was a crack of thunder, then a booming echo as it rolled over them. A few raindrops splattered down around them, then began more insistently. "Gawddamn it," Archwood said, looking up. "Let's get movin', guys. Shit," and they moved fast. Banner saw lightning flash, then another crack of thunder boomed overhead. He and Rick ran to the rerefining rig, climbed inside, and found a roll of five-mil clear plastic sheeting.

"Gonna be a bitch," Rick said.

"You said it."

They stood at the rear open doors of the rig, watching the rain. The Fryman brothers ignored them as they readied the rig, firing up the large generator in the front that was walled inside the compartment away from the oil rerefining equipment. They had opened the side doors of the generator's room, and the machine sputtered, took hold, and roared. The thunder boomed louder though. The Frymans stepped out into the rain to secure the tanker. Banner already hated this job, especially with Dellasandro in charge of the work and screaming at the men.

"Might as well wait until they get that transformer switched out," Rick said.

"Okay by me," Banner answered, lighting a cigarette, feeling tired and worn. "Smoke?"

"Nah. Mebbe later. Sure wish I had brought some beer before comin' up here. Plumb forgot all about it."

"In your enthusiasm to be here."

"Yeah, I know what ya mean."

Archwood and Dellasandro had gone inside an overhead door with the coliseum men right after it started raining. Now Archwood and Bell returned, Bell wearing a raincoat, Archwood still wearing his leather vest and white hardhat. Archwood crooked a finger at Banner and Rick, then motioned to Ringo and Tower, who'd been standing in the rear of their truck, the heavy grounding cables at their feet. Both of them looked miserable, and the job hadn't even started yet. Archwood was already soaked, and looking frazzled.

"Here goes," Banner said, flipping his cigarette on to the ground, and he and Rick climbed out of the rig. Banner carried the roll of plastic over his shoulder, following Rick. Archwood and Bell stood in the middle of the opened substation gate as the four men walked hurriedly up to them. Within moments they were all soaked. They hadn't been prepared for the downpour, nor the thunder and lightning that boomed and flashed above them. They had to shout to hear each other because the generator's noise cut through the rain and thunder.

"All right," Archwood shouted, looking paler and waxier. "They're gonna kill these two end circuit breakers," pointing to both, "then open the disconnects. After that, we get to apply the grounds." He shook his head. "I don't like the idea of switchin' out here in this weather, but we gotta get this work done. All right?"

"Yeah," Rick yelled, amid various silent nods and sniffles.

Banner wanted another cigarette. He followed the others and found himself standing between the transformer and the primary oil circuit breaker. Ringo and Tower laid the grounding cables on the graveled foundation in a straight line. Tower carried the grounding stick and hot gloves, both still in the carrying cases.

It was really raining hard now. Thunder and lightning surrounded them, the thunder cracking low and sharp overhead, followed only a second later by the jagged lightning. Banner didn't want to be here in the energized substation. Neither, he saw, did any of the others, especially Bell, who seemed jumpy and looked scared. None of them wanted to see lightning strike the structure.

The walkie-talkie Bell held crackled: "Ready in here, Ronnie."

"All right," Bell shouted. They all stood around him, hunched over, trying to listen above the rain, thunder, and generator. Banner heard two loud cracks, one followed immediately by another. Mange—dry as a bone along with Dellasandro, Banner thought wryly—had opened the primary and secondary oil circuit breakers.

"I got 'em both open," Mange's voice crackled.

"Got it," Bell shouted into the walkie-talkie, then looked at Archwood. "Okay. I guess I'm ready. Here. Would you mind holdin' this?" and gave Archwood the radio.

"We'll wait here," Archwood shouted. Rain poured off his hardhat. He looked grim and tired. They watched Bell walk over to the primary part of the structure to the disconnect switch by the circuit breaker and unlock it.

Banner looked at the circuit breaker's manual operating cabinet, then turned and looked at the other one. Alarmed: "Shit!" he suddenly shouted, Archwood looking hard at him. "He's gonna open it while it's—"

At the same time the walkie-talkie in Archwood's hand viciously crackled: "Don't do nothin' out there, ya son-of-a-bitch," Dellasandro screaming statically, "this asshole opened up the wrong breakers!" Too late: Bell had just pulled the gang-operated disconnect switches down, and suddenly everything went crazy.

Thunder and lightning exploded at the same time, the lightning striking the ground only a hundred yards away from the substation. Archwood had heard Dellasandro scream over the radio and was taking a step forward to stop Bell, but Bell had already opened the switch. The area lit up brighter than day, the live bright arc of 69,000 volts of electricity dancing crazily through the upper part of the switch rack between the clips and the gang-operated three-phase disconnect blades. The ground trembled and shook, the transformer groaning and surging.

Banner panicked and started to run out of the substation behind Tower but tripped and fell flat on his face after taking two steps, burying his hardhat over his head. He had seen Rick trying to maintain his balance, saw him fall, then crawl on all fours towards Bell. Archwood had just stood rooted to the spot, a look of disbelief on his face, his hardhat jiggling on his head, watching the dancing arc of high voltage electricity. Banner didn't know where Ringo was.

Thunder and lightning struck again.

"What's wrong?" Bell shouted after Rick pushed him into the oil circuit breaker and slammed the disconnect switch shut again. The ground quit trembling. Banner slowly stood, saw Rick's face pale and sweating.

"Jesus Christ!" Rick screamed at Bell. "Jesus," and he shook his head, then leaned against the galvanized column the disconnect handle was on, and began trembling. There was another lightning flash and thunder at the same time, directly overhead, scaring everyone.

It had only taken five seconds after Bell opened the disconnects that Rick closed them again. It seemed like an hour to Banner. He looked around. The substation was still energized. He thought the switchgear relays should have taken it out on overcurrent protection, but they didn't work. The gawddamned transformers were still humming, this time normally, the oil circuit breakers still closed and holding. He shook his head. He found himself shaking.

Jesus.

He watched Archwood walk toward Bell with a deadened expression on his face: pale, white, waxy, zombie-like, and saw him start thrashing the surprised man with his hardhat, beating him savagely about his face and hands as Bell threw them up for protection, surprised by the sudden onslaught.

"You son-of-a-bitch," Archwood yelled. "You son-of-a-bitch, no one does this to me, you son-of-a-bitch. I'm gonna kill you."

Banner suddenly ran over to him, trying to pull him away from the frightened Bell. "Easy, B.S., easy. Take it fuckin' easy!" Banner yelled. Rick was beside him too, and they separated the two men, Rick pushing a still swinging and enraged Archwood away and out of the substation. Banner looked at Bell, who was sitting on the oil circuit breaker's concrete foundation, holding the left side of his swelling face with his hand.

Archwood stopped suddenly, looking at the perimeter fence. "The fuck," he shouted, pointing at Ringo. They all looked and Banner, despite himself, started laughing.

Ringo was hung up in the strands of barbed wire that ran all the way round the top of the fence. The Fryman brothers were standing on both sides of a wooden stepladder, getting a whimpering Ringo untangled. He was hanging upside down now, like the Fool in a tarot card, his ankle still caught. Rick and Archwood started laughing too at Ringo's predicament; trying to relieve the tension. "Shit," Rick screamed, holding his sides. Thunder cracked overhead again. It rained harder.

Then Archwood looked around. His face looked dead, his hollow cheeks accentuating his bony face. "Everybody okay?" he asked, somewhat subdued.

"Yeah," Rick said, sober now, subdued also.

Banner nodded.

Tower was in the rerefining rig, peering at them.

"You okay, Tower?" Archwood yelled.

"Yeah," Tower answered.

"Tommy? Jimmy?"

"Ugh," Tommy said.

"Ditto," Jimmy answered.

"What about you, Ringo?"

"I'll be all right as soon as I get the fuck outta here and in my own bed," Ringo shrilly screamed, still upside down. "I wanta go home! Get me off here before lightning hits the fence!"

"Where's Sammy?"

"Probably beating the hell outta Mange," Banner said.

Jimmy Fryman hopped off the ladder and ran into the building.

Archwood looked at him, then looked back at Bell, who still sat beneath the oil circuit breaker, soaked from the rain. "Shit." He nodded over to Bell. "Rick, would ya take care of him? Tell him I'm sorry I lost my temper."

"You bet," Rick answered, and left them.

"You okay?" Archwood asked Banner.

"Yeah. Shaky, but I'm all tight."

Archwood suddenly glanced at Banner's right hand. "You're bleedin'."

"What?"

"Christ, your fuckin' hand's covered with blood."

Banner brought his right hand up. "Damn," he said aloud, wide-eyed, "how'd I do that?" He looked closer and saw a deep gash in his right wrist, welling blood. Archwood grabbed his arm, pulling the gash apart, inspecting it closely. Banner started to feel it throb.

"There's some glass in it," Archwood said.

"I musta done it when I fell. There musta been glass or somethin' on the ground."

"You're gonna need stitches. Shit."

"Great," Banner said. He hated doctors. Now he wanted a cigarette.

Archwood turned to see Ringo standing upright. "You bleedin' anywhere?" he asked.

"Hell no," Ringo said, miffed. "I just got tangled up is all."

"Well how in the fu—"

"I guess I tried gettin' out by climbin' the damn fence. I didn't see the gate."

"Well Jesus," Archwood said, sniggering, then stopped, looking at Banner. He still held on to his arm. "I gotta take you to the hospital. You need stitches."

"Great," Banner said again.

Rick walked out with Bell, his arm around the man's shoulders. Bell looked warily at Archwood.

"Where's the nearest hospital?" Archwood asked him.

"'Bout twenty miles north on the freeway," Bell answered.

"Thanks." Archwood looked at the man. "I'm sorry as hell I lost my temper. I shouldn'ta hit ya."

Bell nodded, rubbing his face. "It's all right. No harm done. I just didn't know what the hell was wrong. Honest. I'm just a maintenance worker. Not an—an electrician."

Archwood just stared at him. "You shoulda said somethin'. Christ Almighty." He shook his head. "None of this woulda happened if you'da said somethin'. Where's the gawddamned electrical supervisor?"

Bell just shrugged. "Holiday. Day off, I guess." There was nothing else to say.

Dellasandro, Jimmy Fryman, and Mange walked out of the building. Apparently, nothing had happened. Mange looked normal, but Dellasandro was seething. He walked up to Archwood totally ignoring the rain. "You all okay out here?" he asked.

"Yeah, we're all right," Archwood said somewhat disgustedly. "I'm gettin' tired of this bullshit. Looks like these guys are maintenance workers, not electricians."

"Well, where the fuck *are* the electricians?"

Bell shrugged again. "Home, I guess," he said. "All I was told was to see that you guys got your work done."

"Oh my. We can't have the union havin' their electricians workin' overtime, can we?" Dellasandro looked back at Archwood. "Lemme switch this station. I'll do it right this time."

"Rick'll help ya," Archwood said. "I'm takin' Banner to the hospital. He's gotta have stitches put in his wrist."

Dellasandro's eyes flashed. "Oh yeah? What happened?"

Archwood shook his head. "I'll tell ya 'bout it later. I gotta get goin'. Get this transformer out and start workin' on it." He thought a moment. "You know where Gordon Short is?"

"With Lazarus. They're in Philadelphia, workin' there."

"I want him here first thing tomorrow morning. I wanta know why those relays in there didn't take out this station. Call him up," here Archwood looked at his watch, "call him up in a few minutes at that plant he's at an' tell him to drag up. I want him here. That number's in here some place," and he gave Dellasandro the papers he'd been carrying. "I'm taking Banner with me now."

"Is he gonna be able to work when he gets back?" Dellasandro sneered.

"I kinda doubt it. We'll see."

Banner lit a cigarette, holding a compress to his wrist, which was throbbing now from the isopropyl alcohol Rick had poured on it before climbing into Archwood's truck. "See ya later, Jackson," Rick said, grinning and winking, then took off with Dellasandro, who had already started screaming at the men.

They drove to the hospital in silence.

The rain pounded furiously against the windshield, the thunder and lightning still rolling about. The traffic was slow-moving. Headlights were lit against the darkened sky. They finally made it to the hospital and ran inside.

"Glad you didn't bleed to death in my gawddamned truck," Archwood said, and laughed.

"Me too," Banner answered. His wrist really started to hurt him now. He looked at Archwood, then said: "Sorry I screwed up back there."

"Shit," Archwood snorted. "We're all lucky we didn't fry."

"Yeah. If the lightning didn't get us first."

"Yeah," Archwood said. "I wish I had my camera. I forgot the son-of-a-bitch. It sure woulda made a great picture today, huh?"

Banner nodded. "Yeah," he said. "Yeah. It would have been a great picture."

7.

In Archwood's office framed photographs covered two walls, while the third held large detailed sectionalized maps of coast-to-coast American high voltage electrical power grids. Archwood had taken many of the photographs himself: there were pictures of high voltage substations in various stages of construction, with the men who built them standing in a group staring ruggedly into the camera; some with one or two men fitting parts of a substation structure together hanging on the girders and beams to set in the stand-off insulators or potential transformers, lightning arrestors, station service transformers; oil circuit breakers; assembling radiators and insulators on transformers, or setting in a line tower. These were the substations that Archwood and his crews had built from the ground up, hired by rural power companies and industrial plants to do the work.

He also kept photo albums of industrial substations that the company had completed work under contract, and these were lined up in a metal bookcase that went from floor to ceiling in the trailer. He always referred to them whenever they had to go back to one of the plants to work. Each book was noted what substation it was, where it was located, what kind of work was performed in it.

Four-drawer file cabinets around the four walls were loaded with reports filled out by the crews who worked on these substations. Records were kept on individual transformers and oil circuit breakers: the manufacturer, voltage and rating, location, dates when oil was tested, repairs made. There were records also of electrical testing switchgear relays, air circuit breakers, meters, transformers, and insulators.

Archwood's office was crammed, and he hardly ever used it except to give someone a private ass-chewing.

He also kept notebooks on top of the file cabinets, filled with newspaper clippings of electrical accidents that occurred across the country and throughout the world when he could get them. It seemed an almost morbid obsession with him to collect the news articles, show them to his crews for them to study: to see how men, women, and children died; how the events happened in the first place.

Digging into the books one could find anything: a teenager climbing a transmission tower on a dare, then killed after touching a 12,000-volt high tension line; a parachutist electrocuted when he missed his landing target and the wind blew him across three-phased high voltage lines; a 7-year-old girl electrocuted by overhead lines when she climbed a tree near her home, and found lodged in the tree limbs, the limbs and the girl on fire; two young children, brother and sister, and their pet Labrador puppy, electrocuted by a power line that had fallen across a wire meshed fence, charging the fence with 4,000 volts of electricity—the children had both touched the fence, and were found still holding on to it; two firemen dying, the electricity surging through them instantaneously, when the aluminum ladder they were maneuvering brushed a live 11,000-volt power line after they'd been called to fight a fire in a three-alarm warehouse blaze.

And electrical workers themselves: an explosion inside a Commonwealth Edison power generating plant killing a fireman, blacking out thousands of homes and businesses for hours; an air circuit breaker in an enclosed double-ended substation exploding upon being energized, killing two station operators; two station operators killed while switching and missing one step in the switching procedure, hot molten pieces of the bus and disconnects blown up, catching fire; eleven power plant personnel killed when a pressurized steam line broke at a welded seam; an underground cable blowing up in a vault after being mistakenly energized where two cable splicers were busy performing their work, both on fire and skin peeling off them as they were lifted out of the vault, one dying in agony four hours later, the other dead after living with no skin for eighteen days; an overhead lineman blown out of a boom truck after coming into contact with a power line, both arms suddenly missing at his shoulders, and living to tell the tale; Phil Lazarus injured severely after backing into a live 7,200-volt fuse in which the electricity flowed through his skull and blew out his elbow.

"We're crazy for workin' around this shit," Banner said one Saturday night not too long ago in Pittsburgh, as he, Archwood, Dellasandro, and Rick sat in a dark booth in a rocking hotel bar, all of them drunk, drinks sitting in front of them and the surrounding air blue and thick with cigarette smoke.

"Mebbe so, mebbe so," Archwood told him. His bloodshot green eyes flicked to Banner, his shock of blonde hair falling limp over his forehead. "Mebbe we're all fucked-up crazy for workin' around it. Mebbe we don't know no better. But shit, man, look at *you*. College education and readin' books all the time. What the hell you doin' workin' with us then, huh? Why ain't you movin' on, findin' a better job, or, or a better-*payin'* job, huh? Workin' behind some desk somewhere? I know why. I know why. You love this work. We all love this work. You ain't gonna find a better job. You go around and see how other men make their livin'. You see how it is. So why ain't you doin' it? 'Cause you ain't gonna find a more excitin' job to do, unless it's bein' an ironworker walkin' on beams way up in the air, or, or some damn coal miner with nothin' but a mountain over ya. Or a fireman fightin' some kind of gawdawful fire somewhere. Or bein' an astronaut out there in outer space. You're addicted to it just like the rest of us. You love the danger of it all, you like bein' right where it's all at. You like bein' on the edge, knowing how fucking dangerous it all is. The challenge of it, havin' guys tell you you're fuckin' crazy for being around live electricity. So you don't leave, makin' peanuts. Go on, find a better job to do that'll pay you better money. But the thrill, man, the thrill'll be gone, that old rush of doin' somethin' nobody else can do. You know what I mean? After you've done what we're doin' here, you're gonna find that there ain't nowhere else to go. This is the heart of it, this is where it all starts."

Archwood finished his Black Russian, then ordered another. He lit another cigarette and looked out at the people in the bar, silent, almost pensive after talking so much. None of the others said anything. Banner felt nearly sick from keeping up with Archwood drink for drink.

"Imagine, just imagine if there ain't no electricity at all, then what, huh? 'Magine what would happen if all our electricity disappeared all of a sudden and I mean *boom*, now. No spinnin' dynamos, no juice flowin' through the lines, nothin' goin' through the transformers, nothin', man, *nothin'*. Dead. Jesus Gawd, I hate to think of it, ya know what I mean?"

Rick stood up, mumbling something about finding a woman, and left.

Dellasandro looked at Banner with his mocking eyes, smoking a cigarette, silent.

Archwood shook his head, drank the Black Russian, waved his hand to the waitress to bring another round for the three of them.

"Ya know," he said, "people nowadays are just used to havin' their electricity. It's hardly a hundred years old. It ain't like the old days anymore. Oh I 'spect that there're a few who remember what it was like to live without it, but they ain't very many around. Not in this country, unless you're Amish. But now the people, oh yeah, the people, they gotta have it. They're used to it. *Addicted to it* more 'n likely. They just flick on the old t.v., turn on their stereos, the old light switch, bingo, like magic, the light's there. They don't know where it comes from or even how it all works. They don't know there's somebody on the other end of it, makin' sure everything's going okay. How it gets from there to here. They don't want it taken away from them. D'you blame them? I don't, no sir. I don't want it taken away either. But imagine it has. Then what? 'Bout six weeks later, chaos. Nothin' but chaos. Cities on fire. Starvation. Cannibalism. Tribalism. Smell of death everywhere. People around here'd be *killin'* each other for food, eating their pets. Look around," sweeping an arm around the bar, "look around, and tell me how many of these sorry bastards would make it if all the electricity was taken away. Forever."

Archwood took another swallow of his drink. He sat silent for a long time, as if lost in drunken thought. Banner and Dellasandro stayed silent too. The music was loud inside the bar; Archwood had to talk louder to get himself heard.

"Ya know what," he said. "It'd be so fucking easy to destroy this country of ours, and you wouldn't have to bomb the cities or poison the countryside. All you'd have to do is destroy all the power plants and the substations of those power plants and the major tie lines of the electrical system. Shit. And it wouldn't take much to get it all together to do it, ya know what I mean? Christ, you know what I mean. Mask, gloves, bolt cutters, pipe wrench, that's all you need."

Archwood fell silent again. "But I always thought, ya know, on how it'll all work, how everybody can get it together. Just tie the whole fuckin' world together. Just tie the whole gawddamned electrical systems we got and tie 'em to other countries. Span lines everywhere. Cross borders. Oceans. Deserts. Jesus."

He stopped and looked up at the dark ceiling. "That'd be one job I'd love to get hold of, you know. Span the power lines from here into Russia. That would be the start. Wouldn't that be a *son-of-a-bitch*? Wouldn't that be *the cat's ass*?" Archwood shook his head slowly, stared into his drink.

"Gawd that'd be the job to be on, wouldn't it? Just *thinkin'* about it gives me the willies. But I tell you what, yes sir, if that ever came to be, if the decision was ever made to do somethin' like that, I'd sure as hell make sure we'd be in on *that* bid, you bet. If we didn't get that job, you bet your ass I'd quit what I'm doin' now and go work for the outfit that'd be doin' it. Shit. That'd be like layin' railroad tracks across the country, or *buildin' the gawddamned Panama Canal*. Yes, sir." Archwood nodded to himself, now smiling. "Yes, sir, that'd be the job to have."

He belched.

"And you think we're crazy for workin' with this electricity? Well mebbe we are, mebbe we ain't. But there ain't nothin' more satisfyin', lemme tell ya, than bein' in a substation full of raw power, all that high voltage just flowin' through there. Because, man, there just ain't anywhere else to go after you do this kind of work. This is the very heart of it, this is what keeps everything around us going."

He fell silent and drank, then waved his hand to the waitress again. He didn't say another word after that. Banner and Dellasandro looked at each other; Banner finished his drink.

Electric nights in America: give thanks to them for your current life—Thales, Volta, Ampère, Franklin, Faraday, Maxwell, Edison, Westinghouse, Tesla. Witness it, stretching across America: the lit windows in buildings and homes, indicating work and rest and play; streetlamps lighting cities and suburbs and neighborhoods; a lamp post illuminating an old white farm house, keeping out the alien darkness and the still of the night. Heroic workers who are all tied together by electricity give the country the fuel—the light; your life—in their savage, dangerous war to keep America alive, forever burning, ever forward. Generating plants are watched over carefully every minute of every day and every night by these unacknowledged vanguards—and know they always will be unsung. Transmission lines spread outward delicately like a spider's web, threading over the landscape, over mountains and deserts and rivers and the vast plains across the country, carrying electricity, crackling with life-giving power, monitored and watched over every minute of every day.

This is the Ark of the Covenant. *There is nothing new under the sun.*

There is always the pounding rhythm of tires and the roar of the engine as you drive in the night through electric America. Flashing colored neon signs direct you here and there, crossroads lit up by places to eat, to drink, to get gasoline or diesel, to take you further where you need to go—to get you through the night. There is that open free road as you travel through the night where no lights burn, but the million pinprick stars hanging above, casting their own lights to shine on you in frozen space.

But then there's that light burning in the darkness: is it the lonely rural light of a farmhouse, a light shining over a crossroad, the first light beckoning you to the start of a city, or the one that burns within you in the lonely naked American night?

8.

Lightning rolled across the sky.

Miles away Banner saw a city's lights bouncing off the low clouds in a hemispheric dome. The interstate traffic stretched ahead, the red taillights like straight, jagged streaks, while the oncoming traffic's headlights blazed brightly as they cut through the rain. The lights hurt Banner's eyes. He sat in the passenger seat of the Kenworth tanker, slowly smoking, watching the smoke curl lazily upwards from the end of the cigarette. Now he was going home.

What's the Bee gonna think?

Lightning still flashed through the dark thick cloud cover.

He watched as it streaked out of the sky, branching off for hundreds of feet and striking the ground. It scared him somewhat; he had never seen anything like it before in such intensity. The dark land lit up under the persistent storm, and he caught glimpses of highways and suburban areas and trees in the flickering night. Suddenly, way off in the distance, he saw a small blue hemisphere of light balloon out into the black sky above. There were electric lights a moment before; now it was solid black all around. Brake lights lit up ahead of them, then just as quickly disappeared.

"Shit," Rick muttered, and he downshifted the rig.

It was eerie. There were only the traffic's lights now on the interstate, the hissing tires, the engine's roar, the windshield wipers clacking, and the static on the citizen's band radio.

"Did you see that, Mustache?" a gravelly-voiced trucker drawled over the radio.

"Aye, heh heh," Mustache answered archly in a nasal tone. "Pretty spooky, don't ya think?"

"Aye, 10-4. You got that right. It sure is spooky though, don't ya think, that He's puttin' a fireworks show on for us on America's birthday, especially when she's now 200 years old, huh?"

"Aye, 10-4. You said it all."

The citizen's band on Channel 19 hissed back into the rhythmic static. No one bothered to make any more comments. The static hissing filled the cab's darkened interior.

Rick threw the empty beer bottle out the window, then popped open another beer. He handed the greasy bag over to Banner. "Want another mountain oyster?" he asked.

"Uh, uh," Banner said. "But turn on the light a minute, would ya?"

"Sure." Rick flipped the overhead cab light on.

Banner reached up and grabbed the brown package the Bee had given him earlier that morning. He held it between his knees as he pried the staples out of the one end with a switchblade. His right wrist was throbbing steadily now. After he removed the last staple, he dumped the books on his lap.

"Whatcha got there?" Rick asked.

"Books." Banner read off the titles: "*Experimental Researches in Electricity.* Three volumes by Michael Faraday. Original first editions."

"Sounds like light reading material to me," Rick said.

Jackson Banner laughed. "Yeah," he said, and he started riffling through the first volume. "Don't know when I'll ever get to it."

"Ah'm sure you'll get to it someday," Rick said.

Lightning skittered across the sky.

Cigarettes and Coffee
Part V

1.

Jackson Banner climbed into the truck. Rick slid in on the passenger seat, putting the transformer-turns-ratio set on the floor by his feet. Banner started the engine and let it warm up. Sitting made him feel more spent, his soaked clothes weighing him down, his limbs filled with lead.

Up nearly 30 hours, he thought, staring at the rain.

"Turn the heat on, mon," Rick said, teeth chattering.

"I don't know," Banner told him. "I might fall asleep with it on."

"So what? Ah'm friggin' cold." Rick reached over and flipped the switch on full blast. Cold air rushed out on to Banner's legs, and he shivered involuntarily.

"Jesus," he said.

He turned on the windshield wipers and headlights, the citizen's band radio, hearing the reassuring static and tones, then slowly moved the truck away from the shed. The windshield began to fog; he wiped it with his sleeve, smearing it worse. He saw Tiny and Charlie turn on their truck's headlights and was ready to follow them when he saw Dellasandro walk rapidly toward him, his eyes not leaving Banner's face. Banner rolled down the window, rain spitting on him, and kept his foot on the brake.

"What the hell do *you* want?" Banner asked him sourly.

Dellasandro's hardhat filled the open window, rain pouring from it and soaking through Banner's pants. "I ran outta smokes. Whaddaya got?"

"Old Golds."

"Them fuckin' ragweeds? Gimme one," and grabbed Banner's proffered pack. He shook out five, sticking one in his mouth. There was nothing Banner could do. "Here you are, college boy," Dellasandro said through closed teeth, tossing the pack on to the dashboard.

"Back off, you're gettin' me all wet," Banner gritted.

"Say what?" Dellasandro asked innocently, eyes laughing at him; cigarette glaring at him too. "Are you *talkin'* to me, college boy?" he asked, and Rick snorted. "Punch in that cigarette lighter, no use wastin' my matches."

Banner cleared his throat loudly and punched in the lighter, impatiently waiting for it to snap out, wondering what he did karmically to deserve someone like Dellasandro.

"Your truck's a mess, Banner," Dellasandro snarled evenly, almost friendly. "It's a fuckin' black shame to this company."

"Horseshit."

"My my, is that all the vocabulary they taught you in school?"

"Nah. I also learned what the definition of a motherfucker is," Banner told Dellasandro smoothly, looking him straight in the eye. He held the lighter for Dellasandro, who took it and lit the cigarette. All the time his mocking gaze never left Banner. He blew the smoke heavily into Banner's face, who didn't blink.

Dellasandro nodded. "You got balls, college boy, you got balls. It's just too bad Archwood never let me train you my way," he said, and laughed derisively. Then he stared hard at Banner and Rick. "I'll be seein' you girls later. Don't fuck up."

"We nevah fuck up," Rick suddenly piped. "Only on top or from behind."

"Don't get cute, Pitts, or you might find yourself changin' Fuller's earth tanks with me in the rigs."

"Don't count on it," Rick said flatly.

"We'll see. Get the hell outta here. I don't need to look after any more crybabies." Dellasandro looked at Banner slowly from head to toe. "Or any fuckin' *ballet dancers*," he minced, then turned and stalked away, heading for the rig.

"Hell with him," Rick told Banner, his brow knitted.

"Yeah," Banner answered.

Rick continued looking at Banner. Banner impatiently waved at the electric utility men to go ahead, then followed them out the gate, turned right, and sat back against the seat. He knew Rick was still looking at him. He turned to face him. Rick had the beginning of a smirk on his sallow face, then grinned and laughed at the same time.

"What," Banner said.

"Ballet?"

"Yeah. Ballet. So what?"

"Nothin', mon, nothin'," Rick said, fully grinning. "Ah nevah knew, that's all. My oh my," and he laughed and slapped his knee. "I'da like to've been there when ol' Sammy found out, you bet."

"Oh yeah," Banner said, wondering how exactly Dellasandro did find out. "Ah well, screw it. I got other things to worry about."

"You bet. You bet you do." Rick laughed again.

They followed the slow-moving truck as it traveled over the slightly rolling road, its yellowness bright and stark in the dull gray surroundings. Banner wished he were going the opposite way—the direction home—and not having to work in the cold bleak rain near the end of the winter season. They turned off the road and went north on another, both sides of the highway stretching out flat, the Tills Plains roiled with mud and dotted with large arthritic-limbed trees in the distance. Towers carrying high voltage transmission lines stood in the fields too, disappearing in the misty raining countryside. There was nothing to look at for miles around but low-slung black and gray clouds savagely seeding the muddy earth.

Spring was returning in its own fury.

Rick stared out the window, smoking one of his rolled cigarettes.

Banner grabbed his thermos, held it against his crotch, unscrewed the cap and poured the coffee one-handed into the cup that lay on the engine mount. It smelled good to him this time; perhaps because he knew that he was going to go home today. *Home, hearth, and warm loving wife.* He lit another cigarette of the day, finding only two left in the violated pack—*that son-of-a-bitch*—and drank his coffee.

Suddenly he sneezed, spilling the hot coffee in his crotch: *"Hoo Jesus I burned my balls! Ow! Ow! Ow! Ow!"* and Rick started laughing shrilly. Banner reached into his pants to try to soothe his scalded genitals, but the hot coffee had already soaked all the way through. Tears welled in his eyes. "Shit," he yelled. He sneezed again, then blew his nose into his bandana, steering the truck with his knees.

"Gawddamn, mon," Rick said, "you all ain't gonna be in any shape to work Saturday."

"Just my luck, and with askarel, too," and Banner sneezed again. "Gawddamn it, I hope this don't take too long." He crushed his barely smoked cigarette in the filled ashtray, the taste suddenly dry and rank, and rubbed his scratchy eyes with two fingers. "I don't know why I smoke the damned things," he told Rick. "I think I'm turning into a junkie."

"Ah, you love it."

"Uh-huh. Like I love askarel." Banner sneezed again, his chest aching over that one. He sniffed, and accidentally felt mucus go up and out of his nose to the back of his throat. He swallowed it disgustedly, feeling his stomach turn. He drank the rest of the coffee to kill the taste. "Damn it, man, I'm starting to feel bad," he said angrily. "I just know I'm catching a cold."

"Just don't give the gawddamned thing to me," Rick told him. "Ah don't want it. Ah'm gettin' married next week, an' Ah'm gonna need all my strength," and grinned at Banner.

"Uh-huh," Banner said archly.

2.

Banner followed the yellow truck and stopped behind it as it pulled up to the gate of Belltower Substation. Tiny jumped out and unlocked the gate, opened it, and Charlie drove the truck on in. Banner followed them inside.

There was only one transformer in the substation, standing silently beneath a black-painted galvanized steel structure. A primary and secondary oil circuit breaker stood on either side of the transformer, both of them beneath the same steel structure. The dark red porcelain insulators on the transformer and the oil circuit breakers shined in the rain. The primary cables entered the substation on wooden cross-armed poles that marched through a field from the west, and the secondary cables going out of the substation were attached to another set of similar wooden poles that were parallel with the northbound highway, receding into the horizon. A small lone white building housing the switchgear relays stood at one end of the substation. The substation itself was nearly the same size as the one they had just left not twenty minutes before, with a graveled foundation and wire-meshed fence topped with strands of barbed wire forming the perimeter. There were no other buildings in sight, just the muddy fields and low clouds passing slowly overhead. It was quiet too, except for the idling engines and the wind and rain.

"It's small all right," Banner said.

"Uh-huh."

Banner parked the truck ten feet away from the substation structure, in front of the primary oil circuit breaker, shut the engine off, rolled down the window, and listened. The transformer, like the other ones, was dead. "Nada," he said.

"Yeah." Rick nodded.

Tiny suddenly appeared at the window on Banner's side, his rosy face glowing beneath his yellow hardhat.

"Well," he said, smiling, "here she is. The sub's dead. It's just like what you all found back there in the other one. There ain't no oil in it. Whoever did it opened the breakers first, then drained the oil out of it. We came out and opened up the disconnects on both of the breakers. It's grounded for your safety. I'll show you, but you all might want to put on personal grounds yourself. Okay?"

"All right, Tiny," Banner said, looking at the opened disconnect switches parallel to the ground.

He and Rick stepped out of the truck and followed Tiny over to the secondary oil circuit breaker, where the large man pointed to the opened disconnects above them, and the closed and locked red-painted handle of the ground disconnect. The ground disconnect switch was closed in on the line between the secondary side of the transformer and the bus work just above the disconnect clips of the oil circuit breaker. It was set up the same way on the primary side of the transformer.

Banner and Rick decided to put personal grounds on anyway.

"All right," Tiny said. "We'll let you go here. We'll give you a clearance to work on this transformer. When you're finished, stop back by the main substation and get hold of us. We'll come back to check things out, to see your grounds are removed. We'll give you another clearance when you come back to filter the oil or whatever you have to do. Okay?"

"Yeah," Banner said. "I've got the clearance to work on this transformer."

"Yeah. All right. We'll be seein' ya. We're gonna lock the gate on our way out. You can check it if you want to when we leave."

"Okay."

"All right then. Take it easy. And try to stay outta the rain." Tiny guffawed, waved, and walked back to his truck. Charlie hadn't even gotten out of the seat.

After watching Tiny relock the gate, Banner and Rick climbed into their truck. Suddenly left alone, they sat silently and looked at each other.

They heard the electric utility truck's horn as it drove away, its tires hissing on the rainy highway.

"Whaddaya think?" Rick asked.

"I'm beginning to think the ratio on this transformer has worked out just fine, ya know what I mean?" Banner asked, drawling the words out, knowing they were going to do the work anyway.

Rick grinned. "Ah know what you mean. Ah don't wanna get wet either."

"Yeah," Banner sighed. "Me neither. I feel like shit, I'm tired, I'm already soaking wet, and I'm coming down with a cold. I don't feel like messin' with this transformer, not the way I feel."

"Yeah."

"You in any hurry yet?" Banner asked, and Rick shook his head. They both settled in the seats. Banner felt lousy; his head stuffy, sinuses aching. His throat felt raw. He poured the last remaining coffee from his thermos and sipped at the hot steaming black liquid, being damned careful not to spill it in his crotch again, trying to soothe his throat. The coffee was still wretched. He figured that when they'd leave, he'd let Rick drive home; he had been driving too much as it was. He would sleep on the way home. He yawned, stretched, and watched the rain. *What a drab dreary day*, he thought. *It's never gonna stop.* It was silent except for the rain spattering on the ground and the wind blowing against the truck.

Rick yawned too. "Well, shit," he said. "I'll go get the ground cables and some wrenches. We may as well ground it while we're heah. See what kind of music we got we can put in the tape machine, why don't ya?"

"All right." Banner and Rick had installed a cassette tape deck into the dashboard about six months ago and put in two more speakers. Banner lifted a small full case of tapes from beneath his seat and shoved one into the deck. Music filled the entire cab, and he lowered the volume.

Rick climbed into the rear of the truck. Banner turned on the overhead light so Rick could see. He heard Rick rummaging in Banner's toolbox, then shut a drawer, heard him lift the coiled ground cables, and felt him come back to the front. He held two oily twelve-inch open-ended adjustable wrenches in his hand and the ground cables over his shoulders. "Ready?" he asked.

"Not really, but we might as well do it. Get it over with."

"Grab the T.T.R. in case B.S. shows up. Make it look good."

"Yeah," Banner said, opening the door and picking up the heavy case. "Christ this thing weighs a ton," and he climbed out of the truck, setting the case on the gravel. He reached in and finished the coffee in two huge gulps.

"Oh shit," Rick said suddenly, looking back into the truck.

"What's the matter?"

"Ah left the friggin' ladder back at the sub."

"Oh for Christ's sake, Rick, how could we forget?"

"Ah guess in our overenthusiasm to get the hell away, mon," and Rick laughed lightly.

"I ain't in no gawddamned mood to go climbing this bitch," Banner said, angry with himself, imagining Dellasandro having a big laugh back at the substation.

"Well, there ain't no use in cryin' about it now."

"Yeah," Banner said.

"Leave the door open," Rick said. "I wanna hear the music while I work."

"Yeah yeah," Banner said. He stood next to the transformer and read the nameplate information. It was a delta-wye connection, 34,000 volts primary and 17,000 volts secondary, with a neutral ground on the wye. "1280 gallons of oil," Banner muttered.

Rick stood by him, towering above him by a foot, holding the grounding stick. "Let's ground it first," he told Banner. "Then I'll go climb this thing. You give me the T.T.R. after I get up on it and then come on up."

"Yeah," Banner said, silently cursing the ladder left behind and the rain and his forming cold.

After double checking that the primary and secondary disconnects were opened and that the oil circuit breakers indicated open, they quickly applied the ground cables to the secondary three-phased lines and to the substation structure. But no matter how fast they worked, the rain drenched them. Rick took on the appearance of a wiry rat more and more. Banner could only imagine what he looked like.

"Well," Rick said after putting the grounding stick back into the truck, "I'll go climb this bitch."

"All right," Banner said wearily.

Rick put the wrenches in his rear pants pocket, grabbed hold of two of the radiators, and pulled himself slowly up the side, his feet slipping on the wet tubes. He landed on his belly on top of the radiators, eyeballing the jutting porcelain insulators.

"What's the matter?" Banner called out. "Don't ya trust yourself that you grounded the line?"

"Ah wouldn't trust my fuckin' sweet adorable grandmother in a substation, mon, even if she knew how to do the switchin', ya know what I mean?"

"Yeah," Banner said.

Rick grinned down at him, then stood on top of the transformer's metal cover, looking at the insulators and then looking around him. He stood sharply frozen in an instant, pointing at the gate. "Don't look now, but we got company," he told Banner quickly.

"What?" Banner asked, surprised, and walked around the transformer to see for himself.

3.

There were two large black Ford pick-up trucks parked in front of the gate, engines idling, and a man wearing a hunting outfit and bright red hunting cap unlocked and opened the gate slowly and with deliberation. When he swung both sides open, the wheels of the trucks spun faster as they were driven in over the gravel. Banner saw that they were full of men. He hadn't even heard them drive up on the highway.

"Trouble?" Rick asked urgently, frowning.

"Maybe," Banner answered, his heart suddenly beating faster, a sinking feeling in his guts. "I don't like the looks of it." He forgot his cold; the rain; he froze where he stood.

The vehicles rapidly parked behind the truck. Six men piled out of each of them quickly and silently. A door slammed. All the men wielded shotguns. Two of them walked over, raised the rear door of the blue truck and directly climbed inside. There were loud clattering noises as they searched the truck. Equipment flew out the door: hoses uncurling like snakes, boxes breaking open, spilling bottles and Fuller's earth bags into the rain.

The other men stood silently, grouped close together, looking at Banner and Rick with rage in their burning eyes. Most of them had their weapons aimed at the two young men. Banner suddenly became scared, felt his bowels start loosening, and he tried to keep his sphincter under control. The noise inside the truck continued until every piece of equipment and even Banner's and Rick's toolboxes and clothes and Rick's banjo lay spread on the ground. Then the two men who had been inside the truck jumped out. The only sounds now were the idling pick-ups and the music coming from the truck.

"What . . . uh . . . what's the problem?" Banner asked, sounding hoarse.

Jesus.

He hoped none of them had an itchy trigger finger.

Jesus, he thought again.

"Whatta you doin' here?" the man closest to Banner asked in a chilling voice.

"We're gonna ratio the . . . uh . . . the transformer."

"The fuck you are."

Banner didn't say anything.

The silence was highly charged.

The rain never let up.

"Who sent you here?" the man asked.

"It's Boggs, that son-of-a-bitch," one of the other men said.

"Yeah. Uh-huh," other voices commingled, full of rage.

"Is that your machine there?" the first man asked flatly, ignoring the men around him, gesturing with his shotgun at the transformer-turns-ratio set. "Is it?"

"Yeah," Banner said.

"Bring it here. Don't fuck with me. Just bring it here. Now."

Banner picked it up and walked over to the man, who didn't move, and set it on the ground at the man's feet. He decided he wasn't going to fuck with them. Whatever they wanted, they were going to get. Everything was spinning out of control. He wondered where the gawddamned Marines were.

"Open it up."

Banner did and the man stared at it, his jaws clenching.

One of the men spat viciously on the ground.

"Scabs," another man said. "They're a bunch of fuckin' gawddamned scabs workin' up here," and he spat angrily on the ground too, barely missing Banner's boots.

The first man squinted at Banner and then at Rick, who stood quite still on top of the transformer. The rain pelted the man's face, making him look meaner. "Boy," he drawled to Rick in a clear loud voice, pointing his shotgun at him and cradling it calmly in the crook of his arm as if it were a baby, "you mind gettin' off that transformer?"

"No, sir, fuck you very much," Rick said clearly back at him, giving the man the finger. "If you want me, you all just come on up here and get me. Ah got work to do and Ah'm too gawddamned tired to take orders from a buncha assholes like you," and he turned and started unscrewing the nuts and bolts that held the cable to one of the primary insulators.

There was a loud percussion and Banner ducked reflexively down—thought somehow the transformer blew up, remembering what had happened down in Florida: the energized askarel-filled transformer suddenly blowing smoke and flame out through the attached primary and secondary air circuit breakers, sounding as if a shotgun had been fired; the ensuing silence heart stopping and unexpected—then realized it wasn't the transformer that had detonated, but that the man had fired his shotgun.

Rick wasn't up on top of the transformer.

"Rick?" Banner suddenly called; his voice still hoarse. The repercussive sound of the shotgun slowly died away in the rain and out into the fields. His head rang. He stood uncertainly and looked at the top of the transformer. He walked slowly around it, knowing what he was going to find, not wanting to know the truth, having to see for himself; not wanting, he realized then, to die, but to live.

Rick hung upside down, his boot wedged in between two of the tubed radiators, blood thick and streaming, mixing with the rain, down the side of his obliterated head, on to the radiators and dripping to the ground.

Banner numbly stared.

Rick still held one of the wrenches clenched tight in his fist.

He was dead. There was nothing that could be done for him; nothing.

"Jesus. Rick," Banner said quietly. He turned and faced the armed men. "He was getting married next week," he loudly told the man who had killed Rick.

"Mother*fucker*," he yelled. "He was getting *married* next week."

He was in shock, as if all his senses were heightened. It felt as if he were in a dream, his surroundings not real: he was going to wake up from what was happening around him; he was out of his body. He felt as if his entire being was on fire. Banner now understood what it must have been like for those burning horses a few years ago as they tore out of the barn and into the shotguns that he and Old Man Martin used.

He looked at the twelve men, who hadn't moved, and knew what was going to happen.

He was suddenly enraged: *prepare to meet thy God, O Israel*—there was no more time left—there was no time—and he thought of the Bee waiting for him at home. The twelve men looked at him intently with the etched mark of Cain in their eyes. He stood in front of the transformer—nowhere to go; nowhere to hide—hearing the final words of "The Comet, the Course, the Tail" that soared out of the truck, above the far distant sounds of sirens, too far away to help him.

Jackson Banner screamed as he ran toward them.

Screams of Burning Horses was written in Pasadena and Pomona, California, from the summer of 1980 through November 1987

Printed in the United States
by Baker & Taylor Publisher Services